THROUGH THE SAD WOOD
OUR CORPSES WILL HANG

ESSENTIAL PROSE SERIES 134

**Canada Council   Conseil des Arts
for the Arts   du Canada**

ONTARIO ARTS COUNCIL
CONSEIL DES ARTS DE L'ONTARIO
an Ontario government agency
un organisme du gouvernement de l'Ontario

Guernica Editions Inc. acknowledges the support of the Canada Council
for the Arts and the Ontario Arts Council. The Ontario Arts Council
is an agency of the Government of Ontario.

We acknowledge the financial support of the Government of Canada.

THROUGH THE SAD WOOD OUR CORPSES WILL HANG

Ava Farmehri

GUERNICA
EDITIONS
TORONTO • BUFFALO • LANCASTER (U.K.)
2017

Michael Mirolla, editor
Sinan Hussein, cover painting 'I am a refugee'.
David Moratto , Interior and cover design
Guernica Editions Inc.
1569 Heritage Way, Oakville, (ON), Canada L6M 2Z7
2250 Military Road, Tonawanda, N.Y. 14150-6000 U.S.A.
www.guernicaeditions.com

Distributors:
University of Toronto Press Distribution,
5201 Dufferin Street, Toronto (ON), Canada M3H 5T8
Gazelle Book Services, White Cross Mills
High Town, Lancaster LA1 4XS U.K.

First edition.
Printed in Canada.

Legal Deposit — Third Quarter
Library of Congress Catalog Card Number: 2017936265
Library and Archives Canada Cataloguing in Publication
Farmehri, Ava, author
Through the sad wood our corpses will hang / Ava Farmehri.
-- 1st edition.

(Essential prose series ; 134)
Issued in print and electronic formats.
ISBN 978-1-77183-156-7 (softcover). -- ISBN 978-1-77183-157-4 (EPUB).
-- ISBN 978-1-77183-158-1 (Kindle)

I. Title. II. Series: Essential prose series ; 134

PS8611.A7557T47 2017   C813'.6   C2017-901737-3   C2017-901738-1

To my parents.
And to that mythical place: Home.

Through the sad wood our corpses will hang,
Each on the thornbrush of the soul that harmed it.
— Dante Alighieri, Inferno

Freedom from fear is the freedom
I claim for you my motherland!
Freedom from the burden of the ages, bending your head,
breaking your back, blinding your eyes to the beckoning
call of the future;
Freedom from the shackles of slumber wherewith
you fasten yourself in night's stillness,
mistrusting the star that speaks of truth's adventurous paths;
freedom from the anarchy of destiny
whole sails are weakly yielded to the blind uncertain winds,
and the helm to a hand ever rigid and cold as death.
Freedom from the insult of dwelling in a puppet's world,
Where movements are started through brainless wires,
repeated through mindless habits,
where figures wait with patience and obedience for the
master of show,
to be stirred into a mimicry of life
— Rabindranath Tagore

The only certain freedom's in departure.
— Robert Frost

😄

⟫ Chapter One

1 ⋘

THEY ARE GOING to kill me.

My trial lasted three weeks. I was lucky, because some unfortunate souls have to wait for years to hear that same news. I've also read and heard about smoother death sentences, and so to me at least, this speedy decision came as no surprise. This is Iran, after all.

I stood in cuffs as the sentence was read to me and to a roomful of stern policemen, a couple of psychiatrists, a judge and a court appointed lawyer who tried his best, upon hearing the verdict, to appear disappointed. He was a good actor, considering how obvious and predictable the sentence was. I mean, I didn't exactly leave much to the imagination when I confessed to everything, refusing any claims of insanity piled on me by sympathetic relatives and compassionate neighbours who jumped to my rescue. Besides, there was an eyewitness.

No, I didn't ask for anything in return for my confession; no deals were made to spare my life; no stalling or plea bargains. They had asked me a question and I had simply answered truthfully. I thought to myself: Sheyda, why must everything in life be conditional? Why must there always be a give and take mentality even when it comes to the purest of ideals? Why must truth always be prodded with hesitance and a desire for reciprocation? I was accused of being a liar all my life, and in a way, all I had wanted was to redeem myself. The

1

truth will set you free, they say, but believe me, nothing will set you free.

I used to be so sure that death would do the trick, but I have had enough time to contemplate it, sitting in a cell and watching women being led to their death. They should look happier, I thought, if they really were about to soar freely without the anchor of a body. I had wondered why none of them was smiling. Why some of them had prayed before being cuffed and led out of the cell. What could a murderer possibly pray for? Forgiveness? Forgiveness should only be asked from the murdered, and since the murdered were no longer with us in the realm of the living, the very act of asking for their forgiveness was ludicrous and bizarrely funny.

My lawyer wouldn't look at my face. The knees of my dear psychiatrist, Dr. Fereydoon, betrayed him, and he sat down and only got up a few minutes later when I was escorted out of the courtroom. I saw him when I looked back and gave him a little wave and a satisfied smile.

One thing about hearing your death sentence is that it really puts things into perspective. It's not very much unlike a near death experience, though I've never really had any of those, but I've heard all those clichéd stories of lights and tunnels, and of floating upwards to God's headquarters and looking down at your own discarded body. When I looked down at myself, I saw tears in my eyes, and my cuffed hands clasped as if in prayer. I saw tears that the media and the public that day had probably referred to as either crocodile tears or tears of genuine remorse, and palms that may have been described as invoking and fatalistic.

Let me clear the record by saying that my tears were happy tears. My palms were indeed fatalistic. My palms in cuffs, cupping within them the story of my life were symbolic of the twenty odd years I had been forced to spend as a captive sinner under the sun. I looked at my forehead, shiny despite me not having showered for days, and let me tell you: it was as white as a bleached past. I had purposefully clipped my blonde fringe to the top of my head, so that everyone could see my honesty, everyone.

Framed in the black fabric of a scarf, my face was so white it looked almost saintly. I had never looked so peaceful in my life, calm to the ridiculous point of elation, like my mother's face when she died. I searched my back for wings, and there, on the sides of my spine, I caught the glimpse of strong white feathers budding out, slowly, carefully. Afloat in the cold room I looked around at faces, strangers, no one ever knew me. I was an angel, a misunderstood angel. I still am.

Would they bury me with my parents, the Islamic way? Would anyone visit me in the cemetery and sprinkle rosewater on my tombstone? Would they water the weeds or flowers that grew on the carpets of green grass I slept under? Would anyone say a prayer for my lost soul? Would they shed tears for all the unknown injustices of my life?

What was I? Just a face among many, just another name! I was one more broken neck. They'll forget about me like they forget about everyone else, including their own deceased families. I'll be lost in the archives of the prison documents; I will be just another headline in a newspaper that is quickly flipped through, a face that is recognized and spat on: "Ah look: the monster who killed her mother."

Who will be at my funeral? Only those who are glad to be done with a girl like me. No. I only want birds at my funeral. I want them to dump my soulless body in a Tower of Silence to be feasted on by vultures. Just leave me on the peak of a dry and distant mountain, and allow nature to nibble at my toes and ears until there is nothing left. I want to be spread next to red and rotting pockmarked corpses, and let the bald

hideous birds lift me up, then drop me, my broken neck dancing on its way down and my eyes, always looking up. I want
to be shattered and the very marrow of my bones extracted.
I want them to fly freely with me in their bloated bellies, with
my dreams sour on their sinewy rasp tongues, and my hair
still fresh in their beaks. I want my face burnt in their black
angry eyes and my enslaved brown eyes a memory on their
faces. And when they squawk, they'll squawk nothing but my
mournful name.

2 ⟞

I was born a captive.

I was born in Tehran, Iran, April 1, 1979. The day the Islamic Republic was proclaimed.

Months before my birth a Shah was being betrayed by his
people, portrayed as a traitor on the small screens of the world,
delivered with his queen to an exile and a death that transcended the borders of his sorrow and the boundaries of his
nightmares. Months before my birth the history of a nation
was being dissected and chewed on, like the fleshy parts of a
chicken's neck. The carcass of its future thrown out to bearded dogs and crows that cawed from their Holy-Books then hid
behind tall pillars and threw the same books away. A helicop-
ter was lifted and Iran went under siege.

Months before my birth, elderly women were burying the
charred bodies they assumed had once been their kids while
asking God: Why? *Why*? Young men and women who to escape
the outcries of demonstrations had sought refuge in Cinema
Rex and watched *The Deer (Gavaznha)*. They laughed at the
ironies not knowing that they were about to experience them
firsthand. Men and women who never lived to realize *The Deer*

was a last-minute name change, just like the inscription of their names on Death's unforgiving list was God's final thought before bedtime. Men and women who were to be preyed on and hunted, naiveté scarring their faces.

Months before my birth Death was seen in pied clothing on the streets of Iran, calling out the names of children, and playing his magical pipe, luring them away to drown in the river. Pretty girls were putting away their miniskirts and ironing chadors that were as black as their tears. They folded their long cascading hair into old-women plaits. Those were the days of corduroys and Charleston pants, bangles and bell-bottom jumpsuits, headbands and macramé belts, Roman sandals and rainbow shirts and long-haired Europeans holding up the peace-sign as they drove to Kathmandu in green Cortinas and sky-blue Rovers. Those were the days of "Kung-Fu fighting" and "Greased Lightning" and Abba and the Bee Gees. Those were the days of American neighbours with whom we exchanged pleasantries and food and lives and stories long before we drew our swords and took them hostage, and long before they called us terrorists and threatened to sort us out. Those were the days when women were not stoned for being in love, and men were not hanged for having opinions, and backs were not lashed for being exposed, and hairs were not pulled for being beautiful, and dreams were not nipped for being dreams, and wings were not clipped for wanting to fly. But I was not there to see any of that, I was born after. By the time I had opened my eyes to the darkness of this world, a dynasty had been pulverized. A slate was wiped dirty and a state was robbed clean.

I was born captivated. I heard all those stories from the nostalgic lips of those around me and took them all for bedtime fiction. I churned in my bed, ready to sleep, cuddling with a teddy bear that was as eager to hear Scheherazade's modern religio-political retelling of a past of pretty clothing and funny hairdos, where things came in more shades than black, white and gray. A Night among many in the history of this country's a Thousand and One. In this new version the vizier's daughter was modestly-dressed and pious, and spoke in a low and timid voice, because well, a woman's voice was a thing of shame. In this version, Scheherazade didn't care much if she lived or died.

"Ours is a land of fiction, of frictions. And no story is too old to be told time and again," my mother would whisper to me in accidental rhyming. She would pull out of her cupboard some articles of clothing to show me: father's polyester shirt, gold-sprinkled halter tops from the days she went night-clubbing. *Night-clubbing*! I used to close my eyes and try to imagine my saint-like mother in a pink and pleated mini retro dress with platform-soled shoes, chewing the olive of her martini and eying the man who would whet her lips that night, and who, months later, would become my father. My mother who, throughout her life, looked and smiled at everything with the indecision of the Mona Lisa: am I happy or am I sad? Is this what a smile should look like? I am the something, the in-between that has yet to be named. Whenever I opened my eyes and glanced at my teddy bear, it too was smiling its threaded Mona Lisa smile, its eyes wide open, truly shocked. My mother was a teddy bear.

"But here are pictures!" my mother and my aunt Bahar would shove photo albums of proof in my face, pointing at their naked shaved legs or their maxi dresses and their coiled exposed puffy chignons, painted nails peeping from the slits of their sandals.

What they said and what I saw just didn't add up. I'd hold the square pictures in my hand and wonder to myself while looking out of my window: "How did we go from *that* to *this*?"

My mother would tell me: "It actually happened. We actually had that life of *Azadi;* that life of Freedom."

Azadi. Azadi ... That word gave me nightmares. It meant nothing and everything. It was an ideal that couldn't be grasped, like Perfection and God and True Love and Home. It was an ideal that had to be seen, touched, tasted and experienced. It had to be lived through to be proved. It had to be loved through to be true.

"What did it feel like?" I used to ask them.

"It felt ... it felt — " They would stammer not knowing what to tell me, language having left them. Only their eyes articulated what their tongues no longer could.

I was born a captive. And now I am not sure anyone is born free.

3 ☾

> *Yeki Bood, Yeki Nabood,*
> *Gheir az Khuda Hichkas Nabood*

That's how every night my mother started all her stories, with those two lines that made absolutely no sense but which, despite their logical impossibility, sounded musical enough to start me on a night of sweet dreams and restless wondering. An itch would gnaw at the sides of my spine, and by the time the story ended, wings would spring to lift me from the shambles of reality and into a heaven of ideas. And my mother, with a slightly orange face in the shaded light of the lamp, would always tell me: "You don't need wings to fly, all you need is your imagination; all you need is a heart full of love." I'd stare, smitten, at the oval holes of her nostrils, at the few pinheaded black hairs on her rounded chin, which she sometimes made

me tweeze, and I'd wait for her to unlock the door of my cage
and release me: her lovesick nightingale.

Dreams were for free, no one could take mine away. During
the eight years of a war that orphaned children and widowed
mothers, that amputated dark-skinned fathers and beheaded
brothers on both sides of a vicious line called border, I ventured
out of my nascent cage only when the rest of the world slept,
and in the darkness of the night, free from the evils of this life,
I fluttered toward the moon, and only in her light did I sleep.

My mother was an English student whose ambition was to
become a teacher. She learnt English in school, and then practiced it with an American family that had — before the Revolution — lived three blocks from our house. By the time the
Shah was dethroned, our American neighbours were already
back in that distant nosy country, mowing their lawns and
painting their picket fences. My mother had a thing for her
teacher (it runs in the family); a certain Mr. Carl who was,
according to my father, a CIA agent. During the Revolution,
when the Morality Police raided houses to confiscate anything
that they deemed immoral (everything from playing cards to
alcohol but also any pictures of scarf-less women), my mother and father dug a huge hole in our garden, and buried in it
all their books, magazines, and even their own un-Islamic
pictures. That's how memories and knowledge were preserved
in my house. They had to be smothered to stay alive.

When, due to her unplanned pregnancy, my mother had
to drop out of university, her only way of fulfilling her dream
of teaching was through me: I was her only student. I learnt
English very quickly, but it was years later that I perfected my
pronunciation of certain words. For a long time Hawaii was
"Havaii," waitress was "vaitress," and knife, I am ashamed to
say, was "*ke*nife."

4

My second favourite story was the story of my birth, preceded only by the story of *how* I was conceived, a story my mother never told me but one that I heard through the grapevine. One cannot have secrets here, not those types of secrets anyway. They were special stories because my life could have still been saved; at that time it could have gone either way. She could have had an abortion, or could have killed us both. She could have fled the country, as many people had done and were still doing. Life was playing Russian roulette with my fate, but somehow it was always my temple that faced the open mouth of a gun. And each time I made the acquaintance of a bullet, I'd realize that I never pulled the trigger once, it was never me. Someone in my life always volunteered.

She had mistaken her contractions for mere stomach pains, and though her bags for the hospital had been laid and ready weeks in advance, she had only called my father when her water broke. "Be strong, I love you." was what he told her before panicking and dialling random numbers and asking any woman who picked up to please help his wife. When my mother was releasing herself from nine months of carrying me, our black and white TV was standing on its wooden legs like a strange beheaded electronic animal, watching as my mother pushed me out of her and into this world, playing muted news that everyone was following.

A new Sherriff was in town. Out with the new, in with the old!

My mother lay on a mattress that they later got rid of because of all the bloodstains. My maternal grandmother, Nana Farangis, sat behind her, pressing my mother's head to her own heavy chest and wiping with her brown hand a face that dripped hasty pearls of sweat all the way down to her belly. After five hours of shouting and pleading, of alternating swiftly between praying to God and cursing Him for making her a woman, of biting on a pillow, of almost pulling my granny's arm out and kicking the midwife in her breasts so vindictively that my young aunt Bahar had to run and get the poor woman a glass of water, the fight was over and I surrendered.

I emerged, with the combined effort of my grandmother and a foulmouthed neighbourhood midwife, slick and juicy like a pink and purple moist fruit, delicate and ready to burst. I was delivered from the womb of time, from an eternity of darkness to a reality of light, bombs and sunshine, of nightingales that travelled the skies freely, blind to borders while my people perished caged. I awoke to a world where fields were swept by bright red poppies that spotted with longing the green of the earth. Head first, with the bulgy angry features of pressed eyes and a convulsed mouth, my long neck and torso followed, with arms and legs sticking out extended and wiry, promising me the gift of height and a flat-chested adolescence. Finally, a full and rounded bottom which in addition to my lips, the few men I've slept with loved the most about my body.

The first blur I saw when I emerged in my upturned position was the lit TV. I didn't cry, I didn't breathe. I just wanted to hide, to be pushed back into my mother and to stay in her forever. I wanted to go back to sleep in that darkness that was safe. Far away from what was happening. But the midwife delivered to my back three heavy smacks that I was forced to cry despite myself. Physical pain was more real than the intangibility I foresaw of my future. When my father finally arrived from work and held me bundled up in his arms, he cried, and the tears of joy and sorrow that merged and painted his face then, continued to paint my mother's whenever throughout my childhood she had told me that story, a story she always ended by saying: "My lovesick nightingale, the day the world met you was the most painful and meaningful of my life."

Mothers and fathers are ruthless sinners. They condemn many souls to an existence of exile, of failed dreams and marriages, of suicidal lovers and of death and incarcerations, because of their love and hope, because of their selfish needs, as if they didn't know better, as if life hadn't taught them better. Parents are thoroughly and truthfully the worst of criminals.

5 ☾

Do murderers have obituaries?

I imagine mine ...

Ms. Sheyda Porrouya of Tehran, Iran died on the 11th of March 1999 from a broken neck after hanging by a court order from a noose.

Sheyda Porrouya was born on the 1st of April, 1979, the only daughter of the late Rustam and Arezoo Porrouya who were both killed under separate but equally tragic circumstances. Following graduation from Fatima Zahra High School, Sheyda immediately sat for her concour exam (university entrance exam) and passed with flying colours. She spent her first and only year in university studying voraciously, excelling at subjects such as Persian History and Mythology, English and Poetry, and leaving a very strong impression on those students and teachers who had crossed paths with this unconventional and fiery young soul.

Ms. Sheyda was known by one and all as an incorrigible dreamer. Sheyda, the owner of a very unique and congenial disposition, was also an adventurous sprightly thing with endless stories to tell, and a relentless lover who believed with all her heart and being, in the triumphant nature of love and in happy buttery and everlasting endings. Though her early death, brought on by the just decision of a hanging, meant that Sheyda didn't live to accomplish her small dreams of loving the whole world, and in her own misunderstood way, rescuing it, it was her firm belief that we all, each and every single one of us, had an hour to shine, and that her timely death was her hour of shinning.

Ms. Sheyda's interests included an admirably and steadily-growing collection of angel figurines, books, especially ones translated by the mysterious but brilliant Mustafa Jafari. She was a natural and very gifted writer, though none of her writings would ever see the light of day, due to political correctness and reasons that reek of cultural and religious sensitivity. Some of her writings were also deemed as harbouring hate and hostility for the Islamic Regime and thus were burnt after her death. She was a keen observer of both birds and man, noting that in terms of freedom, birds always had the upper hand, or in this very instance, the literal upper wing.

Ms. Sheyda Porrouya is survived by her incarcerated teddy-bear, her faithful rag doll, Laleh, a universe that stops ticking for no one, and her many beautiful and undying dreams.

CHAPTER TWO

1 ❧

"SO WHAT IF she's a little strange? All children have their own way of growing up!" my paediatrician said, offering me a lollipop that I unwrapped and began immediately to suckle on, throwing the orange wrapper on the floor. My father reached down and picked it up. He then gave me a reprimanding gaze which I ignored and replaced with the view of an apple tree outside which stood crucified like the letter T. The branches were heavy with the ripened fruit, and the grass was cluttered with rotten ones. I was sitting squeezed between him and my mother, on a couch of bright brown leather that smelt of vomit and the cries of sick little babies. My parents looked at each other not knowing what to say or do. The paediatrician, Dr. Vafa, with the professional sense of duty and of wanting to put her clients at ease finally said: "What are we talking about here? Imaginary friends? She's afraid of the dark?"

I looked at Dr. Vafa's face and smiled, then looked back at the T outside. With its bleeding arms it summoned. I stood up to leave, but my father pulled me back down. "Sit," he said.

I sat.

"No," said my father clearing his throat, "no, it's a bit more serious than that." He glanced at mother, who was sitting back on the couch, staring blankly at the painting that hung opposite her, which was a miniature set in an expensive carved wooden frame, portraying a group of narrow-eyed turban-wearing hunters spearing a lioness. Maybe my mother sympathized with the beast's wounds, or wished that she was there to save her, to throw herself before the blood-lusting hunters and make them see by accepting their spears into her own flesh, that they were the true beasts. I don't know, but my mother kept her eyes on that painting as if appreciating its cruelty was the reason we were there, sitting in that frigid room. Her black scarf was tied loosely over the hair which, when we were in the privacy of our house, she used to roll around her fingers and chew on.

My mother said nothing, and so my father, with an embarrassed voice, went on to expound: "She's seven years old and still wets her bed, and she — " he looked apologetically at the ground and then impatiently back at my mother: "Arezoo, maybe you should tell her. Say something." My mother violently snapped out of her trance, half-turned to face my father who rubbed tired knuckles into his eyes. A heavy silver ring inlaid with a yellow rock bulged on his middle finger.

Dr. Vafa opened her mouth to say something, but before she could, my mother interrupted her. "Sheyda jan," she said, putting her fingers through my hair, "why don't you run outside and play until your daddy and I finish?"

I stood up ready to dart out, but she grabbed me roughly from my elbow, and then with a palm under my chin she pulled my face to her, lollipop still in my mouth, clicking loudly on my teeth, said: "Don't go past the walls, and don't speak to strangers." She kissed my cheek, and with her thumb, she rubbed off the dark smudge of brown lipstick.

I shook my head up and down then quickly ran out.

I stood under the tree, touching its spine and eyeing the reddest apple on a high thick bough. With my head tilted upwards, I started devising a strategy for climbing the smooth trunk; where to put my leg and which branchy arm to pull on my ascent. After trying and failing thrice, I sat on the moist grass that was still glistening from the three hours of rain we'd had that morning, breathing belligerently with my back glued to the tree, threading grass into my fingers and chewing on my lollipop stick which was beginning to split in my mouth and taste papery. The sweet disturbing perfume of apples rotting around me was pulling me toward a crazed state of dreaminess which I had to shake off before it claimed me. I craned my neck upwards again and tried to talk the apple into falling, crooning the lullabies my mother sang me, promising not to eat it one minute, and then replacing that promise the next with one of munching on it tenderly.

Patiently I waited, as patiently as I would for the rest of my life, for a miracle to happen, for someone to show up and save me or for a solution to drop from heaven into my lap. Then I knew that it was the time for a compromise, so I stood up and wandered in the battlefield of rounded corpses and picked one that looked innocent enough to only cause a mild diarrhea. After grabbing it, I realized that the hidden side was as soft and sticky as a mush of fresh warm mud. My fingers slipped on the dirty brown skin and rubbed deeply into the overripe moist. Closing my eyes and craving apples I bit into the solid side, sugared juice running on my tongue and down my throat, and I sucked it all with a slurp that glued the apple to my lips.

Before the whole chunk was in my mouth, I felt a worm, puffy like an infant's pinky, dangling from my lips, hurrying to save itself and seek warmth in the closest alcove: my mouth. I spat everything out quickly, repeatedly, wiping my mouth and scrubbing my tongue in frightened and aggressive disappointment with the sleeve of my sweater, but only after biting on the worm and tasting the sourness of its severed jellied body. Apple worms taste like puss. Not that I have any clue what other worms taste like but apple worms do.

My parents were taking too long.

When my parents and I had arrived earlier, a blue-eyed boy was sitting outside on the edge of the pavement with his green and yellow parakeet selling the divination of Hafez. The bird was sitting atop a colourful stack of envelopes, each envelope with a poem that predicted the success or failure of your intention (*neyyat*). It was the bird's job to pick out an envelope for you. The boy had been watching me the whole time, trying and failing to climb the tree, trying and failing to hex and chant the apple down. That's what made me want to try harder, his watching me made me crave the apple more. In a way I wasn't much different than my mother. Not my mother Arezoo, but *our* First Mother: Eve. I wanted to save face. I moved again toward the tree, a lumpy stone in my palm. Aiming carefully, I catapulted the stone as strongly as I could in the direction of my apple to clip its stem and missed, time after time. The boy finally rushed to me, his bird and lyrical source of income in his hands.

"Where are your parents?" he asked.

I tried not to look at the bird and fixed my eyes on the apple without answering.

"Where are they? Are they still inside? What are you, mute?" the bird bit gently on his fingers, walked carefully on his arm and steadily made its way up to his shoulder. I still didn't answer.

"If you tell me, I'll get the apple for you." he said, smiling stupidly and showing me that one of his front teeth was chipped.

Defeated, I pointed to the first floor where Dr. Vafa's clinic was.

"You need to learn how to climb. Which apple do you want? Point it out to me. You just have to hold on to my bird, make sure no one steals him. Also, never eat the leaves or the seeds."

"Why?"

"Because you will die."

Before I had the chance to point the apple out, he had already stuffed all his money in the small front pocket of his shirt, and given me the little poetry-filled carton-box he was carrying. He then, whistling, coaxed the bird into jumping onto my terrified shoulder. I screamed when the bird was close to my ear, feathers on my hair. It fluttered for seconds then settled. The boy laughed and told me not to panic, to just act normal. He then took his ugly slippers off and proceeded to climb up the tree. I watched him expertly wrap his knees around the trunk, thrusting himself upwards without the need to grab at anything, but doing it simply by the use of his muscles. His skinny bottom, not much bigger than mine, looking comical as he climbed.

I stretched my arm and shouted a bit too loudly: "That one up there, the shiny one to your left." The bird was hiding in my hair, nuzzling my ears, its curved greenish beak rubbed smoothly against my neck and tickled me into a giggle. When the boy reached my apple, he looked down at me, and from the look on his face I realized immediately that I had made a grave mistake. But it was too late. Eve craved it but Adam ate it. With his legs wrapped around the waist of the tree, he grabbed hold of the branch with his left arm and pulled it closer to him, before snapping the shiny apple off. After rubbing it on his thigh, he took a bite so loud and crunchy its sound rang in my ear all day.

The brims of my eyes filled up with tears then overflew. Fuming, and dropping his box to the floor, I gathered ant-covered rotten apples in my sweater and started throwing them at him. I hated his very sight. The parakeet was panicking, screeching while it hovered over the spilled rainbow-coloured pile of papers on the ground. A couple of apples hit him straight in the neck and belly, but when the last one hit him on his nose, he scowled in pain and dropped like a rock with a bleeding nose and a half-eaten apple.

I ran away.

Fifteen minutes later, I came out with my parents. I hid behind my father's legs, wrapping my arms around him like a frightened koala. I tugged on his pockets so fiercely that he almost tripped. Finally he shouted, untangling himself from my sweaty tentacles: "Baba jan, walk like a human being."

The boy was sitting in the same spot on the pavement, holding a bloodied tissue to his nose. The box of envelopes was rearranged before him, and the bird was sitting, like a bored fortune teller in a carnival tent, waiting for his services in the realms of the phenomenal and unlikely to be needed.

"Hey son!" my father, seeing the boy's nose and dirty shirt said, comfortingly rumpling the boy's black hair, "Everything alright?"

The boy pulled an apple out of his shirt and wiped it clean on his thigh. "Yes." he said with a smile, looking at me with his stupid chipped tooth and handing me the apple. "You forgot this."

I looked at my mother for approval, so the boy said: "She told me to pick an apple for her then ran away without it."

"Well young man, that was very nice of you," my father said. "That was very nice of him, wasn't it, Sheyda?" He then looked at me and nudged me in the boy's direction, "Don't be ungrateful, don't make him feel like he hurt himself for nothing. Go on, take it."

And so I did, I took it quickly, before the boy had any time to change his mind and eat it himself. "Don't eat it now!" said my mother, watching me readying my mouth for a bite, "Wait till it's been properly washed." She reached into her purse and pulled out some money to pay the boy for his thoughtfulness.

"I want his bird," I said, calmly.

"Sheyda jan, you're being silly now," my mother said.

"It's not for sale," the boy answered, irritated enough to make me congratulate myself on the wisdom of having already removed the apple from his hand.

"Why don't you let the bird pick a *fal* for you?" my mother said. "Do you have any questions you need answers to, honey?"

"No. I want the bird."

"Well you can't have the bird. Please young man, let your bird pick something for my daughter," my father said, growing impatient and a little angry. "Think of something, Sheyda. Hold a thought in your head. Make a wish."

"How many wishes can I make?"

"One."

I closed my eyes tightly, and made what I at the time thought was a very important wish. And after the bird had passed its neck over the pile considering its options, it lifted a tiny envelope for me. My mom asked for a *fal*, too.

We paid the boy and left with two envelopes; one orange like the lollipop I had eaten, the other blue like the boy's watery eyes. As we took a cab home, my mother opened hers up and read it, then carefully folded it and put it into her bag. Then she opened mine and read it.

"What on earth did you wish for?" asked my mother, who took the divination of Hafez too seriously, the paper shaking in her fingers.

"I cheated, wished for more than one thing."

"That's fine, what did you wish for?"

"I wished to vanish, or to live inside an apple, like a worm." I said, looking at the apple's shiny surface and trying to see reflections on it. "And you, Maman? What did you wish for?"

My father looked back at us from the passenger's seat, his fingers pressed stiffly around the stub of a cigarette. He answered me blowing smoke out: "She wished that you were normal."

"I also wished for his bird," I said, still looking at my apple.

My mother crumbled the orange paper in her hand, and then irreverently, threw it out of the speeding car.

I never knew what was said in Dr. Vafa's office. But I do have a vague idea, because three weeks later I was staring out of the different window of a different clinic, sitting on a different couch that smelt of expensive perfume, free-association and nightmares. I sat between the same parents who were certain I was crazy. Dr. Fereydoon was and still is my faithful psychiatrist. He was recommended to my parents by Dr. Vafa who spoke favourably of him and of his notable success with tough cases, which I was evidently one of.

The walls of his office stank of shameful confessions and bad memories. It was twice the size of our living room and on his desk were many items that looked very pretty. Items that I thought would look even prettier in our living room, behind one of those glass-front cupboards where mother, in one, displayed her expensive china, and in the other arranged her porcelain collection of angels. This time I sat still for two long hours, waiting for him to offer me a lollipop. He didn't. He kept talking to my father and bombarded me with questions about my toys. I don't remember much else. The most vivid thing is the smell of his couch, but that's because it never changed. There's no getting rid of that stink of memories.

The angel cupboard was always locked. My mother hid the keys, but I knew where to look. Every Friday she'd unlock it to dust and rearrange her figurines, holding each in her hand with great tenderness, shrouding them in a damp black cloth and rubbing their bodies clean. Some were on their knees in prayer while others just looked down at my face, pouring warmth into my eyes and blessing me with extended arms. One played her harp, and a couple were patronizing, never opening their eyes. The key was in the kitchen, in the old and empty ceramic jar where mother kept all the buttons my father accidentally ripped off his shirts while working.

Three days later my mother noticed the black cat, breaking the tedium of white and posing defiantly among the angels. The tail coiled like a whip, and its paw was raised to either slap you or to say *hello*. The face was frozen with a sly wink and it struck out its rough tongue tauntingly. Following me around the room was the other eye which was yellow and hypnotizing.

My mother, with an angry fist, brought the cat down onto the kitchen table in front of me. Busy messily spreading strawberry jam on a crunchy piece of *taftoon*, I looked up from my breakfast with a smile, expecting a thank-you that didn't come.

"When did you have time to take it? When did you even have time to take it?" she cried exasperated, "We were right there with you!"

My face dropped. I licked the bright reddish spoon, clicked it back into the jam jar, and bringing it out with another spoonful, returned to the sandwich I was making.

"You petty little thief, what else did you take?" my mother said, yanking me off the chair and then getting on her knees to look me in the eyes and shake me, "What else did you steal? Answer me."

"Nothing else, just this." My mother's eyes were crazy; I knew that I was in trouble, though not precisely sure why. "I took it for you, for mother's day. Daddy — "

She gave me a slap that didn't hurt, but I began to cry anyway because it surprised me. Quickly, she hugged me while breathlessly repeating: "Sorry my baby, I'm so sorry." Her hair got in my eyes and mouth so I started to cough, exaggerated painful and dry coughs that scratched my throat on their way out. She called me a stupid child then led me sniffing to the bathroom, the spoon still in my hand, dripping jam on the floor as we rushed. She held me up to the sink and harshly soaped my hands and face with a green soap that tasted bitter. I never let go of the spoon. I spat into the sink, pinkish seedy spit and foam. I looked up from her hands. This was her punishment for me: forcing me to watch her tears trickle down a miserable face which stared at me from the depths of the mirror. She was showing me what my actions did to her. At the time, I didn't know which was more cleansing, which was more sanctifying: the water and soap I was being scrubbed with, or my mother's tears.

Now I know.

"Will you tell daddy?" I asked again as she dressed me up, pulling a pair of jeans over my legs and buttoning it above my bellybutton.

"No." she said, and added nothing.

Dr. Fereydoon said that I could keep it. He said that he hadn't even noticed that it went missing. My mother apologized again, profusely, and then squeezed my hand to do the same, to repeat what I had practiced in the cab: "I am sorry I took it without your permission, Sir. I promise to ask next time and never ever steal." The Doctor smiled and told me to consider it a gift for being a brave girl and admitting my mistake. Crimson-faced, my mother quickly rushed us both out of the office.

When we got home, she told me that she was cross with me and didn't want to see my face for the rest of the day. "Stay in your room or I'll tell your father."

I went in and slammed the door, but not before taking the cat with me. My stomach grumbled, I craved a hot cup of milk with one spoon of sugar. I forced myself to cry and managed to extract a few tears which I then licked off my face. Satisfied,

I lay on my bed and watched until the silver of the afternoon turned midnight blue. Then I cried some more because I was tired and couldn't sleep. Finally I did sleep, but just long enough to pee on myself, opening my eyes only when my bladder had pushed the last hot drop out of my body. Suddenly unburdened, my hand reached under the blankets to measure the degree of damage I had caused to the mattress. It came out warm and sticky. With my legs I drove my teddy bear out of the blankets to save it. When it was a safe distance from the crime-scene, I stopped pushing, and it hung from the bottom of the bed with its legs splayed. There was a big hole there, the size of the one the world and I would one day leave in my mother's heart, and I could see that my bear was delivering a wad of cotton.

The door leading from our garden and into our living room opened, the tiny bells hanging on it jingled, I kicked the smelly blankets away and peeped from the keyhole to watch my father remove his shoes, leaning on the wall for support, and lifting his leg to untie his laces. "Arezoo," he called as he put on his slippers, "Arezoo janum, where are you?"

My mother showed up into the compressed view of the keyhole, her bottom wiggling in her long skirt as she walked toward my father. I sprinted back into bed, hid beneath the many soaked covers, glad to be embraced again by that non-judgmental warmth of sodden clothes reuniting with a sodden mattress. Breathing with difficulty the pungency of urine, I held a heavy pillow over my head and started a debate with my teddy bear.

"I am no thief, I am no thief, I am no thief ... He saw me take it but didn't say anything." I kept repeating that, swearing it to be true until I fell asleep. If she was going to tell on me, I didn't want to hear it.

That night, my mother woke me up, suspiciously sniffing the air of my room and carrying on a tray a butter and honey sandwich. "You had nothing to eat all day and there's no jam left," she said, smiling and propping my pillow as I yawned and sat up.

I wanted to ask her about it but didn't. It didn't matter anymore because I was certain that my father had vindicated me. I loved him again. When I removed my blankets to brush my teeth, I released waves of repressed smell. My mother nearly fainted. "Ey Khuda, Sheyda!" she exclaimed, clamping her nostrils. She spent an hour undressing me, washing me in the tub, dressing me in a white crisp nightie which like snow felt fresh and comforting. I then tried to help her flip the mattress to the other side, jumping around it to lift any corner but being of no use whatever. Mother said that it was too late to do anything about the reek.

I brushed my teeth and, when I went back into the room, I saw my mother digging in a pile of clutter under my bed then pulling out the dirty clothes I had hidden there. She held up with two fingers a negligee and three yellow-stained panties, confronting me with evidence I couldn't deny. Ashamed and overwhelmed, I went to my schoolbag and removed from between my books more underwear. They were still damp. I climbed into bed, she tucked me in clean blankets, drying with the back of her palm the wet face I had washed, caressing that same spot she had slapped earlier. She traced my face with fingers that smelt of saffron and sang me to sleep, my favourite lullaby:

La la la la Laleh
You are the flower of my heaven
La la you were my fate,
Sleep O companion of my soul,

Sleep my sweet-voiced nightingale
Sleep my darling, you who will bring me joy
A nightingale sings in my heart
Sleep my blossoming flower
Sleep my precious jewel
Sleep O light of my eyes
Your moonlit face is my paradise
O light of my heart
You are the sweetness of pomegranates.

I lay still, breathing through my nose, my hair smoothed behind my ears and my lashes spiked with teardrops. Assuming that I had slept, my mother switched off the lamplight and turned to leave. I sprang up again and asked her to please do what she did every night. She knelt by my bedside in the dark, looking like one of her angels. She pressed her full lips to my ears and began to softly make chewing sounds. Her breath was ticklish, and I had to titter to shake off the goosebumps. But then as the sounds grew steady, I closed my eyes to this world and imagined being far away and safe, upward, inward, deep in her belly.

"Maman," I said with a sleepy drawl before she left and closed the door behind her, "please, please tell Nana to make me more strawberry jam."

"I've already told her, baby girl."

When I look back at all this, I remember my paralyzed state as she sang, an odd subverting cataplexy, just absorbing the melancholy of my mother's voice, the hopefulness of her movements, the warmth and sweetness of her mint-tea breath. I took everything in with veneration. That night I wasn't sure what it was my mother loved about me or why she had forgiven me. Maybe if I had asked her at the time she would have told me that she loved me because I was her daughter, or possibly she would have blushed not knowing what to say. But then I'd remember her lullaby, I'd remember that I was her fate, the companion of her soul, her blossoming flower. I was her lovesick nightingale.

As a child I struggled to understand what those things meant, and failing to, I'd tell myself that they meant everything because she said those words to me daily. They meant everything, and those few minutes of hearing my mother's voice were our prayer time.

Was it guilt that made her love me, that made her hold me each night? How far people go for you when they are guilt-ridden! They'll do anything. I was capitalizing on her guilt without knowing how I was doing it or why it was working.

The next day I woke up to find that my father had bought me a big bag of diapers and a blue plastic cover for my mattress.

2

A week before that incident, I was facing a shelf full of chocolates while my father stood at the register with Agha Ali, the kind minimarket owner who always slipped me a bottle of Parsi Cola to drink whenever he'd see me playing and sweating on the streets. They were discussing the state of Agha Ali's Iranian-manufactured Samand that had been broken into the night before. Everything that could be disassembled and lifted, including the front seats, was stolen. Radio, engine, windshield wipers, the three mirrors and the Christmas tree shaped fragrance diffuser that was wrapped around the neck of the rearview mirror. Everything! The doors were keyed on the outside and slashed on the inside. The headlights were smashed. The wheels, all four, were punctured, but only after the thieves had rolled the car down the road and away from Agha Ali's house, where they could conduct their misconduct in peace. Agha Ali was distraught, shaking his head and pressing fingers into his temples, his voice rising only to reiterate his sentiments about the thieves who had violated his Samand, but also his personal take on what qualifies as fair punishment for thieves in Iran.

"Their noses should be cut off, so they can't sniff all that powder they are stealing cars to buy."

My father tried to console him, telling him that the police were looking for suspects and that one of his friends owned an auto body shop, and would give him a good deal on spare parts or a new used car if he wanted.

A packet of milk chocolate was torn open, with the pointy tip of a square chocolate bar peeping out of the shiny wrapping. I salivated, imagining a creamy lump melting on my tongue. All I did as the men talked was finish someone else's task: reaching my hand and pulling out of the delicate blue aluminum foil one cold tempting piece. But before I could hide it in my mouth, the two men suddenly jerked their heads at me with inquisitive stares. Four curious and embarrassed eyes floated before me. The eyes kept multiplying until everything in the store had eyes and was looking judgmentally at me. I froze, chocolate piece in hand, and hand midway to my gaped mouth.

"It was open Ammo Ali, *be Khuda* it was open."

My father cleared his throat and started breathing so loudly I could hear the air rustling in his lungs from where I stood. "Sheyda jan, we don't eat things until we've paid for them." he said, enunciating every syllable, trying to control his voice.

I looked at Agha Ali, who was both sympathetically smiling and straining to think of something to say.

My parents had once told me that, when people lied, their

foreheads turned bright red and the word 'Liar' appeared in neon-lights across it. From then on, I always let my hair loose, and hid my forehead behind a protective fringe that fell across my face, even when I had a scarf on.

"I didn't — " Without finishing the sentence I brushed the hair off with my fingers and yelled at them both, "Look. Look. I am not lying."

They just looked at one another, surprised, maybe a little amused by my melodramatic performance.

The piece of chocolate, which was starting to melt in my sweaty palm, free fell from my hand.

I calmly gazed down at my innocent loot, and saw it skittering into tiny sweet particles in all directions, like red hungry ants provoked by touch, carrying whatever they could and running away to hide under shelves, under dust carpets and deep into drains.

I wanted to hide, too. So I let myself freefall on top of it. Landing on my face without as much as an "Aw!", and lying still, only breathing, waiting for my father to go away, waiting to wake up from this stupidity, waiting for someone to walk into the shop and distract the two disappointed men long enough for me to slink out quietly and run home. I lay waiting to scatter into pieces and disappear.

Agha Ali and my father both rushed to me. Picking me up from both shoulders, Agha Ali said: "It's okay Sheyda Khanoom. It's okay azizam. You can take that chocolate you opened home with you. It's just a stupid piece of chocolate, my sweet child. In fact, take a couple extra, it's *Shabe Yalda* (Winter Solstice) and we can all do with more sweets at home."

My father turned me toward him to look at my face, wiping with his thumb two blood drops from my lower lip. And in the way horses are examined, he quickly parted my lips to check my gums and see if I had broken any teeth.

Seeing that I was okay, he let go of me.

I turned my face to the right then to the left, like a Muslim ending his prayers, first to look at Agha Ali who smiled weakly, carrying a chocolate bar in hand and waving it at me, then looking at my father who wasn't smiling at all.

I shouted in my father's ear: "*Be Khuda* it was open." Then stormed out of the shop, the tail of my scarf flying behind me. I waited at the corner of the street.

Suffice to say that he didn't believe me. The only thing my father told me, once he had caught up with me on the noisy road, was that if I were to ever take anything without permission again, he'd make sure I got adequately punished. We walked back home, me with a plastic full of chocolates and other items we didn't need but which my father's shame forced him to buy as an overcompensation for my bad behaviour.

"No place for thieves in our house, do you understand?" He shook my little frame in his hand as he helped me cross the street and jump over a water ditch.

What my father didn't explain, was whose permission I needed before taking things. Something my mother clarified after the black cat incident at Dr. Fereydoon's office.

But my stealing days are behind me. That's not what I am in prison for. That's not why they've arrested me. Sometimes I wonder why my parents never took my side on anything, especially my father who knew what it felt like to be constantly vilified, to be viewed time and again as the evildoer. But no, it was always strangers who stood up for me, who defended my intentions, who understood them and understood me. Maybe it's because these strangers never had to live with me, never had to survive the consequence of being my parents. They could go back home to their own peaceful families and tell their own well-behaved children stories about bad children like me, children who disobeyed God and their parents. They'd tell them what the future held for bad children who grew up into bad adults who stole cars and snuffed white but dirty powder.

It made me wonder if it is true what they say: that those who knew you best were those who saw you everyday, who lived with you, ate with you, travelled and prayed with you. My parents never understood me. That perhaps had always been my one true childhood pain. I wanted to be understood; I longed to be contained by those I loved most. And they longed for something else. They longed to be understood by each other and had no time for me. They longed to understand why and when and how, they wanted big answers to big questions. And I was the smallest question with no question mark at my end.

I went back home that day, and running to my bedroom and looking deep into the mirror, I saw a brown piece of chocolate on my forehead. My loot was stuck on my face the whole time we walked home. I tore the sticky piece off and put it in my mouth. I licked my fingers and wiped at the smudge slowly until my forehead turned red. I was marked. My father had already punished me. He had made a liar out of me.

I wonder now at the wisdom behind that event occurring on Shabe Yalda, the night when the Zoroastrian God of Truth *Mithra* was born. I wonder if the fact that it was the longest and darkest night of the year had any significance on the kind of person I would become.

These things, these little seemingly insignificant things, they linger. I really was forsaken.

3 ☾

They had taken my teddy bear away when they'd found me sitting on my bed with an oversized pair of scissors, cutting into its bottom and trying to shove my head — hoping that the rest of my body would eventually follow — into it. The initial hole between the legs was an accident of wear and tear and was not the result of my own doing, but the expansion in its diameter, admittedly, was an utterly premeditated and conscious effort. Earlier that week, my uncle Dariush had balanced me on his knee, and as I kept busy studying the anomaly of his walrus-moustache, he proceeded to dazzle me with the story of *Ḥayy ibn Yaqẓān*, the child of wilderness, who like Moses was tossed by his well-intending mother into a river that carried him to an uninhabited island. There, a gazelle that had lost her fawn adopted him, mothering him until she died when he was "just like you, seven years of age!" Driven by his curiosity and an early knack for science, Hayy performed, with pointed twigs and sharp stones, an autopsy on his mother, wondering why the heat of her body had left her, and why the gentle drumming in her chest had ceased. He then went on an autopsy spree around the island, comparing animals and plants to himself in an attempt to better understand death, the tangibility of his body and the intangibility of the soul, which he could not grasp ...

My uncle's story ended there, but the real story goes on to explain how Hayy grows into a life of pondering and spiritual evolution, and how after being rescued and taken back into the bosom of society, he finds himself disturbed and mind-boggled by people's intolerance of the mystical realizations which he had attained after a lifetime of solitude and scrutiny. He fails at understanding their irrational devotion to religious activities and teachings, teachings that he, out of concern for his fellow men, tries to stretch beyond the literal sense, only for them to grow impatient and hostile toward him. He contemplates the fallacy and exhibitionism of religious rituals compared to a life of inner harmony and a direct realization of truth. He decides to return to his island, where previously, and away from all the dogma of religion, he had established a more satisfying relationship with truth than he had among people who failed to understand that religion was a tool and nothing else.

Fascinating spiritual hokum, but at the time, the story of Hayy possessed me. And so, one night after losing the custody of my teddy bear to a locked closet, my father found me hovering over my sleeping mother with a pair of scissors, ready to cut her open, and a few weeks after that I was in Dr. Fereydoon's office.

In my defense: she slept without as much as a twitch, her body was cold, and when I pressed my ear to her heart, I heard absolutely nothing.

When I was a child, and it wasn't that long ago that I was, I used to look up into the sky — something I now don't have the luxury of doing — and think about God. I used to wonder why He had chosen to reveal Himself to *some* men and not to others. Weren't we all equal in His eyes? And if it is true that He had endowed His prophets with a pool of virtues inaccessible, unattainable by the rest, then why had He *chosen them* for such curse or honour? He created them special and then seemed to reward them for it.

We were taught these magical fables in school, and I'd sit in class mesmerized with a hand cupping my chin and with eyes fixed on my teacher's lips, picturing the lives of these remarkable holy men — men, they were always men, I failed to notice at the time — who each seemed to have survived a childhood that struck me as strange: they were all misfits who were orphaned, unwanted, abandoned or betrayed; they were the misunderstood owners of hearts that seethed with wisdom and time that was consumed alone, in dreams or deep in meditation. They were also, initially, or eventually, dismissed as mad.

God seemed to favour loners; I thought that God surely empathized because Gods too could be lonely. And the minute I heard that story of Hayy, a thousand knots untangled in my stomach and a rope shot from my head toward the sky and connected me to all those great souls. I was one of them. I was certain that my time too would come. I was certain that God had big plans for me. My suffering was for a reason and the agony of my childhood, that exquisite sense of loss that never left me, had a purpose that would appear like a whale and retch me into the yellow arms of a shore. I was Hayy and the gobbled-up Jonas; I was Joseph wrapped in the darkened echo of a well.

When on a trip to the North, my father had driven us to the shores of the Caspian, I had tossed myself scarfed and fully-clothed into the sea, and made my way through the waves on slippery weeds and rocks that kept calling my name and pulling me toward them. The water ebbed and flowed between my feet and the plastic of my red slippers until the sea withdrew and sank them like red twin boats as I helplessly watched, and the sandy bottom fled through my toes as I splashed with the frail arms of a nine-year-old the heavy waves that hit me.

My father was busy fishing, and my mother had returned to the car to bring more sandwiches and a second flask of chai. I wanted to prove my theory and conviction, that if in the midst of drowning I prayed to God, then He would rescue me just like He had rescued the kindred souls that preceded my birth. He would send His angels to lift me, or the waves would part and a big smiling whale would open his mouth and bid me enter in his belly. The whale would call me his Sheyda soup, but he'd wink at me and let me know with an affable but moral tone that it's all just a story, a little lesson. He'd tell me that he was God's obedient servant and that I was really special. And then, when everyone gave up, when the search for my body faded and my parents' tears dried on their cheeks, when dark crescents appeared beneath their hollow eyes, the whale would spit me back to safety and wave a fin as he swam away.

There was no time for any whales to be divinely summoned, but I did have time to swallow enough water and have a quick little prayer as my legs gave way and as I slipped below the waterline. The sky blurred, the waves turned a page on my existence and I blew a shoal of white bubbles. I drifted into the bottom. It was very quiet inside, peaceful. I was deep in the sodden pockets of the Caspian. But my prayer was hastily answered when a fisherman, who had seen me thrashing in the water then disappearing under it, grabbed the hem of my blouse and dragged me out.

Back with functioning lungs and reacquainted with air, he started panting and shouting. I was both coughing and sucking air in. He carried me on his shoulder and called to my father who, thigh-deep in water and terrified, threw his fishing rod and leapt toward us, pushing against the waves with the rest of his body. I wrapped my little arms around the fisherman's neck, smelling the saltiness of the sea and tasting the oiliness of his wet hair. I looked at the horizon where two blues merged and kissed, and then gazed up into the sky, and knowing that God had heard me, I closed my eyes and smiled.

After wrapping me in some of my father's clothes and leaving my own to dry in the sun, my mother held me for a long time in the car. All four doors were open and we sat in the backseat, with my head resting on my mother's heart, and her cheek resting on my moist hair. I was shivering and had to beg them not to end our picnic, promising that I wouldn't go near the sea again. Instead, I was sternly instructed to sit by my father's bucket and guard the fish he had caught. I sat crying and giving them CPR, carrying each at a time in my hands, mesmerized by their rainbow scales and how, held up to the setting sun they sparkled light blue, yellow and purple.

I urgently breathed carbon dioxide back through their puckered lips, thinking that I was doing them a favour, and feeling invigorated by my act of kindness and tickled at the way they blew up like balloons with my breath, their eyes open wide. Finally I couldn't take it anymore, and the minute my father walked away, I carried the bucket to the sea with my mother shouting after me, hobbling under the weight of five fish, which one by one I hurled into the broken waves, after kissing each and whispering a very sincere "Thank you" to the last. They slapped the face of the water then twisted back to life. Happily, I kicked the bucket with my foot and returned with a bleeding toe to my father to get spanked for throwing dinner and three-hours' worth of effort away.

My father built a large fire, and we ended up eating two bags of chips dipped in sweet garlic yoghurt (*Mast o Mosier*). The family that had parked near us joined, and a couple of local fishermen, including the one who was God-sent, were invited and sat around the fire sharing morsels of their food. I refused to touch anything. My mother later passed tiny paper cups around, and then continued to pour steaming golden chai into them. She added a quarter of cold water into mine and I sat blowing on it until it cooled. The happy sounds of laughter rose, and in no time my almost-drowning in the Caspian seemed like it had never been. Jokes were told and laughed at, and family histories were shared over ripe figs and juicy crescents of watermelon, and when the fishermen attempted to tell mythical stories of mermaids and mermen kidnapping children back into their underwater kingdoms, my father had to motion to them not to because "the little one takes these stories too seriously."

The fire was extinguished, and everyone gathered their belongings to go back to their rented rooms in the local villas where they slept on carpets and foam mattresses in the homes of benevolent strangers, and where they squatted to uncomfortably defecate in the ominous holes in the ground that swallowed their keys and coins, then with focused wrists and with the hopes of not wetting their clothes, they carefully aimed water hoses at their bottoms and longed for the comfort of their secular French-made bidets at home.

The fishermen took my parents away to the shore to show them "the sea worms that glowed like water fireflies." I stayed in my place, waiting for them, listening to the distant sounds of howling dogs and looking up at the sky where I saw the silver of a half moon, and I knew then, that God was peeping at us through the sky's keyhole. For many years that followed, whenever in life I had searched the sky and failed to spot the mottled moon, I slept troubled, knowing that God was busy saving lives, or broken, He had simply pulled a pillow over His head and gone to sleep, because He didn't want to hear all the hateful noise we made.

Darkness draped her velvet veils on everything. Not a star was in sight. The wind blew night's secrets away as the crickets sang then hushed, covering us in a cloak of silence. We walked back to our car beneath the trees, the rescued bucket squeaking in the sunburned arm of my father. Only its old noise guided my path. I held my open palm inches away from my face and couldn't see a thing. Frightened of that annihilating darkness, I faced the moon and sea again. And only then could I see everything. With clarity and for the first time, I saw it all.

I wanted to be loved. I wanted to be loved. To fade in the night's embrace, to be held, to merge with a beloved in the same faithful way sky and sea had. We are as young as our innocence and as old as our sorrows. I am lost in a game of numbers, in years piling to suffocate me and wounds exposed to dry in the sun. But I am stuck, chained to the shadows, and the slits on my soul refuse to heal. The maggots of my past refuse to leave me. Hungry, they eat away.

Though I've since been to the Caspian a hundred times, none replaced the memory of that trip. Never again did I stick my torso out of the rolled-down window in the backseat of our car, listening and singing along to the sad legendary voice of Hayedeh who sang about what a miracle love was, constantly asking my mother to press the rewind button whenever the song *Aroosak* (Doll) finished. I'd thrust myself out of the window, open my mouth and scream the lyrics, my scarf ballooning on my head just like the bodies of the saved fish. The car drove through the cascading wilderness of the mountain forests, my teary eyes reflecting their deep green, the flying wind making it difficult for me to breathe, flapping in my ears, cool on my tongue, and crying, touched by the music, feeling helpless about the permanent winter in Hayedeh's heart, the bitterness she tasted, fully understanding the sorrow of her heart-broken abandoned doll, who like me had a thousand tears in her eyes. And holding tightly to the barely-protruding edge of the window, I'd look at my mother's face in the side-view mirror, the wind drying my tears, and I'd remember what she looked like when she was happy. Then sticking my body inside to search my father's face, I'd find that he too bore the shadow of a smile as he vacantly smoked his cigarette and steered the wheel with one hand. As soon as the song finished, I'd lean to rewind the tape again, and my father would ask: "Why do you keep replaying it if it makes you so sad?"

And kissing his cheek and then my mother's I'd say: "It's not making me sad. It's the most beautiful song I've ever heard."

We'd stop by the roadside to stretch our bodies, or park in misty forests for meals, and my father — to maintain the coolness of our Parsi Cola and minted yoghurt drink — would lodge the plastic bottles between big rocks under the frigid gush of a river, and dip his bare legs inside, his trousers furled up to his knees and his socks rolled into his shoes and placed carefully in his lap. He'd call me whenever he spotted a water snake or a red-tailed bird, and whenever the need to pee arose, he held his jacket up for me as I crouched behind a bush and released myself, burning a wet hole into the mud and fumbling with branches and colourful flower-petals as I did. At lunch time, I'd sit by my mother washing vegetables in a yellow bucket, and I'd watch the maroon almonds of her nails as she speared the shish kebab on skewers, punctuating the herbed meat with tomatoes, onions and the sour mouth-watering bulbs that dropped from our lemon tree.

We were happy, for three days, the three of us were really happy.

4 🍂

When nothing else seemed to work, when no one could tell my parents what was wrong with me, my mother resorted to God. God was her safety net, God and those porcelain angels. My mother the idolater, with her disco days, and her black as night temptress eyes! While her moth-eaten pink retro dress in the cupboard collected dust with the rest of her 70's wardrobe, she went on pilgrimages to shrines and holy sites, and determinedly took me with her, as if on a mission to have me blessed or exorcised.

It didn't work.

We went to Tajrish, to the shrine of Imam Zadeh Saleh,

where at the gates we left our shoes with a lady who placed them in square green lockers, and where my mother picked out, from a big pile of different coloured and different sized fabrics, a long flowery piece of cloth which she wrapped around herself like a chador, clipping it at her heart with two slender fingers.

"*Nazr mikonam barat Sheyda jan*," my mother said. "If God answers my prayers, I will on your behalf give something in return. You just sit still and read some Qur'an."

All I could think of was the poor lady whose job was to collect smelly shoes.

The prayers of many people were answered it seemed, as several stopped us as we walked, offering boxes of pistachio-stuffed biscuits, palm dates, and large blue and white bags of salt. My mother thanked the generous conferrers piously and I, carrying the delicious goods, parroted her words and actions, covering my face with the light scarf I wore, and moving my head in a devout submissive manner. My mother spent a long time praying; I spent a longer time pretending to pray, pretending to know what I was doing and what it was that I was meant to ask God for. I missed God, told Him that I wished that I could see Him, that I wished that He would make my parents happy.

I felt the need for a good sob because my cheeks burnt and my heart banged loudly in its cage. It wanted to break free from all of this, free from the sadness, and free from God Himself. I wanted to sleep on the floor, with my cheek pressed on the cool marble and just listen to my heart sleep. I felt like suffocating, watching my mother stand bend and kneel, then prostrate, muttering the same Arabic verses we memorized without understanding in school, repeating them time and time again and hearing the white beads which collared her wrist being quickly, desperately thumped. When she had finished, I looked up at her face and saw that she was crying. I wanted to get out of that sad repressive place as quickly as possible.

Everyone looked miserable; everyone was praying for a miracle, for guidance or for a blessing. Mothers prayed for the safe return of their husbands and children; girls prayed for everlasting love; daughter-in-laws prayed for an early death to claim their in-laws; spinsters prayed for their knights in shining armour; young men prayed for a way out of Iran; the elderly prayed for the fountain of youth; greedy toothless men prayed for second wives; rich men prayed for their health; and the poor prayed for money.

Everyone went there with a story to tell God, raising their voices in a unified Amen. Everyone prayed for God to intervene, to cast one look, just one look at their miserable lives and to have pity because they themselves could do no more, and because no one else had pitied them. Prayer is an act of desperation. It precedes suicide. It can lead to it. They should all be in therapy.

The highpoint of my journey to Tajrish was walking through the snaking bazaars in which, gold chains and heart and butterfly shaped pendants sparkled from behind the glossy fronts of stores, and where pink and blue shower Luffas were painlessly pinned on the walls. Wigs of different colours were balanced on the heads of beheaded mannequins, and inside the lingerie shops, lacy red panties, sexy push-up bras and garter belts covered the rest of their misplaced and severed bodies.

I asked my mother why was it that mannequins were allowed to dress like that. She told me that they were free to do as they pleased because they had died a long time ago. Their bodies were permanently disfigured so as not to resemble that of a woman; otherwise, they too would have been piled up and driven away in vans. Death in our family was almost always spoken of in the context of release and freedom.

"If you were a mannequin," I wanted to tell my mother, "then you too could dress like that." But my thoughts drowned in the murky pool of the crowds. We meandered through the tight darkened streets, listening to the evening call of prayer break off a gathering of pigeons and sending them fluttering loudly into a dimmed smoky space. We smiled, our dark eyes brightening as a string of orange lights strung on trees, roof-tops and on walls all around us came to life, adding a strange sensual hue to everything, and lighting shadowy corners that reeked of stale rainwater and phlegm. The strawberries were the size of mangoes and their bright color was that of diluted blood, and long and rounded jars of pickled turnip, olives and red peppers were lined-up for exhibition, and strangled above them was a collection of rotund dry limes the colour of sand.

When my mother stood to buy my father some peanuts, the vendor put some cashews in my palm and asked me about my name. I answered him, then stuffed the cashews in my mouth, chewed on their smooth saltiness and tasted the strug-gle of his days, the nagging of his wife, the tears of his children and his devotion to his prayer rug. Slippers and trinkets and toys and flags and cinnamon and saffron and promises and guarantees and discounts and buy one get the other free and the white fuzz of cotton candy that looked like edible aristo-cratic wigs and pale yellow oval talismans with the inscribed names of both you and your mother, and birthstones, each with a colour and texture that said something about you and your life. I am an Aries, I am the Crystal Clear diamond of April; and I am supposed to be innocent. My mother laughed with no amusement and rushed us out of the shop.

At the entrance of the Bazaar, as we started back to the square, a man standing over a wooden box filled with various green leaves was shouting: "Butterflies for sale, for sale, but-terflies." My hand slipped from the grip of my mother's and I ran to him to find an army of caterpillars, striped like zebra crossing, black white and yellow. My eyes widened. "Butter-flies?" He smiled at my apprehension. "Do you want one darling? You just have to feed them and soon enough they'll become butterflies. I promise you." Seeing that I was still scared and too mesmerized by the crawling creatures, he lifted a long leaf that was punctured with caterpillar bites, and let a bored caterpil-lar with its many tiny feet crawl onto his finger, which he then brought near my face. I shrieked and held onto the long man-teau of the woman standing beside me, and then looking up, sighed upon realizing that it belonged to my mother. She was smiling. When he saw that my mother didn't mind, the man continued to move his hand back and forth, enjoying my laugh-ter and the terrified sounds I was making, which admittedly I exaggerated, having been caught in the moment and enjoying the smiles and the pleased glances people passing by were giving me.

"Do you want one darling? Here is one for free."

I started clapping, but my mother, becoming suddenly pale, said no. There's no one to take care of it. Let's go.

Now.

"*Khanoom*, it will take care of itself, just put some leaves and water in a jar."

No.

I stomped the ground, fell and started crying, the heaviness of the day pouring out of me. I only stopped when a compromise was reached. He instructed me to open my palm, and nudging the caterpillar with another leaf, we watched as it slowly, la-boriously, twisted like a comma and exchanged fingers.

"A butterfly, it's a butterfly my little girl." He glanced up at my mother and smiled.

My father, who had dropped us in Tajrish square, said that he'd return to pick us up, so we crossed the bridge to the main street to wait for him. The dark river as if late for something was running loudly underneath us. I wanted to kneel over the stone walls, like my mother had knelt in prayer an hour before, and listen to the river pulsate through the shivering night, offering life to a city with no memories. I wanted it to wash my memories away, to soap me clean, then turn me around and wash me again. I wanted it to smack me thrice on my back, heavily, and make me cough out my imagination and all the other things that made my mother sad, like a piece of bread that had lost its way. My mother was racing her own breath, the air wheezing through her nose, talking to me or to herself, repeating in anger while stealing quick and nervous glances over her shoulders: "Where is your father? Why is he late? Why is he never with me? I am — "

I started singing, the memory of the caterpillar's soft legs still fresh in the landscape of my hand.

"That son of a bitch, that dirty son of a bitch slipped a finger in me," my mother whispered to the sorrowful river and whispered it again to the amnesiac night because I, her little one, was faraway dreaming.

Melodiously, obliviously I sang.

She took me on a less memorable pilgrimage to Mashhad in Northeastern Iran, where she cried at Imam Reza's mausoleum and prayed for my sanity and the salvation of my soul. It was my first and only trip on a train, a serpentine rusty old thing that in twenty-four hours drove us through four seasons of weather and panorama, from mountain peaks that wore like fedoras their white reflecting snow, to gold-rimmed flowers that glistened under the sun. Clouds that floated in clear skies, following our holy journey like clenched fists that suddenly tightened, and crushed crystals of rain which pelted the iron roof like bullets, before drifting, those pillows for sleepy drunken Gods, slowly and calmly drifting away from us. The vagrant autumn leaves left their homes on treetops and were blown into the train's eyes by a mellow gust, as if in mourning for things to come.

The shrine was crowded, with tides and tides of people teeming like ants in their underground realm. She led me by the hand through the many courts while I struggled to keep up with her fast pace as the blue and black chadors of women brushed against my cheeks and left in my nose the whiff of sweat and tears. I was always watching. I watched the lost confused eyes of other children, who snot-faced and wanting to be somewhere else shook their heads at me in silence, a language we understood. I watched as the hairy-ringed fingers of men scratched their crotches, and as their white and yellowing shirts towering above me came between me and the light.

The light that was golden. Golden minarets and a golden dome right above the gold-fringed tomb, the sacred tomb of Imam Reza, the man for whom grateful gazelles wept, and before his poisoning with grapes, ominously banged their hoofs, because he had once saved one of their kind from the cruelty and arrows of one of his own. We treaded on cold marble, like millions had done before us, and inside the mosque warmed our feet on the expensive carpets where people slept and prayed and waited for miracles, and all the while the heavy stink of shoeless socked feet surrounded us from all directions. Once we were in, I gazed up at the chandeliers that sparkled like diamonds, my birthstones. Within those Turkish-blue walls decorated with Arabic calligraphy, religious men had called the Shah's father *The New Yezid* and days later had met their death.

On our way out of the shrine, an armless beggar masquerading as a holy man with a mat on the floor blessed me and asked my mother for payment. My mother dug into her bag, and retrieving her purse, pulled out all the paper money she had, thrusting the crumpled wad into the only hand the old beggar owned. Coins jingled in my mother's purse, she unzipped it and pulling a 100 *rial* coin and flipping it to tails, she pointed at the depiction with one finger and said to me urgently: "This is where we are, can you see it?" She then moved my face toward the mausoleum and holding the coin up she juxtaposed the two. "Can you see it now?" She shook me.

"Yes," I said, my nose dripping.

She then turned her purse upside down and emptied it onto the beggar's beaming mat.

The coins dropped on top of one another, chinking: *ding, ding ding.*

"A blessing is a priceless thing ...," the beggar crooned.

CHAPTER THREE

1 ⟨⟨

FOR ONE WHOLE week after my arrest, no one but Dr. Fereydoon visited me in jail. But unexpectedly, uncle Dariush and
his son Navid showed up and asked to see me. Up until then,
those three had been my sole visitors. But I tried not to take
things too personally; I knew very few people to begin with;
few among them liked me before any of this had transpired;
and fewer among them still would have wanted to spend any
time away from their blissfully-ignorant homes visiting a mur-
deress. Uncle Dariush's wife, Hilla, was too afraid to come,
but of course his excuse was that she was out of town. Out of
town where, he didn't say and that was how I knew that he
was lying. Uncle Dariush was the type of man who always
volunteered information, even irrelevant information. He was
as transparent as a soaked white shirt. His honesty was both
his vice and virtue, a man of many friends, and just as many
enemies. Frankly, I don't understand how he has managed to
outlive my father, how he is managing to outlive me, considering his unapologetic outspokenness and his passionate con-
tentious opinions, his secularism and hatred for all things
Arab and Islamic.

"My Holy Trinity is dead," he used to tell me. "God, the Shah
and the Country." When he said few words, or toiled to pick
his words like fleas out of thick coarse hair, that was when I
knew that something was wrong, unnatural. I was upset when

I didn't see his wife with him. After all, I had, throughout my childhood, felt particularly close to her, having spent many days playing with Navid whenever they had visited our house, chasing him around the garden with a hose and sprinkling water on the curly but meticulously gelled hair he took so seriously.

After complaining to my mother, and untangling his black mane then reapplying gel, Navid would soak a towel and chase me around the garden, twirling it in his hands and noisily slapping my bottom as I tried to keep my balance and run at the same time. Tiny cold splutters would fly in the air, glittering in the sun like the jewels of a crushed pomegranate, then land on my face and drip along my legs to reach my feet. Frequently, I'd slip into the full pond, hitting my head on the stone angel as I did, and then climb out to his satisfied fits of laughter, dazed, soaked and in tears, with green leaves and drowned wasps stuck on my clothes. I'd topple over flowerpots or flip, head first over the rails, and then his mother would come and haul him scowling by the ear inside, where she sometimes smacked him, and made him sit like a gentleman between her and my uncle for the rest of their visit. The few times he had attempted an explanation, complaining to his mother about the many hours he had spent in vain in front of the mirror, his mother would twist his ear harder and tell him: "You are two years older than she is, and you should never, ever hit a girl."

There was something very delicious about watching Navid get hit. I doubt very much that this peculiar sadism of mine was directed at Navid himself, because I have nothing against the poor lad, who during our childhood suffered at my impish hands just as much as I had at his. The source for my joy and gratification expands to include all creatures of the male species, and goes deeper, much deeper than juvenile sadism or satisfied vengeance. My mixed fluctuating contempt for men is that of my mother, Eve again, not Arezoo.

Navid my cousin was my first kiss, the proof that love and violence always go hand in hand. You can only ever truly hurt those you love. You must love them first to hurt them, to damage them beyond any hope of recovery, and for your actions to burn and linger, they too must love you back. Love always bears its own punishment, carries it on its shoulder, like its twin brother.

Aunt Hilla always took my side, and that game of taking sides empowered me, made me proud to be a woman. Her absence had made no sense. What could I have possibly done to her? What did she have to fear? Her son and husband were present and I was in cuffs. A hundred eyes were on me, and besides, I only killed those I loved. And as sweet as aunt Hilla was, saying that I loved her would be a stretch. But she was close to my mother; maybe that's why she didn't come. Checking on me would have been a betrayal to her friend.

On the day of the visit, Navid sat quietly by his father. He didn't say a word, but simply nodded his head at his father's questions or shook it to dispel my answers. I don't know if he was shocked or just scared. Maybe he thought that he was dreaming, and his dream was slowly turning into a nightmare. He stared vacantly at the table between us as the words poured from my uncle's lips. He then put his hands in front of him and held the same entranced stare, as if he'd never seen his hands before, or a table or a chair. He moved his open palm back and forth to his face, and for a minute I thought that my darkness was contagious, and felt like advising him to wait until midnight, and to hold his hand up to the moon, which like a silver lamp would show him, just like it had once showed me, everything he needed to see.

Uncle Dariush asked me if I was okay.

Yes.

He asked me why I had done it and I told him that I simply had to.

Why?

Because things had got too much and because it was the right thing to do, the only thing left to do.

Are you lonely?

A little.

Are you afraid?

Of what?

Of what's going to happen to you.

Why, what's going to happen to me?

Well, you might be locked up forever, does that scare you?

Yes.

What about death, are you afraid of death?

No.

Do you regret it?

No.

Do you need anything?

Just a watch, a watch and a picture of the open sky!

A watch?!

And a picture of a cloudless sky!

He shook his head without saying a word, licked the rough hairs of his moustache, gestured to Navid and got up to leave. You take care, he finally told me. We will pray for you.

I wanted to tell him not to bother, but I didn't. My secular uncle wanted to pray for me. Now that was really something.

When, during the Iraq-Iran war, fathers and sons were torn from the bosoms of screaming women to defend the honour of our country, I remember my cousin Navid who was fourteen years old at the time hiding in our house, crying for days because the neighbourhood boys, the grimy dusty ones I always saw him playing with, were being dragged out of their homes at night to fight at the front. Knowing that his son's turn would surely come, uncle Dariush hastily purchased two one-way tickets to Syria for both Navid and Hilla, while he chose to stay behind to look after his little shop in the bazaar. He asked his wife to pray for him and pray for Iran at the Shrine of Sayidda Zeinab in Damascus. After nine months of being away she returned without having done the single thing her husband had asked her, saying: "I don't know how to pray anymore." To which uncle Dariush indifferently answered: "That's fine. We are past the stage of prayer, beyond being saved. Hilla jan, the Trinity is dead."

I expected more guests after the verdict was announced, but I haven't seen my uncle or Navid since that orphaned visit two weeks ago. I still didn't get a watch, or that elusive picture.

2 ⟞

The first ten days in prison were the most difficult, and it was during those infinite hours spent with frightened huddled bodies that I would have appreciated visits the most. There simply were far too many things to adjust to, and I do not mean hard mattresses and cold gray walls that wrote down your every breath and read them later to an audience on the other side. Nor do I mean the smell of guilt and innocence ground under the shivering dirty feet. It wasn't the limited space which made me cautiously stretch my arms and legs so as not to bump into any of the wretched beings that shared a living space with me. After all, I was a tender girl, tall but with delicate bones that like twigs could be snapped in half, and after witnessing the many fights between my parents, I was one practiced in the art of sleeping in tight, dark and uncomfortable places.

No, the reasons for my discomfort were altogether different.

It was a sort of a cultural adaptation process really, one that took you through the stages of honeymooning, culture shock, recovery and finally that sought-after, that craved stage of integration. I admit to having somewhat romanticized the idea of captivity. I thought that I'd fit right in with all the outlaws, the rebels, the misunderstood, the disgruntled and the lonely, but that's not what happened at all. The source of my culture shock was the strange company that shared a cell with me. And it was one of the few instances in my life when I felt scared, really scared, looking at women who had killed and stolen and then killed again, out of need, but not always. It was like looking at my face in the mirror. I saw in there what people on the outside must see when they look at me: desperation I think. What a deformed face it had!

There were skinny girls with flat inferior bottoms, and women who were obese with dangly mushy breasts that never sat together but fell sideways like unacquainted hills, with each nipple pointing in a different direction. There were also pretty ones, though life has taught me that no one is ever really ugly. There are simply those whose beauty was less extravagant, less loud, those whom you had to spend a few extra minutes on because God didn't bother to. You had to study their faces and search the depths of their eyes. That kind of beauty was my favourite; I always was one to enjoy a bit of a challenge, and that perhaps explains why my lovers ranged from the stop-and-stare stunning to the unfortunately homely. Sometimes beauty hid in deeper, farther places.

I discovered in prison that many of us Persians have sad … no, melancholic eyes. Our eyes are wretched because they reflect thousands of years of ruin and glory. Our eyes are not only doors to our souls but doors to the souls of our ancestors, their pride and disappointments, and they are keys to the souls of all those unborn Persians who'll one day dust our graves. I thought about my love, my Mustafa and my fixation on black eyes, and I realized how silly a fixation it was, considering that most Iranians had eyes that were as black as midnight's, or owned deep brown ones, like two stirred cups of tea that swirled round and round. Eyes that made you stand out of breath, simply glaring in patience for something to happen, or to stop happening.

We were all expected to wear chadors inside our cells; otherwise we would receive brutal kicks to our faces each time the bearded warden performed a surprise visit and found any of us uncovered. I was in a room with prostitutes and drug addicts, those were ruthless, almost killed me to get my socks. I shared an existence with expecting mothers with rotund bulges and impatient angry ones with sore breasts that dripped milk while their young and easily amused children played by their extended feet. There were a couple of political prisoners, activists or journalists, I don't know, but they were accused of the ambiguous crime of terrorism; the one right crime for every occasion, the one size fits all of political transgressions.

Political prisoners were the unfortunate recipients of "special" treatment. They were usually locked up together in different units, but occasionally, perhaps as punishment, they'd get transferred to our unit for a few days. Many disappeared within days of their arrival. Those who made it back alive were deformed beyond recognition, their heads bent out of shape like battered watermelons, and their black and purple nails fell off their swollen fingers like the dry scales on a turtle's shell. One of these ladies had gray short hair. She only came to life when she was dragged out of the cell, cursing and calling to God to see what His religious and practicing followers were doing to her. "God is dead," I wanted to call after her, "And we killed Him." But then I remembered that Nietzsche was also dead and that we were all going to die.

She would scream saying that the world knew about her, heard and read her story. She always returned empty, empty of voice, empty of struggle, and empty of hope. The teacups in her skull were empty. There was nothing in there, but a carved and noiseless suffering that ate away at her soul. She had nothing else to fear, the worst had passed, if only for the time being. Her city was ravished and the storm had moved on to her neighbours. She would just sit as far away from everyone as she could, settling in a corner, facing the wall and weeping silently, comforting the dark-pink swelled up face and her black contuses, hugging herself tightly with shivering arms. She looked like she needed someone to hold her, but she trusted no one and so soothed herself with an embrace from her own bruised arms.

She reminded me of my mother, the helpless fragile way in which she trembled, and though she was much older than I was, I wanted to mother her. I felt like wrapping my arms around her, and singing her to sleep, maybe my favourite lullaby. One day they took her and didn't bring her back. This was the only day when she left without an iota of a struggle. I don't want to think about what happened to her, to them, before dying. Being sprayed with bullets and then having a single one planted in your head was the easy part of the process. The hours of horror that preceded this were what most feared.

Every morning newspapers would be delivered, and there'd be a long list naming those who had been executed the day before. I never read anything.

Our guards too were women: young, ugly and pitiless. I never truly realized the extent of brutality women were capable of exhibiting, especially toward their own kind. I never grasped how they could tear at another woman's hair, knowing that it was the crown of her head, or how they could scar, with eighty perfectly-calculated lashes, the naked innocent backs. How they nonchalantly led women to their deaths or into dark interrogation rooms to be raped, munching on apples as they walked, and mocking their beseeching wails. Weren't they women themselves? Had their hearts turned to stone? Hadn't any of the prisoners reminded them of a distant aunt, a sister, a mother, of themselves? It felt like treason, they were doubly insulting, those slaps and kicks that came from women with vaginas, with developing milk-secreting breasts, with wombs and period cramps and fallopian tubes. How could we turn on each other? We were all victims in this country, in this world. All women, in or out of prison, victims of men and their men-Gods!

The prisoners would grow irrationally excited at the arrival of a new face. A new face meant a fresh reason to talk about old stories again, and they really enjoyed that, like hissing masochists uncovering their old infected and self-assuring wounds and orgasming with pleasure. Not that they needed an excuse to talk, as most of them seemed more than happy to speak to themselves, or to the sleeping ghosts on the frigid floor. Hearing their stories is what initially scared me; their stories made me feel like I didn't belong here either. Imprisoned all my life, I felt out of place in prison. It made no sense to me. Where exactly was my paradise? Where was that secret resting ground where I would finally lay my head and dream of no other place to be? Where was that comforting pillow that would imbibe my tears and sing them back? It took me a few days to remember that my place was out and away, not out of iron bars but out of flesh and ribs. And only then did my mind rest and forehead cool.

During the day, all we heard was the symphony of backs and feet being strapped and lashed, and the unbearable screams that ensued. The pauses were short-lived, mere seconds for the torture-weapons to swap hands and for the guards to catch their breaths, wipe the sweat off their brows and rub their exhausted muscles. Five times a day we heard the call to prayer, amplified by speakers in our cells, and five times a day tired and hungry women stood up to pray or to pretend to at least. Not once did I move, not even when a woman offered to teach me. "I know how to," I said to her. "I just don't want to. My Holy Trinity is dead."

There was a TV room that we were allowed to visit sometimes and a courtyard which had been locked since my arrival. I had no money to buy anything from the commissary. The sounds of heavy snoring, which the first night forbade my sleepy lids from shutting, later became background music to my nightmares, and whenever the snoring stopped, I felt the need to run my nails on the walls, scratching the back of a stony monster and shuddering in pain until the snoring broke out again and released me from silence. Silence that made me think, think about things that I had no right thinking about. Not after the deed was done. Silence is the real terror, it's the ultimate threat to your sanity. Silence is what forces you to stop looking at the world, and take a deeper look inside, at your rotting massacred soul, and at the ruin that life has made of you. You break the mirror and instead look with eyes rolled inward at your own lacerated face.

You long to hear sounds when you are in prison, you wish for tinnitus, mosquitoes buzzing, insults, clanking ringing sounds of iron doors being dragged open and shut, mice scuttling along under hairy flowery pillows and heavy mattresses, nibbling at socked feet, cockroaches whizzing their wings and flying in the blackness of the room, groping with their antennas and landing on faces and under smelly armpits where they sleep, and where they are usually found in the morning, squashed. Grumbling hungry stomachs, nasal sounds of mortals sleeping, sibilant hisses of sinners repenting, recovering from recurring nightmares, words, meaningless words like *sorry* and *didn't mean to* and *tomorrow*, meaningful words like *no* and *yes,* and *love.* That silence was the blanket we all dreaded but had to sleep under; it was the anticipated journey of a bullet to the back of your head. It was you, blind-folded and on your knees, waiting, waiting, waiting for that sound, for that gun to be clanked, for that trigger to be pulled.

One of the girls, a drug-addict around my age, who was being trialed for drowning her two young children and awaiting execution, told me that I would get used to it, the silence I mean.

Though she herself cried every night, she was right.

Looks can be so deceiving. This particular girl had the greenest most beautifully-determined eyes among us. I called her *Sabzi*: Greenery.

I thought a lot about Mustafa those first few days, and how, had he been alive, he would have visited. I am sure of it. He would limp in on his crutches, sit across the table and pull out his pipe, before looking around and hiding it in his pocket again. He would whisper to me his complaints about the glaring white neon lights in the waiting room. He would reach his hand across the table, and hold mine, for seconds, squeezing it hard to show me that he cared, that he understood. Mustafa who watered the dead and dying trees, Mustafa who taught me the meaning of my name, only he would have saved me, only he would have wanted to.

Life makes you do things, things that if you were dead you wouldn't ever consider doing. This is my ingenuous argument against life. *Life: it makes you do things.* That should be God's caveat, His one line of advertising. Right there is the summation of my philosophy. You *have* to do something. You can't just be, unless you want to escape and become austere, masking your escapism with another charlatanry of benign submission, esoteric veils and silly arguments about what a nothing this life is and what an everything God is; you have to *do* and as you do you are faced with choices, choices that have consequences, and sometimes, occasionally, quite often, you may not make the right ones. And that's when you have to pay. You always pay. One way or the other.

I think everyone should spend a few weeks in prison. It's as enlightening a place as any cave in Mecca or any silent meditative spot beneath the far outreaching arms of a Bodhi-Tree.

3 ◖

I don't want to give the false impression that the numbered days I had spent sharing a cell with other women were in any way a thing like I had expected. Nothing prepared me for what I had seen there. At first, the prostitutes hit me and took my blanket. They referred to me as the Crazy One. But soon after they got to know me a little, I was fondly renamed *Jendeh Khanoom*. According to the angry souls who picked that description for me, the term of endearment which meant Lady Whore, suited me perfectly, because according to them I was a polite whore with class and I was so well-mannered. They, in fact thought that I was the most well-mannered among them, excelling in the art of *taarouf* or the exaggerated self-deprecating politeness that Persians are so famous for, repeatedly saying, reason or no reason: "Thank you, you are too kind," "I beg your pardon," "But only after you" and "I am your sincere friend."

I was called Lady Whore so often that the guards finally picked up the name and started teasing me with it too, except that they would add my full name to it and bark Lady Whore Sheyda Porrouya before collapsing onto their backs in thighslapping laughter. Within three days, my real name had become so out of use that, when I was called Sheyda, it took me a few seconds to realize that I was the one being addressed. A few more weeks in here, I thought, and my whole identity would be annihilated. Maybe that's the point of incarceration: Erasing you from the world's memory and from your own memory in fragments, first your face, then your name, then your identity, until you realize that you never really existed in the first place. Who will mourn you then?

This issue about names reminds me of the time when one of my lovers had told me, as I lay my head on his naked shoulder, that in China, it was believed that for a person to fool his fate, the first step was to change his name, thus altering the luck attached to it. It was a scrambling of stars. Feel free to judge me, but a drowning woman will clutch at a straw. The process of tricking fate, according to the Chinese who have truly dreamt up a solution for every conceivable and relevant problem out there, was to choose a different name, no need to resort to legal bodies and make any legal modifications, but simply to choose one and have five hundred people use it to refer to you, calling it out loud to your face.

It took me ten weeks to find five hundred people who were kind or crazy enough to call me Beatrice, the name I had chosen for myself. The same lover had told me that I didn't look Persian enough, so we started, at my request, looking at ancient civilizations. I wasn't going to demote my status from a civilized Aryan with thousands of years' worth of history to some unknown inbred race. He suggested other nationalities: Greek, which I cringed at, thinking of that narcissistic homosexual buffoon, Alexander the drunk, Alexander the midget, the burner of books and cities. Egyptian, which amused me, and appealed to my extravagant senses of regal burials and which aligned nicely with my obsession with death, but which I wasn't dark-skinned enough to reasonably qualify for ... The

Indus Valley? My eyes were too big to be Tibetan and not big enough to be Indian. No. Roman, I said, Italian. I would be Beatrice the Florentine.

But anyway, some of the benefactors who had helped me with my name change were cleaning ladies and students in my high school. A few relatives succumbed to my nagging, making me, for several weeks, the butt for their jokes. But the vast majority were people on the streets, whom I had to stop and explain to that this was a literal matter of life or death. I picked the name Beatrice because books had been written for her, and poetry dedicated to her memory. Dante's Beatrice, Beatrice whose name meant *Voyager through Life*! I certainly felt like I was a voyager, a voyager with snipped wings. I wanted, like her, to be someone's saviour, it was a name with a great musicality to it, one that sounded so Shakespearean, that looked so pre-Raphaelite. I wanted to lead into heaven, to guide and get lost with my lover into its nine spheres. Of course, I was entirely ignorant at the time that Dante's Beatrice died, like I would very soon, in her twenties.

The name Lady Whore, while not my first choice, grew on me. And I began to really see it as a term of endearment, in a place where other women were being called far viler things. My first choice was *Shashoo* (bed wetter), because, well, it was true. After my first night in jail, I started wetting myself again.

Wicked wicked life, despicable slimy gutter, in or out of prison!

4 🍃

Hanging.

There are worse ways of dying than hanging. You could be stoned to death, or crushed in a car accident. You could fall;

surprise the world and tumble down a rooftop while removing snow off a satellite dish, or trip out of a window feeding a sparrow. You could be clearing your throat to cock, spreading your rainbow feathers, slip into a neighbour's garden and be strangled by a little girl. You could be dragged to the backside of this jail and shot, under the open sky while a wall of tiny incarcerated eyes you had spent time with watched from slits and barred crystalline squares. The last thing you hear could be the echoing whine of the bullet inside you, or possibly, the startled flapping of scared wings.

The best way is to die with your whole family. To all of you, just leave together. Snap out of existence toward the finish line like sprinters, charging with your arms flailing, grinning at the cameras. Though I must say that hanging in Iran can be just as despicable to watch, and no doubt to experience, as any stoning. I wonder if they are going to drop me and hear my neck snap and head separate the old-fashioned way or if they will winch me up on a crater, strangling me by the neck like a stray dog and watch me suffocate from my own resurrected desire to live, to break free. Justice Will Be Served!

I prefer the second for two reasons. First, it is fair. And second, I want to be beamed up into the sky, like Jesus and unlike Judas, who rustled shamefully with the tree that held him. I want the horizon to be the last thing I see. Let them winch me up. It's more a testament to my belief and to their cruelty. I'll submit to my destiny without a struggle. I will show them.

I don't like surprises. At least I know how and when. How many people have that luxury?

I realized last night that, for an atheist, I use the word God a lot. Perhaps I am an agnostic, but who cares? Don't get me wrong, I am not getting soft in here. Jail is not changing my convictions. I am not reverting to the wishful-thinking ways of my childhood. Imprisonment is not affecting my sanity in the same way it has affected some of the other sinners in here, whom I've seen sitting for hours thumping beads and reciting from their Holy Books. The truth of the matter is that I don't think I am a sinner at all. I have been sinned against. Dismiss the G word as a bad habit, a very bad habit, one that's almost built in my DNA; that I more or less picked up before my birth, like a child smoking simply because his mother had puffed away while he swelled in her belly. It's in my blood you see.

To tell you the truth, and just for the sake of clarification, because I know that once I am dead, everything will be taken out of context, not that being alive makes that much of a difference but still: it's not that I don't believe in God, it's simply that I doubt His kindness. I am suspicious of His motives. There is no logical (or illogical for that matter) evidence to prove that God truly is who He claims to be, or what His followers claim Him to be: omniscient, all-hearing, merciful... In fact, all evidence points in the opposite direction.

I remember how a long time ago, there hung on the wall of Dr. Fereydoon's office a beautiful piece of carved wood. Inscribed on it in English were the words 'In God We Trust'. And each time I read it as a child, I had wondered why the sensible doctor displayed such a misspelled piece of art for all to see. Finally, growing impatient, I pointed out to my mother that there needed be double O's for the sentence to be correct, "In Good We Trust," I said. And that's when with a smile, she taught me that Good and God were one and the same, just spelled differently.

I look around me in this humid mouldy cell where even insects which should be thriving in such filth are suffering, and I wonder about God's whereabouts.

God is redundant to me, that's all.

Two years ago, in an attempt to reconnect with the dear

almighty, I went to a Sufi circle. The event took place in an apartment that was overheated and overcrowded. The apartment itself, furnished only with bare necessities, was located on the third floor of a dilapidated building that seemed to reflect the asceticism of the Sufis dwelling inside. Removing my shoes at the door, I made my way, warily, into the dimly-lit stuffy seating area, fearful of being singled out and recognized for the cynical infidel I was by the unenlightened colours I emitted, my unholy energy or what other unnatural means by which the spiritual claim to gain access into the hearts of people. I sat between a row of many women who, leaning their backs on three walls, had already made themselves comfortable, fanning their sweaty faces with magazines like a harem of bored housewives perched on shiny red cushions.

There was no need for scarves to be worn as we were all women and indoors, but a few seemed adamant on hiding their hair, as if we were unknowingly in the presence of invisible religious spirits that carried the XY chromosome. Most women however sat unbuttoning their overcoats, loosening their scarves and sitting plainly with colourful V-neckline tops and tight skimpy jeans. The fourth wall was where the musicians stood, moving their legs and necks like restless horses and carrying, like full moons, their large pale traditional tambourines, and waiting patiently for the room to pack and the event to start.

On a horizontally long but short-legged table in the centre were edibles, such as soft palm dates, biscuits, dry figs, and boxes of *Sohan Asali* (pistachio-crusted honey toffee) that looked so tempting I had to get up and get some. All were brought in by people who, again, came to pray and give food away in exchange for answers. I felt embarrassed for being the only one to ignorantly walk in empty-handed and the only one to — on top of my apparent stinginess — greedily help myself to handfuls, even taking extra for my mother. So I left some money on the table, and retreated to my seat quietly trying to feign a look of modesty. Once I had settled in my corner, the elderly woman next to me told me with an amused fat chuckle that I didn't have to pay for the food I ate; it was free. I shook my head smiling and threw a fig in my mouth. Nothing is free.

I strained to control my thoughts, my hopes, and my un-religious fantasies, avoiding eye-contact and directing my nervous smiles to the walls to be picked up by all and by no one in particular, lest anyone be encouraged by my false display of friendliness to approach me for small talk. I tried so hard that I am certain I must have appeared constipated, because a few of the girls who were darting in and out filling teacups asked me with a concerned look if I was alright or needed anything. One pointed to the ladies' room without uttering a word.

Finally, a white-haired Sufi woman walked into the room, accompanied by three more who followed her reverently like a succession of seasons. All four were entirely dressed in white loose garments and everyone in the room stood up upon see-ing them and raised their voices with their salaams, shower-ing them with their incoherent blessings, praising God, His prophet, Ali and his son Hussein. The white-haired woman said some words of wisdom or poetry, about the heart being God's throne and love being the one true vehicle of ascension. She then led everyone in the room into an hour-long session of Remembrance, heavily repeating *Ya Hu*, the Divine pronoun of the Sufis, as her disciples whirled in front of her to the steady drumming of tambourines, and to throats suffocating with prayer and breathing. The musicians moved their in-struments above their heads as they tapped the translucent goatskin with their wrists and fingers. The rings and chains circling the wooden frame crisped our souls into a haunting, ritualistic dance, and in the darkened room, the dancers reeled with shut eyes and thirsty arms stretched out to heaven, *give us love Ya Hu, so we can in turn give it.*

The room vibrated with fatigue, the fatigue of this life, the fatigue of always wanting. It swelled with longing, for answers, for divine ears and for a truth to be out there somewhere. Women were chanting, shaking their heads like drunkards, tapping their hearts and crying, their tears burning permanent wrinkles on their drooping cheeks.

"Like pigeons, like white twirling pigeons." excited and through my tears, that was all I could say to the same woman who sat sobbing beside me, as the dancers whirled me and my pain into a delicious state of oblivion.

"Everything whirls," said the Sufi woman in a defeated voice, looking in my direction as if she had heard me. "Everyone, everything!"

5 ✿

They had to separate me from the rest of the prisoners because of my crying. My bladder was crying, but so were my eyes, involuntarily and in my sleep.

There was no place for me to hide my crime, or hide from it. The first time I woke up at night to the realization of what I had done, I quietly turned the mattress around, sleeping soundly on its other side. By the third night it was entirely soaked, my urine leaving yellow sticky patches on the thin green carpet beneath the mattress. The sharp smell was accentuated by the lack of air circulation and the mustiness of unshaved armpits and unchanged garments. I longed for the blue plastic covering my father had bought me. I longed to be in my bed, far away, to be a child, free to pee without strangers hitting me.

The first few days, they whipped me, as if whipping would enhance the work of my bladder. I never gave them what they expected and wanted: a show of supplication and begging. That's why they flogged me harder. But when I took my punishment in silence and seemed to enjoy it too much, the guards, mortified and visibly shaken, stopped.

I limited my intake of liquids, yielding only when my body absolutely demanded it. I stopped drinking water. I would go for a couple of days without it, my body sustaining itself on the thick green lentil soup we had for lunch and the dry tomato sauce I licked off plastic plates. But somehow my bladder always found something to squeeze out of me. The inmates started complaining, not only from the smell, but because I'd pee so generously the spilled puddles usually extended to neighbouring beds. My gifts to that cell were the large dark carpet stains. But then the crying started, loud and desperate doleful crying that first angered the women then scared them. No normal human being made those noises. No woman. I was keening for my parents in my sleep, waking up each morning with both ends of my mattress soaked. They told me that I would sway in the dark, move my arms like a shot bird, turning in circles on the floor, face-down, bumping my head into the wall until I passed out. I'd remember none of it in the morning, but see the bruises. I'd see my nails on the floor, whole, dead, bloody. I started collecting them just as I had once collected marbles.

According to the testimony of dismayed eyewitnesses, I used to sing too, a modified rendition of that childhood nursery, Humpty Dumpty the creepy suicidal, replacing Humpty Dumpty with my name or that of my country: *Sheydanty, Iranty*. I was clearly, despite my being unconscious, very intent on getting the rhythm straight.

All the king's horses and all the king's men,
Couldn't put Iranty together again...
All the king's horses and all the king's men,
Couldn't put Sheydanty together again ...

It sounded like something uncle Dariush would appreciate.

Everyone within earshot was being deprived of sleep — guards, inmates, mice. At first the women complained, asked me to go out (where?), to get lost (where?), to shut up and drop dead (I tried both, alas!), anything. But then they stopped. They stopped calling me Lady Whore. They started sharing their food. They returned my stolen blanket, and even the now smelly and holed socks they had violently stripped off my feet.

Some held my hand when I slept, caressed my hair. And when I told them about my mother and why I had killed her, they tried to understand. Some of them laughed, and I knew that those had perfectly understood. One of them sang me lullabies, the same green-eyed girl who had killed her babies. This one called me a liar, she said: "You don't have it in you to kill." And I found it strange how much tenderness those criminals were capable of. We are all angels, misunderstood angels in an unfortunate world that's intolerant of wings and halos.

But they moved me anyway, to this luxurious cell, where I pace in small little steps, all day, waiting for my death or for any other visitor. I don't pee in my sleep anymore, despite drinking like a thirsty elephant. Dr. Vafa had told my parents once that there was little proof to support the argument that children wet themselves to get attention. There was, according to her, a genetic element to it. When she asked them if there were any problems at home that could justify my emotional stress, they said no and dropped the subject, never asking her or anyone about it again.

There is an attempt at a hole in the wall near my face by the bed. It's big enough to make me wonder if this had simply been laziness or thoughtfulness on the labourer's part, who simply couldn't be bothered putting all his effort into building a prison, or if anyone had naively tried to dig his or her way out of here. I try to imagine the people who had slept in this bed before me, all the restless breathing into this same hole, all scratching it with their fingers, wondering about who was desperate enough to first initiate a project of such magnitude, each prisoner adding to its width by every night placing a clenched fist inside.

My first night here I glued my ear to the wall, like I would to a conch shell, and from the strange dug wound in the wall I heard the soothing Caspian, calling my name and the names of strangers, whispering secrets, dreams and curses. I sat kneeling with my eyes shut, and listened. I giggled and some-times cried. The guard thought I was praying. I *was* praying, but not to his God, but to the spirits of all those who had passed before me. Will I be thought of in the same way when I am gone? I hope that no one ever sleeps in this bed again.

I had asked the guard, a male this time, to put me in a room with a view, just a window for me to look out of. Not that there was much to see beyond these walls, but I hungered for the sun. There was the great mountain that reminded me of train-rides to Mashhad, and there were a few dry trees that, like everyone, dreamt of being someplace else, witnessing hap-pier endings. He told me that unless I wanted to swallow a penis from both ends, I should stop acting like this was a five-star hotel. "*Jendeh Khanoom,*" he said with a wink.

How much evil can one swallow? I stopped talking alto-gether.

The white paint on the ceiling and all around cracked and fell, like the skin of a burnt witch. Sometimes, during the

night and in the light of something distant, shining through
a faraway window in the corridor, I'd see motes of white paint
peel themselves off and slowly descend, like flakes of dandruff
in a rush. Green and white tiles gave the cell the chilly abandoned feel of a bathroom. The toilet bowl made me want to
stick my head in it and retch a river of yesterdays and a map
of tomorrows.

They would have moved me here anyway, even if my tear
ducts and urinary tracts functioned perfectly. My execution
is in nine days. Why they are being so relaxed and unrushed
about it is something I don't understand. But they usually isolate
before killing. It's not too unlike sacrificing sheep really.

I am dying soon, so I suppose that I won't live to see the
final stage of cultural adaptation: integration. Well Sheyda,
worse things have happened in this world. Worse things are
still happening.

⤳ Chapter Four

1 ⚓

MY FATHER WAS a human winch.

On my first day in school, when I was asked the question "What does your father do?" that was the answer I gave, after an hour of violent sobbing, for being separated from said human winch.

"*Hammal,* dukhtarakam, *Hammal,*" my father corrected me with a chuckle, biting off the head of a carrot and lazily pointing the rest of it at my mother. "Arezoo, why aren't you teaching this girl anything?"

He then aimed the same orange wand at an invisible blackboard that floated somewhere before our eyes and drew letters in the air. I followed the wand with my eyes as it:

Circled the seahorse of my father's nose.
Drew a tear out of my mother's eyes.
Stood as erect as my menacing fingers.
Curved like the hook of a butcher.

"*Hammal;* your father is a labourer, a load lifter." he finally said.

He never in the least seemed to be embarrassed by that job. If anything my father was unreasonably proud. And as I later came to understand, he had good reasons to.

My father, Rustam, was the product of a working class family, perhaps a rung below working class, and yet, in an untraditional way one that was also entrepreneurial. The son of a fisherman from Rasht, a city by the Caspian, well-known for the sharp unforgiving intellect of its thrice-a-day fish-devouring inhabitants, and better known for its pretty green-eyed long-lashed women who make for good attentive wives. His mother wove straw hats and baskets which in summer she sold to the hordes of Tehrani tourists who fled the smoke-clouds of the city and the political turmoil that was chipping away at the rest of Iran. Tourists, who tunnelled through mountains of gray snow and plains of green tangles to reach the clear blue of the sea, and to spend long weeks with their families or hasty weekends of lust and wanton in the arms of their lovers. Though it wasn't her name, I used to call my granny Khorshid (Sun), because the straws which threaded her fingers resembled plaited sunrays.

Grandma Khorshid surveyed Rashti girls, trying to pick and reserve in advance local pretty ones that would make good wives for her sons, and even better daughter-in-laws for her and her husband. This she did years before any of her sons had even grown moustaches. Her hat and basket making business flourished, and soon she had enough money to swap her small stall in the street for a shop she rented and eventually bought. Her business expanded to include inflatable beach balls, floats, souvenirs, toilet mats, summery bags, pieces of fake jewellery that were occasionally mistaken for valuables, and regularly stolen by misinformed children and glamorous crows alike.

She also sold fluffy cotton-stuffed teddy bears and rag dolls (like my Laleh) which confused and curious sparrows used to peck holes in, and which wailing cats in heat made passionate love to before being chased away with curses and flying slippers. The nests of Rashti birds were filled with delicate April-coloured straws pulled out of the hats in my grandmother's shop.

On the rare occasions when business took a hiatus (in extreme and bad weather), she would offer to personally read futures in confused thick black patterns found in the small silver-rimmed Arabic coffee cups which she sold in overpriced sets of six, in addition of course to selling the black coffee grains that swirled inside them.

Her husband, upon realizing where the money was, put an end to his fishing days and remained by his wife's side, watching her run the show, playing second fiddle and settling for the small parts of sweeping, piling, lifting boxes and selling coffee.

She'd sit gazing at the mesmerizing brown bubbles that the settled coffee grains burped, then she'd watch as her clients sipped and swallowed their bitter thick drink, sucking their tongues and teeth as they finished and quickly turning the tiny cups upside down on the saucers.

"*Vey vey,*" she'd say, staring fox-eyed deep into the jumbled patterns of roadmaps and imagined faces, and then, with her wrinkly mouth and her purple-lipstick-stained teeth, the white hair she refused to dye messily tied with a thin ribbon at the back of her head, she'd add: "I see a man ... a dangerous man." She'd then be silent to inject the psychological element of suspense, and the group of girls surrounding her would reach for their throats and gasp, looking at each other then at the victim of this reading who would shake her head knowingly and sulk: "He's married, isn't he?"

"*Vey veyy,*" my granny would repeat solemnly, and take the story from there, using sounds to express herself; *Bah bah bah* to display pleasure in what the coffee Gods showed her, and invoking a different God or one of the Imams by inciting

Khuda Ya, Ya Ali or *ya Abulfazl* whenever disasters appeared in the murky cups.

In the heat of her small house, she'd sit sweating with her long colourful skirt pulled all the way up to her waist and rolled up into a bundle on her lap, airing her thighs. I remember her sport sneakers. Her skinny old legs in sport sneakers, like garden sticks in wide pots. And gray curly pubic hair sticking out from the edges of her green floral panties. I remember the smell, beneath the kitchen table where I chased ants and marbles on the floor and where she counted her money. The smell of moist body parts, of untouched triangles and the lust and longing of her fisherman husband, of swollen arthritic feet, of sweat traversing the back of her knees, racing to the finish line of her socks, the smell of rebellious womanhood, of once upon a time a girl, of forgotten femininity. I remember the smell.

God how I remember it!

She had a very large fan base of devoted divorced women, widows, and spinsters who sacrificed time and money they didn't have, and who gladly made a few detours especially to consult her. There were peak seasons, as my father had once explained to my mother, with every political upheaval, with every natural disaster, whenever war reared its head, whenever death loomed on the horizon, they'd come running to his mother, who would welcome them and the crispness of their Tehran-handled money, who would hug them when they sighed and who had a tissue ready to dab at their faces when hot tears fell.

They praised the accuracy of her clairvoyance, which always shocked more than surprised her, because it was all masterfully fabricated. Their compliments made her marvel at her own skill, even if that skill was a dishonesty to be ashamed of. But I suppose that, once you've lived to reach the age of seventy, life can become tediously repetitive, viciously predictable, like watching clusters of rain-clouds skidding sideways on the arena of a darkening heaven. The same faces, symbols, and meanings repetitively concealed then revealed, spitting snarls and blowing moist kisses at you.

Life becomes a soap opera with five-thousand episodes worth of déjà vus; where the same thing happens but to different generations of strangers who look awfully alike because of all the incestuous fucking of their ascendants. Sometimes she herself couldn't believe the nonsense she was telling, the nonsense that people received without a breath of questioning: every woman had a dark mysterious man in her cup, or a pale wench with an aquiline nose and an evil mole somewhere on her face, who was built like a bulldozer and plotting the woman's ruin. Different women would exclaim variations of the same thing: "Oh, my mother in-law!" Or: "Must be that peasant aunt of his who's trying to snare him for her daughter!" Every woman was hexed by a jealous friend or a rival, each was the victim of evil eye.

The fact that their lives were what they were because these women themselves were luckless creatures, doomed at birth, was something that none of them wanted to accept. They'd readily believe in the powers of magic and candle-burning, in the possibility of capturing love and breaking up marriages using menstrual blood and hair locks and burnt incense and cauterized pictures. They'd believe in unicorns and tittering leprechauns if they had to, but they would never, never believe that God had already handpicked their fates for them, that the book that held the secrets to their pleasure and wretchedness was already written, turned to its last page, read every night, and that God or luck, coincidence or the stars or whoever, whatever set the world to chaos, had already decided who gets born where and why.

Decisions, decisions!

My father used to talk about this and laugh, but let me tell you something: there is nothing funny about it. It is sad, the most tragic kind of sad. It is sad how in this country we are always searching for salvation, searching for someone to rescue us, and how we often look up at our captor, that divine prison ward, expecting salvation to be delivered by Him, He who has enslaved us. We invoke holy names; we flip through poetry books; we drink coffee we don't like — the bitter repressive religious coffee of our once-conquerors; we visit shrines and desperately hang onto the green and silver latticework that covers them.

We look in black eyes. Oh. We search for faces, we search in faces.

We drop notes into wells, and in cemeteries and at the tombs of our loved ones. We knock the pebbles of our burnt Empire on the sealed stony gates of their undergrounds, and there we cry our prayers, and ask them to please, *please*, deliver on our behalf, to please ask on our behalf, because by proximity, being dead means being closer, closer to that source, that source of salvation. It's not funny because hope is all we have, in this land of poverty, of opium and unemployment, of sin and theocracy, in this land of mullahs and naïve Shahs, of people who idolize their rulers then hate them, this mortally wounded land of traffic jams and secrets, salvation is the only thing to look forward to.

It's the most tragic kind of sad.

"*Dukhtarakam,* nothing to be sad about, it's black comedy, so tragic it's funny." my father explained.

They'd leave, offering grandma Khorshid urgent promises of word-of-mouth publicity and lavish presents upon the manifestation of favourable outcomes, and they'd drive away in their coughing sputtering cars with hopes that their problems would be solved, so that they'd never have to see her greedy face again. She'd wave coffee-stained fingertips and count the dirty money before tucking it in her bra, and pressing it on her creased brown skin, to sleep on hairy black nipples near her heart.

My granny was an expert at selling what people wanted, and when what people wanted was lies or half-truths, she was glad to deliver before anyone else could. A woman with no scruples when it came to making money, it was thanks to her, as my father always reminded us, that not only did we have a roof over our heads, but that we had the privilege of referring to ourselves as homeowners. It was her money that bought a house for each of her sons as a wedding gift. Uncle Dariush's house a mere ten-minute walk away from ours.

"You come from a line of storytellers." father had once told me.

He might have as well said a line of liars.

He spent his mornings fishing with his father, and then selling the slick creatures in the market to butchers or to people on the streets, who walking or with feet pressed lightly on the brakes of their deceasing cars and with heads stretched out of scrolled-down windows, would yell questions about his smelly merchandise. He'd fill buckets with clanking ice-cubes and sit with his fish under a wide white and yellow umbrella beneath the merciless sun. And on the emaciated spine of the umbrella, a carton-board sign displaying a badly-drawn downward-pointing arrow would read "*Mahi foroosh*".

When his mother's business boomed, he only fished for fun, or whenever they had craved barbequed fish with juicy slices of sour lemon. He would spend his afternoons with his older brother, my uncle Dariush, sitting on a large stool chatting with customers, swooning over city girls with their skinny bare legs and the ripe nipples that defiantly sprouted out of their sweaty tops like buds in springtime, pushing out of soil. Uncle Dariush joked with my mother, telling her once what a lothario her husband was as a young boy, running after girls, spellbound by the glow which the sun had left on their bright pink faces, wanting to lick humidity off their ankles, and wanting to gently suck the triangles of skin between their slender parted fingers.

"My mother had to tell him to stop scaring the poor women away," my uncle said laughing. "He was bad for business."

"Don't act so innocent, Dariush," said my father without looking too bothered, patting my uncle twice on his back. "Agha Dariush here, *masha'lla khodesh kheyli heez bood*, he didn't leave me anything, he had a new woman on his arm every week."

My mother whispered with a flushed face: "Don't speak like this in front of the child."

And so it was, that my father, who constantly dreamt of city girls, seized the first opportunity to go to Tehran when he got accepted into university there, finally breaking free from the stink of fish and imaginary futures. He shared a room with two young men who were sex-crazed and alcohol obsessed, and spent two years getting stoned and studying law, which he had to drop out of after impregnating my mother, for fear of scandal, and for wanting to do the honourable thing of marrying her, because — to the distress of my grandmother who tried her utmost to stop that nightmare of a wedding from materializing — he actually loved her.

They had to keep the pregnancy under wraps, so the wedding was a rushed improperly planned affair, an occasion that my maternal grandfather who abhorred my father refused to attend, and one where my embittered grandma Khorshid, who hated my mother for trapping her son using the oldest trick in the book, sat gravely with painted frozen eyebrows and a mouth sealed like a healing wound, refusing to talk to anyone.

Months later, the Islamic Revolution took place, and the universities were shut for two full years, rendering useless an entire generation of students, something that made my father feel better about himself, since everyone he knew was now with him on the same sinking ship, forcibly driven out of education, unemployed in a country that was falling apart. A year after my birth, when the war with Iraq broke, thousands of missiles fell on Tehran, digging thousands of graves, painting thousands of holes on stone and iron canvasses, burning thousands of fears and sounds into memories and carving hearts with brown and rusty blades that broke inside Iranian flesh and melted there.

We moved to Rasht where we lived, hidden for three years, because of the risk of my father being summoned to fight the Iraqis at the front. He *wanted* to fight for his country, side-by-side with all the young men who foamed at the mouth with patriotism, who picked up arms to put those Arabs back in place. He wanted to be one with those children of Zoroaster, the off-spring of Cyrus the Great: Persians, proud, superior and forever Persians. My parents were among the millions of Iranians who, dissatisfied with the way the Shah was running the country, had stood on rooftops at night shouting "*Allahu Akbar*". My night-club-going sinning parents shouted those religious words into an abyss that throbbed with desperation and echoed, chanting the Shah down. They supported the Islamic Revolution, and with blood they signed on the dotted line. They wanted change, change at any price, and that's what they got.

"*Allahu Akbar*," my mother shouted, with me wobbling in her belly, dreaming about a better future.

I always heard my father arguing passionately with uncle Dariush, whom he in private hypocritically referred to as *ghar-bzadegi* (Westoxified). "At least now," my father used to say, "our heads are bent to no one, we bow down to no one."

He always said it in a proud rasping voice that I felt was tinged with more self-consolation than truth.

But for the first and only time — to my father's surprise and slight relief — my mother and his took each other's side and begged him not to go to the front, harping on the strings of sympathy, because after the death of his father, who had passed from a heart attack, Rustam and Dariush were the only men our family had. "What if something, God forbid, happened to you? Who would take care of your wife and daughter?" said his mother, in her croaky old voice.

Though I have perfect recollections of my more recent visits to the North, I was too young to remember much about those three years we spent there. I have, for instance, retained random stills that very possibly may have been gleaned from the piles of photo albums stacked under my mother's bed and not from distant memories that exist in the compartments of my cluttered mind. I remember the sun shining on my face at a certain angle, like holding a piece of broken glass under the sun and watching rainbow colors scattering on your face, stinging with long sharp glints of yellow the irises of your eyes. I remember the sound of the Caspian that forever lives in me and ebbs and flows with my every breath. I remember the music of cone shells, whispering secrets about white men with machineguns and dark cold places where snow fell and covered everything even sorrow.

What I remember well enough to recount are the endless episodes of Caspian drama my mother, throughout her whole life together with my father, was insistent on reminding him of, such as: "When your mother said this to me ..." or "When she called our daughter ..." Whenever I had flipped through photo albums and looked at the pictures of my parents, I'd shut them quickly, feeling distressed enough to vomit the gold of elusive sand and fields of careless paddies, slippery weed on gray skull-shaped rocks, misty forests with green-reflecting waterfalls and a battalion of stars that were always scattered in those pictures with us. It was as if the regrets of my parents and their overwhelming grief seeped into me from the waxy archived pages of a past that haunted us like a devil that refused to be exorcised.

But he took solace in his job. He felt blessed to have had it. My father, the law school dropout was proud of a labourer's job because he believed in working his way up, his parents had shown him the way. The big house we lived in was a badge of honour. He didn't belong in the city, but the hard work of his parents had earned him a permanent spot there, and now his time too had come to prove himself, prove that he too could make something out of nothing for his wife and child.

My father had a labourer's body. Under shirts and rolled-up sleeves, his toned biceps tightened whenever, like a bag of wheat, he playfully lifted me to his back. A button would split, shooting under a couch, and I'd have to walk on all fours, groping without seeing, and pull it out, then toss it into the ceramic jar with the other buttons which like us, owners of the house, dreamt of seeing the light again. My father went through a series of small irrelevant jobs, until an old friend put in a good word and secured for him a modest clerical position in a chocolate factory. After the double pain of expensive dentist appointments and being forced to see his daughter endure the agonies of having three decayed teeth removed, he had to cut off the supply of chocolate, toffees and bubble gum he had made the habit of returning home with every day.

Rustam the fierce, after each fight with my mother, would look back at me crying and cowering behind a couch and tell me, before bolting out of the house without returning for days: *"Mamanet hamishe gardane mann ba pambe miborreh."*

Your mother always slits my throat with cotton.

I always felt that part of why my father had resented my mother was because she always got what she wanted from him in a way that can only be described as passive aggressive. The source of resentment was also partially her stopping him in his tracks, a twenty-two-year-old who still dreamt of women, success and money. It seemed that he was always cornered into making decisions. He never appeared to have a choice or a say about his life. It seemed that the only two choices he had made were loving and leaving: leaving Rasht and loving my mother. From there on, he was forced to leave his university, forced to marry early, forced to return into hiding, forced to become a father, forced to keep me and then live with me, accept and love me.

My father and I had one thing in common: like me, love had made him do things, stupid, silly and passionate things, things he wasn't sure of. But that's how love is, that's how love makes you: reckless, elevated, drunk with madness and folly. It traps you; it sets you free; it gambles with your mind, makes you chase shadows in a labyrinth; it sticks you into honey and offers you as a treat to ants and flies; it ties you to the tail of the devil, to the back of the wind; it flogs and flogs you, like a carpet in need of cleaning. Love is a shackle of heavy chains. You can never break free with your wings intact, with your head or your soul in place. You will always be in pieces.

Choice is a luxury, decisions, always decisions.

It's as good a time as any to mention now that my father died years later in a car crash. He died three months after being promoted to the position of a Distribution Manager, and after gifting himself a scooter, something he had always dreamt of owning as a youth. Riding it, he went far and fast into the oblivion that is death. He drove into that place, where no decisions needed to be made. Yes. Rustam rode his scooter, and two cars crashed them (him and his scooter) to pieces. The cars and their owners survived. I suppose you could say that my father died crushed. That's what my mom used to say anyway. He would have found it funny, poetic in the extreme. My father always loved the irony of life, even when he was its victim.

My father, who looked dapper, strong, proud in whatever he wore, who loved my mother but sometimes hit her, then cried then hit her some more, who parted his hair to one side of his head and gelled it like the school boy he never stopped being and the lawyer he never became, my father who was in a fight with the world, who always bought his cream-colored suits from mule-driven carts and took his tea with one small spoon of sugar, died crushed, like a pesky sad fly.

I laughed when the news was delivered. I laughed then fainted. Black comedy! Rustam, my father, always gave unforgettable lessons.

2 ✿

What more can I say about my mother? Perhaps I can start by saying that she died three times in one lifetime. The first was when I was born, the second, on her thirtieth birthday, and the last was when ...

Her death on her thirtieth birthday was metaphorical. Despite all the insanity, alienation and havoc my existence had wrecked in the lives of my parents, some forms of social normalcy once existed in our house. Birthdays, for instance, used to be joyous occasions, celebrated with family and a tight circle of friends (none of whom were mine). All until my mother turned thirty and realized that she wasn't satisfied with her life. Nor was she proud of what she had achieved, which was understandable, because, unless marrying a load lifter and bearing his unhinged child could be considered worthy achievements, my mother had accomplished nothing.

She decided that after thirty years of being alive she had accumulated too little: guilt, porcelain angels that couldn't save themselves let alone save a house, a wardrobe of useless yesteryear fashion and inanimate memories that rooted her to an Iran she wanted to both recover from and forget. So we stopped celebrating birthdays, not just hers but ours, too. The years started piling and no one was there to count them, no one to tear the numbers off calendars or blow the flames of unattained dreams, no one to taste the icing of our shame.

The last birthday I had celebrated was my tenth. My parents got me badminton racquets with the hope that I'd miraculously stay out of trouble, or alternatively, that I'd one day find someone worthy of friendship to play with. I disappointed them, but I did learn how to entertain myself, chasing the shuttlecock around the garden, and often striking it hard enough to send it flying over the stony walls, and depending on whose neighbour's house it fell in, I would either run wearing a scarf next door, and loudly with my slipper worn on my hand, bang at the gate and retrieve it from Mrs. Ghasemi, the lady with green fingers, or allow the concerned hens of Hajji Khanoom next door to peck at the dead feathers to their hearts' content.

My mother was twenty years old when she gave birth to me. As old as I am now! At the age of twenty my mother had lost her life; her selfishness ended so mine could start; and at the age of twenty my journey of self-interest was in its final stage. Except that I was leaving no prisoners behind.

On birthdays, my mother was extreme and extremely confused. She would spend the entire day in the kitchen stressfully cooking, sweat beading her forehead and moisture filming her eyes as she made a meal fit for kings. Saffron rice that made you hover around the pot like a dazed sprayed insect, just to catch satisfied whiffs and glimpses of the long yellow grains. Juicy soft lamb that melted in the mouth and which one could still taste long after the lump had disappeared. Stew with fried onions, split-peas and eggplants, all marinated in tomato sauce and seasoned with pepper and turmeric. Tomatoes sliced in half framing plates of roasted chicken. *Baghali Polow* with tender and buttered Lima beans served with yoghurt, and *Ash e Reshteh*, the thick noodle soup which was so filling my father always saved it for the end.

I'd sit by her side near the stove and watch her fingers quickly working, chop chop chopping the colourful ingredients that went into the salad before expertly tossing all in a bowl and squeezing on the delicious concoction the substance of a whole lemon. She would then give me the peel to sourly suck on, and try not to smile at how ridiculous I looked with my lemon-peel lips and watering eyes. Her hands moved on the chopping board as if to the rhythm of a war drum, horizontally and vertically, working at the vegetables with vengeance.

"I am sick and tired of cooking," she'd say. "Sick and tired."

The rich scents of the spices travelling deep into our nostrils, filling me with a desperate nostalgia for places I've never seen and times that no longer were. My mother would ask me to open my mouth, and then place on my salivating tongue a white salted piece of chicken, which I would ravenously chew on and urgently swallow before reopening my mouth like a greedy fledgling and waiting for her to notice me.

When the cooking was done, my mother hid the candles, the balloons, the paper lantern garlands, and the frilly glittery cone hats which I used to cover my mouth and nose with and run around the house beating my arms and screeching like a deformed extinct bird. And if my father returned home with cake, she refused to have any and just sat at the table with her face cupped in her palm, watching us eat with a mortified expression, as if we were feasting on her remains.

Unless my father wanted his gifts to my mother to be passed on to aunt Bahar, he had to carefully time when he offered them. The perfect time was three weeks before or after the day itself. Still, aunt Bahar's closet thrived at my father's expense. Any gift that was deemed too sentimental was quickly disposed of. My mother never stirred when my father gave her things; she never undid a frown, or stopped the corners of her mouth from drooping.

Somehow my mother's lips started looking like they had been super-glued to her face, and only later did we realize that this acquired pout, this new addition to her features, was simply life's gift to her on her 30th birthday. It took effort to neutralize, and a greater effort still to reverse or return life's gift. Whenever my father saw his gifts around my aunt's wrists, draped over her hair, spilled out of her bags, he would look at my mother, then back at me and under his breath whisper one word: "Ungrateful."

My last birthday gift to her was a miniature flower basket, filled with rounded colourful milk-chocolate pills produced by the same factory my father would one day work in. I haunted Agha Ali's minimarket until he took pity on me and gave me a bagful of them before sending me away. Not a single piece touched her lips, the basket with all its contents went into the glass-front cupboard, and there it should still be today, tempting the diabetic angels.

She acted the same way for our big days, except that, for us, she'd completely disappear into her room, leaving my father and me in the kitchen, eating what she had spent all day making. We would then pile the plates in the sink and go to bed, toothpicks in hand and with our full bellies jutting from beneath our blouses. And when we woke up in the morning we'd find the kitchen glowing, as if my mother, along with an army of helper-elves, toiled all night as we slept.

After a few years of this behaviour, my father stopped trying, and my mother stopped all types of preparation. All birthday festivities were completely annihilated in the Porrouya household.

I knew that her own mortality had finally dawned on her. That's why I never complained about not celebrating my birthday anymore. I was happy to be done with what I thought was a frightening ritual. One day the planets would shift and make me fall in hate with numbers, and I didn't want that. It always surprised me how it took some people *that* many years to be done with birthdays, to be done with celebrating a day which all my life I had perceived as a milestone to be mourned. It surprised and saddened me, witnessing hope being chased that far into the horizon, only to see it outrun those I loved every single time.

When my father died, I remember locking myself in the bathroom at night, calling out to him and waiting to hear his heavy footsteps behind the door and his fingers flicking the lights on and off and off and on again as I sat on the cold white tiles. I waited for one of two things to happen: for his voice to angrily boom with insults or for a monster to climb out of the bowl and flush me with a loud slurp deep into the earth's black gurgled throat before spitting me out of its other end. I was no longer a child, but I was sure that only a secret passageway that went through the gutter would lead to the other side just as one equally smelly must have led us here.

As ashamed as I am to admit it now, I tried to negotiate a deal with God, any God who listened, asking Him or Them to please let it be some other girl's father, a candid camera episode gone too far or a mistake on the hospital's part. I am not sure what I would have done differently had my father then returned to life, or what I would do if I was told today that I had one more hour to spend with him. I'd probably hold his hands for a very long time. I would hold his hands and appreciate the roughness of his palms, scathed by years of manual labour, of carrying things for other people. I'd hold them longer because they are no more. I'd ask him to lift me with his taut arms, and despite my long legs he'd let me climb on his muscular shoulders and move me around like a sack of grains. I knew my father. He was kind when I least expected him to be.

If I had one more day with my mother, I'd comb her hair for her, just as she had for so many years combed mine. The silver curly strands that the comb held on to would remain with the brush in a drawer in my room. I'd inhale deeply from her scent and lock it into my lungs. We'd both look far into the mirror, unafraid, me with my lost brown eyes and her with hers: black, angry and fragile. And if I saw her tears I'd bath in them, I'd gather them in my palm and perform my ablutions and pray. I'd drink them and anoint myself. If I had five more minutes with my mother I'd ask her: "Why? Why didn't you wait for me?"

I have been mourning my mother my whole life. She too did things when I least expected her to. My mother was brave.

Chapter Five

1 ✍

"IF GOD IS, as you claim Him to be, Merciful, or by all accounts Just and Understanding, then He, the dear almighty, would respect a person's choice of wanting to put an end to a story he has no interest in finishing. I dare say even, that He wouldn't at all be offended, if this gift of life is crumbled and tossed back in His divine face."

That's how, for many years, several of my high school classes began and ended: with me offering an opinion on God to any teacher who'd listen. I was seventeen years old, and in the eyes of almost everyone who knew me, emotionally unstable, a failed suicide, and a shameless heretic.

"What diatribe!" Ms. Marjan, my spinster of a teacher, scoffed. "What blasphemous philosophical rubbish! You might be allowed the freedom of speech within these walls, but don't go pushing your luck."

What she would have liked to tell me was that the gallows awaited people like me. That it was only a matter of time until I, like many people my age, swayed from a noose, to and fro, like the tireless weight of a pendulum, with the sad face of a ruined Persian landscape behind me, weeping for her children.

When Ms. Marjan wasn't accusing me of blasphemy or madness, she always referred to anything I said as a diatribe, a harangue. But neither one of us took offense because by then we had been accustomed to that little game we played, the game where she asked me for my opinions pretending to want to hear them, and where I made a genuine effort to reveal what I believed to be true, pretending that I did not know how she'd react.

What I appreciated about Ms. Marjan was her integrity — how she never, despite all that had happened, felt the need to disguise the contempt she had for me. She wasn't really winning the game of pretenses and I respected her for it. She would pretend to listen, but asking her to pretend to like what she heard was another story altogether.

"Where could you have possibly learnt to speak like this? Where would a girl your age get such horrible, horrible ideas from?"

"From life!" I said, moving my arms theatrically and smiling, "I am a student of life."

The girls in class giggled. The single scoff I heard came from the seat in front. That was where Ms. Marjan's pet student sat.

Nature always cared about me. Outside, raindrops started their southward pilgrimage. A few landed on my face through the metal bars of the open window. They affectionately marked my cheeks in the gentle way a kiss would. With the pink tip of my tongue, I licked a tiny fresh drop off the corner of my mouth. A sparrow fluttered on a branch, shook the rain water out of its tiny bulk, and collapsed a little neck to a puffed up breast the color of clouds. I could see that there were more under the leafy branches.

I swear they recognized me, the whole host of them. From the very beginning the birds and I had this strange affinity; I understood them, and they empathized with my struggle more than any one of my kind ever did. We used to share our lunch together. I used to spend recess watching them squabble for the bits of salted crackers and bread soggy with cheese and cucumber. I had to make different arrangements when the young cleaning lady begged me to stop because they shat all over the place, and salted crackers and bread soggy with cheese and cucumber bird-shit was apparently hard to clean. Eventually, I skipped lunch altogether, because it was rude to eat while others hungrily watched you nibbling at food that they themselves craved.

There in that class I was free to speak my mind. No one seemed to care. There, I was deaf to all things but rain. There, I had learnt that there exists a certain inverse correlation between headaches and pretenses: the more you pretend the fewer headaches you'll have. But you don't have to take my word for it; try it yourself. Next time someone yells at you, calls you crazy, perverse, demented and delusional nod your head and pretend to understand. Pretend to be sorry when you don't know what it is you did wrong and harmony will reign again.

When you don't want to retaliate and avenge a wounded ego — and by doing so only condemning your conscience to the nocturnal bites of guilt, pretend simply to be timid and let an insult slide and slip on the carved shell of your pride. People might think you are a coward, but if they are at all clever, they might suspect in you the budding signs of enlightenment. And if you are a woman living here, in this besieged country of poetry and pomegranates, pretend to agree with the Morality Police who pull you to the side in the malls and lecture you at length on the length of your *ropoosh* or the colour of your veil: 'Too seductive,' 'Too suggestive,' 'Not Islamic enough.' And I assure you that you won't spend the night in a cold cell with dead cockroaches for company, or an hour in a dark van pleading with thick eye-browed women to stop smacking you for answering them back.

"Why should death be feared? Suicide is your birthright." I remember saying with a heartbroken finality.

In the silence that followed, I heard the sleepy drizzle of raindrops on the trees outside, and in my mind I heard the words my mother had given me that morning: "Daughter, on your way back, don't forget to buy some yoghurt." As if yoghurt for our lunch of tuna and rice that day had been all she had wanted. But I knew better, because, when you spend years pretending and believing that everyone around you is more or less doing the same, you stop looking at people's faces and learn to read their eyes instead. You learn to read the invisible nothings that march between lines and eyebrows, stacking up in secret to form from nothing a something that very few people can see or read.

My mother's forgotten eyes had told me: "Daughter, please come back. I will be waiting for you ..."

"Well, now then. Thank you for sharing that with the class, you may have a seat!" Ms. Marjan sighed, putting a conclusive and natural end to the discussion, and I knew from the heaviness in her voice that the only reason I was not sent off to the principal's office was because my dear Dr. Fereydoon had pleaded with my teachers to allow me to speak my mind, and to not stifle my dark energy.

"Set her devils free!" was his exact phrase.

She didn't seem particularly happy about that arrangement, her inability to drag me by the collar — as she used to do when I was younger and the difference in our sizes worked to her advantage — to Mr. Masoodi's office. Though, to tell the truth, at the time I wouldn't have minded the hot cup of chai he had the habit of offering me. I distinctly remember his words to my mother who, when this whole dilemma started, sat on the red couch in his office refusing to touch her cup.

"Oh, but of course, I perfectly understand! Sheyda is such

a bright young girl," he said, looking her straight in the eyes. "Things have simply been too much for her and it is quite normal that her studies would suffer. But I know with confidence that she has more sense than to repeat her mistake or to allow the past to ruin her academic progression. Please don't worry; I'll personally keep a close eye on her."

He had then looked at me with his calm black eyes and smiled, wrinkles deepening around them and making him appear much older than he really was. He spoke about me as if I hadn't been there in the same room with them, and he spoke with such certainty that I for a moment doubted if it really was me he was talking about. His ability to oversimplify the complicated always struck me in the softest saddest places, and I, at that moment, appreciated it like nothing else, simply because my mother was there, and hearing those words meant something to her.

I quickly looked away.

If people fail to catch your gaze, if they fail to see the true you and the truth in you, does it mean that you don't exist? That you are somehow somewhere else?

Ms. Marjan with a sudden thwack shut the frayed cover of the book before her, then pushed it to the side with all the other notebooks that needed grading. She tightened the knot of her yellow headscarf under her neck, and then gently tugged it back on her head to reveal an unevenly dyed thatch of copper that matched hideously with gray eyebrows. She looked at me and mumbled something to herself, then returned to the notebooks.

But it was okay, I didn't mind. My other teachers had been more forgiving. You see, it was a little game we played. I talked, and she pretended to listen. I blasphemed to unload, and she pretended that it didn't matter. The rest of the world giggled then pointed fingers, pretending that they had never entertained thoughts like mine, and that, deep inside, they all had never wanted to do what I had done. Albeit, more successfully.

Life went on, *c'est la vie*, like the movie, like the song.

The birds used to follow me out of school.

By the time the crumbs of my half-a-day old sandwich touched the glistening pavement, there were six or seven sparrows pecking at them with faded yellow beaks, and hovering behind me in stealthy pursuit. Sometimes, a pigeon would join. But it was a rare occurrence, because pigeons in this country are not as brave as they are in other parts of the world. A student in my class, that bitch from the front row, had once showed us some pictures of her in London being pelted with blue extremely well-fed pigeons. I had wondered at the time if they'd shat on her. I hoped they had. Here, pigeons like people are mistrustful, and have more to fear than hunger.

The sparrows ate my trail. No one found me, no one but them had ever followed me.

2 ℭ

I am now twenty years old. But, if there existed a calendar that kept track of my sorrow, then on its dirty pages one might find a number of significant milestones. The one milestone, however, that marks my real descent would be blowing five white candles on the cake of my biography. It was love that sent me spiralling into a space of madness where I plucked stars and planted them deliriously on trees and carpets. It was love that stepped on my despairing nail-bitten fingers and pushed me off the riverbank. And it was love that turned away when wild with passion and with withered flowers I sank into the bottom, silently. It is love. It will always be.

Five years ago a stranger who wasn't a complete stranger asked me to do him a favour. But our first meeting preceded all favours. In the chaos that is life, the beginning and the end intermittently swap places.

The first time I'd set eyes on him, I was ten years old, climbing the long iron door that is the signature of almost all Iranian houses. I clutched with slippery but experienced fingers the top edge and prayed to God that I don't fall or get spotted spying. Naturally, it would have made more sense to open the door and observe in a bond-girl fashion through a carefully measured chink while the new visitor to our neighbour's house unloaded the trunk of the car — a white familiar Paykan. But the squeaking of our old entrance exercising its rusty joints would have attracted attention, and a scarf-less young head with scattered blonde hair would have attracted it even more. I never was a fan of the spotlight, like all terminal voyeurs my preferred place was always in the shade and the shadow, behind the lens, on treetops. So I balanced myself, bobbing head, held breath and on tiptoes and quietly watched as a strikingly handsome black-bearded man walked on crutches into the gates of the open garden opposite to our house, while another much older man carried his belongings — an elegant brown medium-sized suitcase and a folded wheelchair.

A group of young children spilled out of the neighbour's mossy house and into the streets, preceding an elderly lady who walked carefully behind. The children scampered and danced around the bearded man like moths and bees around a mayflower. Was this black-eyed stranger a pilgrim? Were these his kids? Was he, God forbid, married? I felt a pervading sadness in this man, and I liked it. I liked it because I understood it. His pain felt familiar, old, nurtured. It made me want to save him.

It was spring and beautiful, and I remember telling myself then that I would marry him, even if he couldn't walk.

Before disappearing into the house, he looked back in my direction and waved a brisk hand with a smile that told me that I wasn't as camouflaged as I had hoped. My grip on the door loosened with the flush of blood in my cheeks. I tumbled down with a screech and, without dusting myself, ran home through our tiny cherry-blossom strewn garden, stepping in purple gum on the way and forgetting a slipper somewhere. I ran in and hid, my chest heaving and my temples sweaty. I ran in and hid. Slightly mortified, mostly embarrassed.

"His name is Mustafa and he is a cripple," my father told me when I'd asked him at dinnertime. My mother was busy skinning and slicing a cucumber.

I looked at her and asked: "What's a cripple?"

My mom shushed us both, biting her index finger and arching her eyebrows so far on her head they merged with her curly hairline. "That's not a nice word, what if they hear us calling their son that? Poor poor Mustafa, such a good man! Sheyda jan, he is — " She paused for a moment. "Injured."

I learnt then that he wasn't born injured. But I also learnt that he'd never walk straight without his crutches again. "He was hurt in a suspicious accident: he fell off a roof, or was pushed." My father, stuffing a whole boiled egg in his mouth, and splattering tiny wet bits of white and yellow mush on my fascinated face, then added: "No one knew and he never gave a straight answer!"

"He jumped!" I said, wiping my face clean and giving my

bewildered parents a ten-year-old girl's take on the story. "Maybe he just woke up one day and jumped."

My father blinked, and then with great difficulty, he swallowed.

The children were not — thank God — his. They were his students, his old students, from the days when he could stand up in class and teach.

What did my Mustafa teach? He had taught English to third graders and gave private lessons in French to university students. He also taught love, and this he had done, with a lack of partiality, to people of all ages. I mean to say that in his spare time — whenever he'd had any — he had taken upon himself the task of translating from Farsi, among other things, the love poems of Mawlana Rumi. A true labour of love which meant that his name could be found in tiny fonts stamped across large books that enclosed between their heavily ornate and decorated covers, in addition to mystical secrets and divine love, an array of colourful Persian Miniatures of kings wielding swords on horseback, or long-haired brown-eyed maidens offering the wine of their lips to handsome travellers.

I had no knowledge of any of this at the time. It would be years later when I found out, scanning the spines of books in a bookshop. Pulling one out and seeing on the cover the small familiar name that jolted me back to my childish self, as if those days had never passed, and as if by a form of miracle every memory remained intact, preserved in the attic of my brain like old toys and schoolbooks, waiting to be needed again. I traced my fingers on the protruding names of mystic author and keen translator, goosebumps invading and conquering my skin. Perplexed, I opened the book, quickly read the translator's note, and shifting my gaze to the first verses of the first poem, I read:

When the rose is gone and the garden faded
you will no longer hear the nightingale's song.
The Beloved is all; the lover just a veil.

The bookshop owner, a sturdy man with a neatly snipped moustache, glasses and no hair was busy putting some books in a bag for a customer. When he finished, I looked at him and asked if he had anything else translated by the same man. He squinted looking at the book in my hand, and then opened his mouth and let out an "Ah" of recognition before pointing with his index finger to a middle section in a corner that was designated for poetry, translated to and from Farsi.

Thomas Hood, George Eliot, Hafez of Persia, Gibran Khalil Gibran, William Blake, and the entire volume of Baudelaire's *Les Fleurs du Mal* which I returned home with, not having sufficient money to buy — as I would have ideally liked — everything. That night I slept with the book under my pillow, hoping that the name on the cover would induce dreams just as easily as it had induced memories.

It was unnecessary; book or no book, the dreams returned. When you truly love someone, you always carry them in you; they are tucked in the folds of your being. It's just a matter of unlocking the vault, cleaning up the cobweb, and letting some sunlight in.

After our first meeting, I started seeing him daily. Every morning walking to school I'd find him perched on his wheelchair with a dark blue blanket covering his legs. He'd be pensively watering the plane-trees that lined the streets in front of his house. He'd water everything in fact, even if it was dead or looked dead. That's when the intensity of his devotion struck me. After all, you'd have to be quite mad or helplessly devoted to spend any of your time on anything expired when most people hardly wasted any bothering with the living. And I knew that Mustafa was not mad. Not at all, Mustafa was devoted and a little hopeful.

Of course his garden was always tended to first, and within weeks of his arrival it looked like the spread wings of a butterfly, emerging out of a cocoon. Flowers of the most exquisite colours grew with pointed leaves and with their tangled branches draping over the rims of their heavy pots. Grapevines came to life around the marble pillars of the house. Mysterious types of creepers bejewelled with flowers of deep red, deep yellow and light purple were snaking around a tiny fountain in which centre Cupid held his bow and arrow and aimed squarely at my heart. Even the bird bath, where sparrows splashed in pools of fresh dew and raindrops, was held up on a bed of roses like a tray of offering to the Gods.

I observed this daily ritual of his from my spot on top of the door. The days of my mother suffering to awaken me every morning and of me playing sick desperately to avoid going to school or, to delay at least that which was inevitable, were over, because ever since his arrival, I'd be up and ready in a blink just to have enough time to climb my iron nest and watch. And then, when it was time for me to leave the house and become visible, I'd clutch onto my heavy school bag, fix my gaze to the ground and walk speedily as if no one else was there. In peripheral vision, I would always see a pale hand rising up to greet me in slow motion, like on that very first day.

During the afternoons after school, I'd still spot Mustafa, sitting behind the window on the furthest end of his gray house. It was the only window that overlooked the active street where young children chased footballs of striped and hard plastic, and where supermarket delivery boys rode their faded bikes with plastic-bagged groceries dangling from the handles, their bike bells ringing intensely to frighten the malnourished stray cats which had become so desensitized to the horrors of life on the streets that they refused to budge. Many of these cats dallied around with a limp or missed the tips of their tails.

Mustafa could see directly into our garden from where he sat, and there was no need for me to climb any doors to see him, because from where I stood by the white rails that separated the front of our house from our walled yard, there was nothing to hinder my vision either. But he never looked in my direction, not even when I wanted him to. He was always gazing upwards, occasionally sideways to follow the journey of birds that hopped from one branch to another, and when he glanced down it was usually at honking cars or at elderly couples bickering or holding hands. He never looked in my direction when I was conspicuous and desired him to, only when I was running away from him or sleuthing, as if he wanted me to know that nothing in this life is ever really obscured. Someone can always see you.

That was the first thing he had taught me.

By asking as many questions as would any child with a curiosity for life and with an overly active imagination, my parents became somewhat intrigued by my obvious fascination with the man next door. My 'childhood crush' they called it. It seemed to amuse them more than anything. It was a madness that was both benign and bearable, and they didn't think much of it at the time, understandably as I was clearly too young and innocent, and Mustafa was injured, harmless and a "rare breed of man, a true gentleman."

The children went there frequently, to study or to visit, often carrying cakes or biscuits their mothers had baked for Mustafa. I was extremely jealous and felt betrayed by everyone. I, more than any of those children, deserved to be there with him. After all, according to my logic, I was the one who lived across the street from his house. I saw him first. I had tried desperately to think up and imagine any excuse that would make my mother permit me to cross to the other side and play under his window, or to deliver an item, a saucer or a cooking pan, a bowl of soup, anything. But no, none of my tricks worked. It was best to remain quiet about my love — that was the decision I had reached, growing sick of all the tasteless mocking. "What does a little ten-year-old girl know about love?" cigarette in mouth, my father used to tease.

I didn't know what to answer then, but I know now. She knows enough.

So I started doing my homework for school in our garden, just to see his figure suddenly appearing behind the wide frameless window. Not being able to discern the details of his face, but just having the memory of seeing it in the morning and knowing how beautiful he was. I'd spread my notes and books and pencils and papers, trying to look all focused and professional, playing to perfection the role of a diligent student while all my attention was transfixed on the dark figure in the opposite house. My heart always beating fast for fear of my mother realizing why her reckless little one had suddenly grown so fond of homework, my ears straining in the hope of hearing my name for one reason or the other escape his lips, my breath held tightly to my chest, and the rate of my blinking reduced to detect the slightest hint of movement on his side.

I'd stay in the garden until dusk, when the sky turned her lights off and people turned their lives in. And I'd see, in peripheral vision again, his dark silhouette rolling back on his wheelchair, and disappearing, like that, in a second. A curtain would roll down, and thick orange light would come to life behind it. I'd gather my books like autumn leaves, and go inside myself to have dinner.

One could say that, when the weather was kind to us,

Mustafa and I did things together almost daily. Our lives were synchronized, like husband and wife.

3 ◟

Our walled garden!

So many of my memories are still there, buried under the weeping cherry; so many of my secrets are embroidered on her ruled leaves, and the shady sides of her tender blossoms. She wore her fruit like red and shiny earrings, and dropped them into my open mouth as I stood below her many arms, my greed facing up. I used to colour her narrow neck with crayons in winter; I'd choose different colours for her finger-nails (like mommy did), then bury my crayons there, deep into the brown mud, and wait with them for spring.

Sometimes she looked bare and lonely. I knew exactly how she felt, I understood it perfectly, and I was sure that my crayons, feeding colours to her roots, were the reason she, when the weather improved, wore her best attire. I used to snap her branches, swat at her skinny arms with a stick until our next-door neighbour, the kind Mrs. Ghasemi whose house was to the right side of ours and who loved trees, told me that trees felt pain, too. "Use a ladder and pluck her gifts gently. The tree will pray for you."

Sometimes, when I sat with my books, pretending to write, waiting for Mustafa to protect me with the shielding warmth of his face, I'd hear Mrs. Ghasemi singing in her gar-den, and despite the thick walls between us, her voice would be as clear as the water she was splashing in her driveway, the dry taste of dust and water rising, adding a cooling humidity to the afternoon. She'd sweep with her yellow and red straw sweeper, the muddy footsteps of her three children.

When she climbed the three stony stairs that led back to her house, I heard the rubbery sucking sounds her wet slippers made, and dragging a hose behind her and waiting for the sun to slip coyly behind buildings, she'd stand on the patio that overlooked her verdant kingdom, and would wash its dust and thirst away. Cold water from the hose would occasionally land on my warm exposed neck and my dry neatly-tied hair, tearing my attention from a distant second-floor window to a flowery garden behind me, where a hose was being aimed high enough to reach the crowns of treetops and tickle the empty nests of birds.

"Auntieee," I would shout with a little spasmodic shiver, and hunch protectively over my fragile books. "*Akhee* auntieee, auntieee, what are you doing? You are making me all wet! Aim lower, aim lower akhee." She'd laugh and tell me that a little fresh water never killed anyone. "The trees need their shower just as much as they need a drink."

To our left lived Hajji Khanoom, the octogenarian who occupied the second floor of the house with her son and daughter-in-law, and who didn't mind trees at all but whose real passion was chickens. And I don't mean eating them, but mothering them. Her name was Ravan, but she had made it very clear to my parents and to everyone who knew her, that under no circumstances were they to ever call her by that name. The formal 'Hajji Khanoom' was more than fine. Nana Farangis, who for a few years had been friends with Hajji Khanoom, explained to my mother that the reason why the old lady abhorred her name was because, throughout her childhood, the mean kids in school had called her Ravani: *Crazy.*

When my mother and granny realized that I was hiding under the table (I had giggled upon hearing the word Crazy applied to someone else other than myself), my mother drove her foot to my bottom, and prodded me until I was forced to leave the warm shelter which the plastic tablecloth had created for my spying convenience. I crawled breathlessly on my stomach, and then rolled onto my back, my eyes following the eights a plump black fly was making around the ceiling's neon lights, and I laughed open-mouthed, pointing at the dizzy fly and repeating the words: Ravan Ravani, Khanoom Ravani!

"How many times have I told you that it's rude to eavesdrop? Ha?" my mother said. "*Kesafat pashu, pashu bebinam*, get off that dirty floor, you filthy child, and go get ready for bed. I'll come and tuck you in soon." My grandmother silenced her daughter by giving her a reprimanding look for cursing me, then she said to her, really designing the speech for my neglecting ears: "Sheyda is a good girl, perfectly capable of keeping secrets, aren't you, honey? Aren't you *asalam*?" She bent down and scooped me back up to her ample lap, where I sat, burying my face in her neck, and tittering some more as she tickled me.

Hajji Khanoom had a coop built for her chickens on the roof of her son's house where, she said, they would be safe from preying cats and impolite children, and every morning going to school I'd see her from our garden, sprinkling handfuls of seeds that were propelled from her clenched fists like the dried exploding pods of a flower scattering potential progenies. They'd hit the roof's floor noisily, asynchronously, like the pearls of a broken necklace.

Her friendship with my grandmother ended when my father threatened to twist the neck of her fearless rooster, and feed him to the black neighbourhood cat. The rooster which, every day, arrogantly strutted the walls that separated our houses, and which hours before dawn broke, with a hoarse voice that would eventually be stifled, proceeded to perform his daily gig of disturbing the neighbourhood to an audience of starry-eyed hens which he would loudly rape after the show. You couldn't see his eyes through the many layers of his fleshy red earlobes, his quivering wattles and angry comb.

He always looked at me with one eye, yellow, indifferent to my existence. He'd walk to our half of the wall and skilfully stick his body through the long black iron spikes, legs first, like a lady in nylon stockings, and curiously he'd poke his head, measuring the inferiority of our garden compared to his. Then he'd look at me, in a disgusted manner, and turn around, giving me full view of his small and filthy bottom. He'd spread his tail like the fan of a Spanish flamenco dancer, and squeeze out of his pink aperture and on our side, very elegantly, a long paste of steamy black feces, before relaxing his muscles and prancing away.

He also often crowed during the day, and as if entirely aware of his immunity due to his owner's threats of vengeance if anything was to happen to him, or to simply spite his true nemesis, my father, he'd stand gloriously on a protruding stone on the wall, extend his orange neck, spread the green feathers of his tail and rapidly flap his large wings, fanning dust and little insects and scaring the hens and sparrows as he crooned, *kokko ko kooooooooooooooooooooooooooooooooooooooooooooooo ooooo,* and every creature, alive or dead would patiently wait for him to explode or run out of breath.

I hated him because he couldn't fly.

"He sings like it's a bloody competition," my father said to my mother. "Why does she keep chickens in her house? We are in the city not on some farm in a village! I've yet to see another house in Tehran with a chicken coop."

One day, when he had finally had enough, he shouted at the old lady as she was feeding her hens: "That goddamned rooster of yours has the flu, give him some medication, or put him on a different diet!" He then smiled guilefully and said:

"Or just throw him in a stew pot and get this issue sorted once and for all!"

All civility (the nod of acknowledgement in the morning, the *give my regards to your granny, my old friend*), however, entirely ended when one afternoon Mr. Rooster was found dead in our garden. He just slept on one spread wing with half-opened mistrustful eyes. I thought that he may have died putting on a show for his harem of cackling hens, or giving them perhaps, a skydiving class. There was no blood, no signs of struggle. My father and I carried him by his yellow scaly feet and took him next door.

Hajji Khanoom held the rooster, wrapping her hands gently around his body. "May God have mercy on his soul, he is a martyr!" my father sniggered, and then when he saw how upset she was, his tone changed. "I swear, Hajji Khanoom, we just found him like this, not one feather was plucked out of his body; there are no scratch marks or bite wounds. He was just lying there."

She stood at the gate of her door, half-concealed behind it, with a scarf carelessly thrown over her hair. She looked at us as if we had killed her firstborn. She then slammed the door in our faces, and never spoke to us again.

"Why didn't she believe you?" I asked my father that night. "You were telling the truth."

"I know," he said, "but people will always believe what they want to believe."

"What do you mean?"

"I mean, Sheyda jan, it's easier to believe that I killed her rooster than believe that that ugly old thing expired on its own, probably deafened and deflated by its own singing. It's good to have someone to blame."

"The black cat did it," I told my father and smiled.

"What black cat?"

"The black cat you said you'd feed the rooster to if he didn't shut up. I always see him watching the hens, sitting on the wall with his claws held up, waiting for one to get close enough, and then escaping when the rooster attacked. Perhaps he finally got brave." I held out my claws and lunged at my father. "Meow!"

My father laughed and said: "I made that up, azizam; there is no black cat."

A week later, Hajji Khanoom had another rooster.

Those were our neighbours. Between Mrs. Ghasemi, Hajji Khanoom and Mustafa, the time I spent alone in the garden observing all three substituted for my lack of friends. All the houses in my neighbourhood looked the same: fountains with stone angels, walled gardens, large iron doors and patios with discarded slippers. Some had beautiful trees while others had noisy pets; in one lived a handsome cripple, and in ours lived a crazy child.

It was on one of those homework-in-the-garden days that we both, Mustafa and I, witnessed another death of a bird. A pigeon was executed this time and that shared experience bonded us together in the uncanny way death usually does. The wretched creature — the pigeon, not my Mustafa — was balanced on a branch with two or three of her pigeon friends, conversing in soothing coos and quieting only to bury her beak into a feathery chest and to shut her eyes and rest a little. I only realized that they were there and marvelled their benign camaraderie when I had spotted Mustafa admiring them, wondering at the time what it was that he admired so religiously, jealous of anything that could grip his attention so fiercely, distracting him even from the restless commotion taking place beneath his window, and the passionate ardour burning in the garden across, and fearing also, that this

107

entity was another girl, or Heaven forbid it, a woman closer to his age.

Ah, the relief: only pigeons! A single white pigeon that cooed while her drowsy gray friends slept! And so we looked on, both of us, the cooing lulling us into a state of calm, the light of the gentle afternoon setting a perfect background for our love story, and only the rustling of leaves to remind us that this perfect moment was not a farfetched dream but a joy attained in the lucid simplicity of everyday life. Thus was our state when it happened, when a stone piercing the air struck the pigeon. The stone appeared from a mysterious place beneath the trees, a place that neither one of us could identify. It was as if the very earth had sucked in its cheeks and forced out a bitter seed it could not digest.

The pigeon not yet realizing what had happened attempted the most natural reaction: to fly, just like her friends had flown. She fluttered drunkenly for seconds, then submitting to her faith and to the laws of gravity, twirled toward the ground like a broken kite. She fell straight into our garden. I gasped, dropping my books and tripping over the heavy iron chair, my hands mechanically reaching for my heart. Mustafa helpless behind the window and visibly distressed shouted at the hidden assailant. I heard the scampering of feet, shameless profanity and a sting of laughter which frightened me.

When I held her in my hand she was still warm but dead. Her body was completely limp. My fingers slipped into the white feathers. The eyes were slightly open and her skull shattered. Her little pinkish feet were clasped tightly around nothing. I cannot rationally explain what I did next, but my actions sprang from an absurd spontaneity I wasn't aware I had, one that I no longer possess. I opened the garden door, forgetting that I had no scarf on my head, and crossed the street, holding the white corpse to my heart, bloodying my dress and caring nothing for consequences. And before I had any time to compose myself and ring the square buzzer, Mustafa, struggling on his wheelchair, had slowly opened the gate to his house and was looking at me. I was finally face to face with the man I loved, with the black eyes I dreamt of nightly, and the reality of this unplanned, this almost coerced meeting forced out of me a passion so tearing and sudden that I threw the dead bird into his lap, my eyes filling with tears again, and I said breathlessly: "Look at her, she's dead!"

I was disgusted by the perplexed look on his face. How subdued he was! I screamed an insult loud enough for his parents and the whole neighbourhood to hear me: "You useless cripple! You are no good!"

Mustafa's distressed look suddenly left him. His shoulders relaxed as his long fingers ran on the pigeon's wing, caressing her as if she had been still alive, his face calming with every stroke, his brows and eyes untangling as if they'd found in the softness of the corpse something to be happy about. And that strange sense of tranquillity, the one I would always feel when near him, overcame the hubbub in our hearts and minds, and then like a tide swept us both. We just stood there. He rolled his wheelchair closer to me, then stretched his hand and softly whispered: "Let's go inside and bury her, Sheÿda."

Alarmed by his knowledge of my name, I withdrew my hands and made a move to dry my tears and blood-stained fingers on my dress, but he shook his head and led me to the water faucet inside the garden. He pulled up the green hose and turned the faucet on. Clear cold water came gushing and he helped me wash my hands and flushed hot face, wiping snot and saliva with the hand I refused to take.

"Do you remember me?" he said after I had calmed.

"Yes," I answered, sniffling "yes of course, I see you every day."

"No," he responded with a smile, "I mean, don't you have any older memories of me?"

Only then it occurred to me to ask him: "How do you know my name?"

"I carried you when you were born, and I used to visit your house daily to water your father's garden before I moved. You used to always have a confluence with your teddy bears in the garden! Do you remember? Ah, but of course you wouldn't, how absurd, you were too young!" His face which had grown cheerful for a minute sank with the last words.

"No, I mean yes, I remember, I remember you." I told a heartfelt lie just to make him happy. He knew what I was trying to do but found compassion in my effort. He smiled.

"I am sorry I shouted at you. It was unlady-like," I said.

He didn't hear me, or if he did, he successfully pretended otherwise. "Let's go bury her. If we bury her there" — he pointed to a corner on the left — "under those rose bushes, she will turn into a rose, a beautiful white rose."

He rolled his wheelchair then as if he had abruptly remembered something, he stopped and told me: "My name is Mustafa. Do you know what Mustafa means?"

"No."

"It means The Chosen One. Do you know what Sheyda means?"

I shook my head.

"It means: Lovesick."

He stretched his wet hand to me again, and this time I held it tightly in mine.

Now when I look back at those days, I realize that birds, several types of birds, had always been around; they were always a part of my life. It seems, though, that I was the only one aware of their existence, or more truthfully, they were the only ones aware of mine.

After that day and that shared intimacy, we regressed to being voyeurs, neighbours who knew each other only to the extent that observation as a pastime permitted. Autumn quickly followed, and with its paintbrush stroked hues of red and gold on skies, clouds and leaves, plaiting even brows and wrinkles on young and old faces alike. The days became shorter and darkness lingered, and each morning, instead of my revered fleeing from Mustafa's eyes, I fled my house to the sounds of straw brooms sweeping with dull and monotonous strokes the dry breakable leaves, with the elderly neighbours and caretakers stuffing them into bags and doing God knows what with them afterwards. Some leaves were burnt; I knew that because I smelt it.

The door to Mustafa's house remained shut. God was his gardener now. Sometimes when I returned home, I could still catch the sharp whiff of burnt leaves which always made my throat dry, and I'd know that somewhere in one of our neighbouring houses, a tiny fire still scorched and crackled at the bottom of a black barrel, eating away what was left of its dinner, and ever since, it has been this smoky smell of anything being burnt that always reminded me of autumn and Mustafa.

But I dreamt of him, all the time. At every possible chance I had, at every available moment, awake or asleep. I had imaginary dialogues with him. We discussed flowers and birds, and in my dreams he could always walk, or stand up straight and carry me. I dreamt that we stood behind his window and watched together the passing couples, the stray cats and the dusty children. And on the days when fate forbade us to meet, he'd drop me flowers and perfumed love letters from the cracks in the window, and I'd run to pick them up, press them to my face and inhale deeply, not caring for artificial perfume but only for Mustafa's scent. Urgently, I'd search the white pages for dents where I thought his fingers may have been, and then I'd hide them in my pockets to kiss, read and reread later, before bedtime, early in the morning.

Those dreams were delicious. I saw him in every set of black eyes, and when male visitors extended a hand to shake mine, I felt traces of Mustafa, the slender softness of his fingers, the calm grip that made me safe. TV shows about gardens made me squeak and clap happily; any mention of roses, especially white, made me blush. But pigeons, pigeons of all colours always broke my heart. At nighttime I'd close my eyes, knowing that my love was a stone's throw away, huddled with blankets and pillows, drifting to sleep, perhaps, hopefully, thinking of me. That thought would energize me, oil the wheels of my imagination and my heart would beat with unrelenting fervour, forbidding me the relief of sleep. I'd toss and turn, like an insect in the agonies of a slow and painful death, until dawn broke and sleeping made no sense at all.

In dreaming, I had to compensate for the wasted time winter had snatched away, ending with its hail and rain our romantic summery rendezvous, me in our garden looking at him, him framed by a frameless window, looking at life. Climbing the iron door became a useless activity as there was nothing to see across the street, except flowers wilting then freezing in the hail, and trees dripping thick and heavy raindrops into the soil that was no longer red but a dark upsetting black.

Each outing under the rain meant undressing to take a shower afterwards or at least spending twenty minutes with my head under the hairdryer which was something I dreaded, the hot air pinching my ears and scalp red as mother harshly combed the tangles out with her fingers, and me straining not to yelp each time a hair got caught in her ring and was carelessly uprooted. I stopped going out into the garden, and Mustafa too appeared less frequently behind his window, until one day I realized that it had been three weeks since I had last seen him. That realization sent me into such panic that I cried for days, not knowing what to do or how to answer to my parents who had no idea what was wrong with me. They eventually called the doctor telling him that my forehead was on fire. That was the wrong diagnosis because it was my heart that was set aflame. But no one knew, not even the old doctor who gave me some pills and cold syrup to drink.

After the first weeks of winter, when bit by bit my cheeks recovered their paler shade, it was the steady tapping of raindrops on glass that relaxed me back into a reposeful sleep. Like studied shots of tranquillizers, they arrived at exact intervals and promised that spring would be back and with it the face of my beloved. I'd doze off, repeating in my head that delightful promise, and I'd sleep, perfectly still, like a heart that never knew pain.

Mustafa was the love of my life. Winter took him away.

When the rumours started, the children stopped visiting Mustafa.

Winter was long, and even the energy well of a hyper child like myself was bound to dry up eventually. I was determined though to keep my love for him alive, and what helped me in my conquest of memory were the many stories that circled our neighbourhood like a restless tempest that wasn't really going anywhere, but determined to dance between cement and concrete, attracting an audience, then gobbling them up.

There were many rumours. Various types of fiction, dreamt up no doubt by full-time mental cases and insomniacs who had nothing better to do. There was no truth to any of the stories; I know that now as much as I had known it then. But Mustafa's quiet withdrawal made them worse and the unyielding silence of the gray house didn't help at all. Of the many types of rumours, the best way to feed the flagrant imaginative type is to remain silent about them. To neither negate nor confirm, by word or action. Those were no ordinary fires that could have been extinguished by disregard, the rumours around Mustafa were the scalding tongues of a holy fire that reached into the sky and fed on themselves. Trying to put them out would have been like going against God. Who would want that? A lost battle, an injured soldier in a lost battle!

God never picks on anyone His size. The second lesson Mustafa had taught me.

Mustafa was a good teacher, a good teacher who had been accused of a terrible thing. Terrible enough to make someone seek a precipice and tip himself over it with a resignation more frightening than the deed itself. The rumours were old. When years later I had asked Mustafa about the accident and his legs, he confided in me, saying: "If life is a bus ride then one should have the freedom to get off at any stop he chooses. But life is not a bus ride, or a train ride or a joyride or a roller-coaster ride, and one is not free, because one never chooses to get on this bus on his own accord to begin with. God put you on this bus, chose your luggage for you. And sometimes He stole your wallet and change. They'll teach you that He does this to test your faith and love for Him; they'll teach you many things. Never believe any of it."

At that time, I croaked "blasphemy!" in the same way Ms. Marjan would later continuously do in class whenever I spoke, but deep inside, I knew that he was right. And when I went home that night, I prayed hard to the God I was losing faith in, asking Him desperately to give me an answer, or a sign that He was really up there, that He heard me praying. I threatened to profane myself, to commit acts that were spiritually detrimental, wrong and obscene. I asked Him to strike me dead and stop me from breaking rules that to me seemed utterly forged. That to me meant absolutely nothing.

No answer. No sign. There are times in our lives, difficult as they are, when integrity demands that we be completely honest with ourselves, that we shatter the vase of lies passed down to us from our parents and their parents before them, and knowing by doing so, that all we have to rely upon in this world are ourselves, our innate moral codes of right and wrong, our mental and emotional assessments of what constitutes a sin and what weaves the fabrics of a virtue, and occasionally but not always, we must, we simply have to rely upon each other.

We are quite alone. Helplessly so! Mustafa's words, not mine.

That night for the first time in my life I touched myself thinking of my love. That night I broke my hymen.

They may not have heard it out from my own parents' lips, but Mustafa's parents knew exactly what people in the neighbourhood had named their son, and were familiar with all the stories woven around him. But they acted like they didn't, as if 'The Cripple' epithet belonged to someone else who lived next door to them, someone imaginary, a ghost that wandered up and down the street every night and morning. They kept pretending until Mustafa's father passed away, heartbroken and in his sleep. After that there was no need to pretend. By the time this had happened their house had become well-established and known by one and all as the abode of Mustafa the Cripple.

"He died in his sleep, in his sleep, the lucky man!" my father who would make a habit of stirring this subject said. "One moment he breathed life in and in the next he breathed his soul out. Best way to give it up." Father, envious of our elderly neighbour's calm demise, flicked his cigarette twice then added: "I hope that my death will, like his, come by this easily."

As I've already mentioned, it didn't.

And so, eagerly, I waited for spring and spring finally obliged. After months of being engulfed by the sullen darkness of winter, thin shafts of sunshine evaded the clouds and cast the elongated morning shadows of trees and electricity cables on our house. The air became fresh and crisp, and walking out to our garden in the morning I'd squint in the sun and rub the remnants of sleep off my face. I'd look up at the clouds slowly clearing, and let the sun warm my skin, then skip smiling with an inner hope of opening the gate and finding my love tending to the trees and flowers. But Mustafa never appeared. Not once. I tried to go out at different and irregular times, to surprise him, to catch him sneaking a peek into our garden, or at the streets, but he was never there. The streets were empty and no one sat behind the window. Was he avoiding me? Was he upset by my negligence? Was it because his father had died?

We were approaching the end of March and Norouz was just around the corner. Soon everyone would gather in the streets, setting the flames of our enduring heritage and our ancestral faith and jumping over them, giggling when the flames warmed the soles of their shoes, and screaming playfully when the fire licked the tail of a scarf or the sleeves of a jumper. Surely, I told myself, Mustafa would come out then, with the arrival of spring, to look at the fireworks or at the resurrected gardens.

The day my mother set aside for the festival's cleaning was the day I saw him. All the doors and windows of our house were open, and a cool wandering breeze had found shelter in our house and decided that it liked it enough to flow briskly and inspect the rooms, clearing the dust and heaviness of the stifling winter. I was sitting in the kitchen, with a light jacket over my shoulders. My mother was on the top rung of a ladder, spraying cleaning detergents on a shelf and then wiping it smoothly with a wrinkled striped piece of cloth, the spray nozzle hissing twice then the heavy silence of wet cloth on wood.

It was a Friday and the smell of dust was clogging my nostrils. And my mother kept asking me to make myself useful, to stand at the bottom of the unreliable ladder and hold it still for her. I sneezed continuously and told her that I was busy combing my doll's hair. It was then that I heard the sound of our neighbour's Paykan being fired-up and with it the voice of my father rising and falling to wish someone a safe trip. I threw Laleh to the side and ran with sickness in my heart. Mustafa was leaving. Again. To the same place he'd come from. Where was he before? When would he return?

This time I stood in the street, knowing that he could see me. I stood without scarf and without shame. As the car was slowly driving off with my first love story in it, I gave a sob and a little wave. He smiled tiredly, rolled up the car's window, and looked away at the trees.

My father, wearing drab brown trousers and a shirt missing a button, walked toward me and shooed me back into the garden. "Go in and help your mother, child." He put his hands on the back of my head and gently evened my hair. I ran in before he could see the shrinking wet trails my tears were forming.

4 ☙

That was how I had first met Mustafa, how as a child I had said goodbye to him. The wait to see him again lasted five years, and that's when it all happened, and when it did I never had a chance to bid him farewell or adieu. Our story was over very quickly, like an emotional burst of summer rain or a good unexpected sob when you really need it.

I had returned home one evening from my uncle's house to find my mother asleep in the living room. Her head was resting on a richly embroidered cushion on the couch and her mouth was slightly open, as if she'd fallen asleep mid-yawn or mid-song. All the lights in the house were on, and so was the TV where a Turkish prima donna was animatedly performing a Mozart. When the door closed behind me, my mother momentarily opened her eyes and closed her mouth, giving me the odd impression that she couldn't keep both mouth and eyes open at the same time. Seeing that it was only me, she swallowed the dryness in her mouth and then nuzzled the pillow like a lamb would nuzzle a bush before chewing it, and went back to sleep.

From the empty teacups and the bright swirly peeled skins of fruits arranged on the table in front of her, I knew that we'd had guests. I realized that my mother had dozed off watching television, possibly, telling herself what she always told me whenever I insisted that she take a break, and managed to secure from her a hesitant acceptance: "Sheyda, I'll rest my head just a little bit, then I'll get up and finish cleaning." Or sewing, or cooking or whatever else it was that she did.

Of course she'd be so drained she always ended up sleeping for hours, sometimes through the afternoon and into the night, waiting for my dad to return. And I'd gladly finish doing what she herself was too tired to. I picked up a sugar cube that played chameleon by trying to disguise itself on the white and turquoise patterns on the carpet. I took another one from the saucer, rolled it in my palm then threw it in my mouth. Slowly it melted, rough but sweet. When I returned with a blanket to cover my mother, I had to remove from her feet black sparkly slippers. They only hung by the toes which were swollen, manicured and wrinkled.

When I had turned all the lights off and was groping

blindly toward my room, careful not to bump into anything or make any noise, my mother turned her face to the back of the couch and said: "He's back."

Tired but curious I stopped and turned around. "Who is back?"

My mother took a deep breath. "Who else, your childhood crush, your Mustafa!"

The sugar cube melting on my tongue acquired with this revelation the taste of honey. Do you think I slept that night, or any night since? Thankful for the gift of darkness I excitedly asked her, trying my utmost to rein the passion in my voice: "Is he, well, is he still injured, Maman?"

"He is," she said, "more than ever ... we all are, honey."

That night, I heard my mother weep. And my father, wherever he was, stayed out all night.

It was my mother's idea.

The study was dark, not due to the lack of natural or artificial light but simply because the curtain — a soft gold paired with cream gauze — was pulled over the only window. It was early afternoon and, despite the window being sealed, I could still clearly hear the chatter of young boys dribbling soccer balls on asphalt, and young men on motorcycles putting on a show for heavily made-up girls who had to feign indifference, lest they all got arrested. I felt like a match in a box. The room was lit simply by the streaks of light that seeped in through the keyholes in the hardwood doors and the tiny slits beneath them.

The whole place was silent but for the regular tick-tock of an old brass mantel clock that gave the wrong time. In this house, time travel was possible. Outside these walls it was four in the afternoon but within this time-travelling machine, it was five in the morning. I was tempted to stand up and straighten it out, set it back to working order again. But I was concerned about how it would look if anyone was to walk in on me probing and prodding around the house on my first official visit. So I sat still and tried to look at something else. Time was running away from me, and there was nothing I could do to stop it.

When I heard movement behind the door, I sat straight in my chair then crossed and re-crossed my legs. I held my breath and fixed my eyes to the door knob and watched for any breaking of light patterns behind the doors. I was taken by complete surprise when it was the door to my left that opened and not the one I myself had entered from.

He was and will always be the most beautiful man I have ever laid eyes on. His beard was trimmed closely, and his hair was still a solid disarray of black threaded now with occasional silver that appeared at irregular places. But something else was different about him, something more subtle, a darkness in his eyes that transcended their beautiful colour. Something in the way he sat erect on his chair, with a fierce and sour determination.

He rolled toward me on his wheelchair, navigating between the sofa, chairs and table, the wheelchair floating silently on the carpeted floor, his eyes glowing with recognition the closer he got to me. I didn't know whether I should stand up or remain seated, so I heaved my shoulders up, in a position that suggested a readiness to swing either way.

"So, my dear neighbour wants to improve her English then?" he asked rhetorically to break the ice. "Oh, don't get up please, there is no need! You may not remember me but —"

"I remember you perfectly," I said.

He stopped his wheelchair in front of the sofa, and then shifted his body to it so quickly and expertly that I had no chance to offer him help. "Please forgive me if I lie down. It's more comfortable for my legs if they are stretched and not bent. I hope you don't mind receiving your classes in this deranged unorthodox way! Perhaps you are aware of all the problems this has caused me, the rumours, namely." He smiled amused as he lifted each leg and stretched it before him. Then with his arms he pushed himself back and reclined on a green pillow pressed on the arm of the sofa.

"No, I don't mind at all," I said, much too awed to add that I would have liked to stretch right there beside him.

"The saint patron of birds," he said, smiling. "Like Francis of Assisi, do you remember that? How upset you were?"

"I do. Vividly."

"Where is your aunt, Bahar, I haven't seen her. How is she?"

Casually I told him: "She's doing very well, very happy, engaged to be married."

"I see," he said taken aback. "Congratulate her on my behalf when you see her."

"Maybe she'll invite you to the wedding." I smiled. "You can congratulate her yourself."

"Yes. Maybe ..." He looked away. "Did you like the garden? The roses?"

"Beautiful."

"Yes. A bit neglected now, but still beautiful. How long has it been? Seven years?"

"Five. It's been five years."

"Well," he said, clearing his throat, his right hand resting on the wheel of the chair, rapping on its rubber with his three middle fingers, "in that case, let's not waste any more time and get started immediately. It is my understanding that you are hoping to improve your speaking skills. Therefore, I will as a rule forbid the use of Farsi during the hour. Whatever you don't understand, we will find words in the English language that best describe, clarify or substitute. And one more thing, which I hope you won't mind ..."

"Yes?"

"We will be talking in the dark. No lights."

"Perfect. Good, as you wish," I said. "I mean to say that that's perfectly fine by me."

I looked forward to those classes. An hour five days a week taught me that Mustafa had spent those lost years in England, where he had pursued a second degree in Literature and where accessible to him were the best doctors and physiotherapists in the world.

"Falling on purpose is only a good idea when you know for certain that you won't survive the injuries," he once told me. "I miscalculated and that's why I must walk again."

If it was his destiny to remain alive, then he wanted to gain back the use of his legs. He never lost hope that he would, which was admirably optimistic, considering everything the doctors had told him, which was, in a nutshell, that it would never happen. "Death is imminent at all times. And that's what makes life so beautiful: that it passes, quickly, and ends for us alone yet goes on for everyone else whether we live or die. How dispensable we are and how easily replaced! Life is an ongoing heartbreak, it's a Shakespeare!"

Mustafa had returned from England with more than English propriety and one more degree to hang on his wall. A few strange quirks and unconventional tastes had snuck into his bags and slept there. He was resolute on not allowing our classes to be inflicted by light, and so the windows remained covered and the inside world of this gray house concealed. No one could peep into the curtained keyhole of the living room window. He said that darkness helped clear his mind, and that light threatened the potency of his thoughts. Sometimes, he'd stutter his way through a dialogue, as if he was having it with himself. Thoughts were competing in his mind, racing to roll forth on his tongue and often arriving at the same time.

In all those years, and from afar, I had never seen a cigarette stub touch his lips, but when our classes started I realized that Mustafa was a pipe smoker. After every class, he'd ask me to open a tiny drawer in the bureau by the door and pull from it a pouch of English tobacco. The drawer, once open, would diffuse a serene heavy smell that filled my nostrils until I slammed the drawer shut again. He'd spend a few minutes filling the chamber with a wad of leaves that looked like dirty whittled wood, tamping three layers, lightly, tightly, then lightly again, and with a satisfied look about him he'd sit back, close his eyes and calmly light it, as I watched and savoured his every move, his every expression, his lips biting gently on the wooden lit question mark and the curve of the bent pipe supported on his chin.

He'd inhale deeply and puff out smoke that smelt old, like our memories of each other. How I loved the smell, and how I loved smelling like him when I returned home. I smelt ashy, elegant and a little sweet. It was a smell that slowed down everything — my thought processes, my heart beat, my desire to get back home and touch myself indecently. It made me think of what he had taught me, of the almost-touch that never happened, of his lips pressing to form an O that could have just as easily been a kiss. In the dark room it was just Mustafa and I, with only the haze and smoke between us. Dreaming. And each time, just before the hour ended, with the pipe still hanging from his mouth, he would, with his long and slender index finger, rap a new word's pronunciation on the hard cushion of the sofa:

E re me tic
Nuc tur nal
De co rum
O da lisque
Co al esce
E le gy
Boud oir
BOOD WAA

BOOD WAA: a word that could have just as easily been a kiss.

One day when he saw me so reverently watching him smoke, he asked me if I wanted to have a puff. I made such a fool out of myself, biting the scaly finger of the pipe hard to keep it from falling. When I had attempted — in my desperate way of wanting to appear like I knew what I was doing — to swallow the smoke, I coughed until my eyes reddened and tears ran down my cheeks, my lungs bursting with the aggravating smell. Though there was no need, Mustafa asked me very politely not to tell my parents about it.

He'd point at random objects in the room and ask me to describe them in English: a painting, the stone mantel, anything on the desk. He'd probe me about myself, my interests and dreams, most of which I had to censor because they included him and lewd acts involving him. What made me tick? What made me laugh? He taught me idioms, like: *Barking up the wrong tree* and *Beating a dead horse, All came out in the wash* or *Hit someone for six* and my favourite: *A diamond in the rough.*

Those were happy days, when after each class I'd cross the street back to my house on fortified feet, a cheerful ring to my voice, and a sparkle in my eyes. "How was your class? Is Mustafa feeling alright? How is his mother?" my mom would ask upon my return, and I'd just wave the questions off with a blush and a smile: "Perfect, useful, such fun, yes, she sends her regards!" I'd lock the door to my room and remove the ribbon off my hair. I'd sigh deeply massaging my scalp, and undressing fast I'd lie on top of the cool sheets and touch my body with steady fingers. Alone at last with the image of Mustafa burnt inside of me, and a soft pillow between my legs. I was happy, my life had meaning.

The last day I saw him, he casually said to me: "This might be our last class. I will be leaving again soon."

I could not believe what I was hearing.

"No. Don't leave me," I said on the verge of crying, "Please, take me with you."

"Oh no!" he gasped, realizing for the first time what was going on in my heart. Then so as not to embarrass me further, he smiled, a smile full of guilt, and it occurred to me then how I had never seen Mustafa laugh. When he was amused at my awkward behaviour, moved by my sincerity or genuinely found funny a joke I had told him, he just smiled, never too broadly. As if fearful that anyone would mistake his smile for actual happiness.

"I just thought that you might want some company," I said, trying to justify my reaction. "Travelling can be very lonely."

"Living here can be lonelier," he said without looking at me.

Impatient and a little encouraged, I saw this conversation as the best opening for me to confess my love for him. "But you are not lonely, you have your mother, and —" I looked down at the carpet and whispered: "And you have me!"

"In a few weeks my mother will be moving to a nursing home. She is very old and I have burdened her enough. She needs to be looked after, cared for, and I am useless as a son."

"Don't say that. Why a nursing home? I'll come over every day and help you and your mother. I'd love to."

"You are very kind to offer."

"But if she goes, who will take care of you when you come back?"

"I have thought about it, and I won't be coming back. It's going to be sad, leaving this house, but I trust that you will take good care of the garden."

"No, don't go, you have me," I said in a panicky voice, getting off my chair and walking to him. Mustafa was stretched on the sofa, hugging a pillow. I kneeled down by the sofa and with my palm cupped his knee and rubbed it. "Look, I am here for you." I then looked into his eyes and with all the passion in my heart repeated, emphasizing every word: "You have me, Mustafa."

Mustafa visibly discomforted by the invasion of personal space and at the same time, touched by it, put his warm hand on top of mine. He held it tightly, and then slowly removed it and placed it on the sofa. "You are too kind to offer." I could feel my eyes — which up to that point had been thirstily following my hand carried in his, hoping that he would place it on his chest, or lips or anywhere else on his body — welling up with tears. My pride was violently slashed.

I nearly said it, almost spoke the words that had tormented me for years, the words that had been simmering since that first day I saw him, and filling the void of my existence. The words I had practiced a million times in front of a mirror, and whispered breathlessly to a pillow between my legs: "Mustafa, I am so madly in lo — "

"Sheyda jan, it's best to mention now — to avoid future embarrassment and awkwardness of any sort — that I spoke to your mother and made it very clear that I refuse to accept payment for these classes. I appreciated having someone to talk to and your parents are like a family to me. I love your father like my own, and you Sheyda jan, you are like my little — ”

"Can I open the curtains please?" I stood up suddenly, feeling very bitter.

When he sat up to object I moved quickly across the room toward the large window. I yanked the curtain to the side. The light tore at my eyes, but once the sting had left me I realized that I was looking straight into our garden. That fact disappointed me greatly. I don't know, I suppose that for all those years I had the romantic notion that the window out of which Mustafa always looked was his bedroom's. And standing there, I could see despite myself why he had never bothered looking at our house. It was a very sad thing to look at: white, plain, bare of flowers, perversely uninspired. A washing line stretched across the small garden from one end to the other on the patio, so that when my mother — who when I had opened the curtain had already finished hanging the wet clothes — turned back to get inside, she had to duck her head and pass beneath an orange scarf that quivered in the wind, beckoning like a hung and flayed sunset. Undergarments and socks were placed to dry on the rails by the soil-filled pots in which something was supposed to grow but never did.

"On a second thought, maybe it's best to keep them closed," I said, drawing them quickly and walking away. "You stay in the dark, Mustafa, but I need to go home, if you don't mind."

When I was back in our garden, I turned to have one more look at the gray house, and it struck me then that the house of Mustafa the Cripple looked like a Cyclops with a shut lid.

For weeks I cried, but I never went back.

The news of his death hit me for six. Mustafa finally managed to successfully kill himself a few nights after his mother was taken to the nursing home. He didn't survive any injuries; he didn't have to. He swallowed a bottle of sleeping pills and, like his father, died in his sleep. One moment he breathed life in and in the next he breathed his soul out.

I was hospitalized for a week after trying to do the same, except that I had opted for a more dramatic coda that I thought was more befitting of our love story: gashing my wrists in the shower as I had seen a woman do in some movie. My wounds had only hurt when my arms weren't underneath the shower head that rained crystal-clear needles down on me. It was as if one pain cancelled the other; the scorching ebbing of water and the painful flow of love and blood evened each other out. I watched my wrists weep ruby tears, and felt the arms of a soothing dizziness wrap around me. And just before I passed out, I saw black eyes and Mustafa's face.

Dying can be very lonely and I didn't want him to be alone.

I think about him here, in the darkness I am in. Sometimes I wonder if roses grow on his grave, but then I remember that Mustafa is in the heart of every flower and that as long as my love for him lives, death means nothing. As long as traces of him exist, Mustafa stays.

5 ⚶

Those days, weeks and years following Mustafa's and my father's deaths were very difficult. People made it more so. Wherever I had gone and whenever I had passed, there were constant whisperings, pursing of lips, clucking of tongues and tsk tsk tsking. Pointing fingers jutting toward me from behind black chadors like miniature misplaced erections. Some were curious, many were judgmental. Frowning angry faces, too.

Those always increased the closer I got to my home and neighbourhood, where people recognized me and had knowledge of who I was and what I had done. But at all times above my head, the birds flew; at all times, above and around me, the sparrows followed, looking out for me, keeping me safe.

A hundred times I had walked those roads, which spread before my eyes, revealing the manic way in which life generally signified options: right left, backwards, upwards or down in the open sewers. I remember insignificant details, for instance how I had once seen a green *joobed* car by the road, stuck in one of those sewers that ran in lines by the sidewalks carrying, in addition to water, anything unfortunate enough to fall inside. The front right wheel of the car was jammed entirely, and the unlucky owner was at the front, trying with both his arms to winch up the green body just enough for his young son behind the wheel to drive the vehicle back in reverse. I've lost a handful of things to joobs, those faceless all veins and appetite monsters: slippers, dolls, and once a schoolbook which I had chased after and rescued, the blue ink of my handwritten notes spreading into large dark blotches and rendering unreadable many of its pages.

Each intersection I had memorized by heart. I had walked those streets endless times, knew where the trees were leading me. Every weekday, my mother had to wait an extra couple of hours for my return from school, and every weekday, I had to remember to buy her yoghurt.

Five days a week for two whole years, I walked and the birds followed. The journey from school to destination lasted twenty minutes on foot. I would arrive, press the square buzzer and hear an authoritarian voice ask who it was, and upon recognizing my voice, losing its serious edge and letting me in. I would turn to thank the birds for ushering me that far, then walk through the beautiful garden that smelt of damp grass and lemon trees, manoeuvring my way through dirty puddles. A door would open, and Mr. Masoodi's tall figure would appear, and splitting open a tangerine he'd ask me to hurry and get in from the cold. He'd smile, open his arms wide to catch and kiss me, and in the blackness of his eyes I'd see Mustafa, always looking, at me, over me, and deeply, oh so very deeply into me.

It's true. Why won't anyone believe me?

Chapter Six

AT FIRST, MY visits to Dr. Fereydoon's office were an intense exercise of lying while keeping my face straight. Back in the day, I — most of the time and merely to keep things afloat and interesting for the both of us — felt the need to reactivate my imagination and resort to my wit whenever our conversations grew stale. I never ran out of material. I'd like to claim that the smoothness of the last few sessions I had before ending up in here was proof that practice made perfect, but I know better. The doctor had simply, despite his sincerity, grown as sick of me as I had of him. I can't really blame him. In my younger days, he was tactful, careful with the words he employed as he cross-examined me, asking me to draw pictures, discuss dreams and as I grew older, to keep lengthy journals, which he later read to himself, shuddering no doubt at the extent of my perversity, or perhaps feeling slightly aroused by it. I don't know, you can never be sure about these things.

We even role-played. A lot of pretending took place in his office and I liked it. Like an actress on stage I felt glamorous, but then the short-lived glamour would pass and I'd return home with a terrible amount of self-loathing and vehemence. He was convinced, utterly convinced that I was normal and faking it. He had told my parents that my only fault was having a soul prone to drama and a heart rich with mischief. I also was, according to him, blessed with the imagination and the quixotic softness of a creator, a writer or an artist of some kind. No major traumatic occurrence had permanently marred me, no event of particular significance could adequately justify why I had acted the way I did or why I continued to.

Upon further investigation, and after making me take endless tests of emotional and intellectual aptitude, he claimed with a chuckle that I fared better than half of the doctors in the facility, with a mind capable of complex analysis and a heart that rattled with the seeds of humanism. He noted, slightly alarmed, that my irrational fixation on men with black eyes could easily be explained as a reaction to the tragic loss of my love. It was a coping mechanism; my mind and heart were still busy processing the shock. Death was the most unsettling, reality-shifting tragedy of all human experiences, and a certain period of mourning and for convalescing was to be expected. It could be years for some people, as he said would clearly be the case with me. That was especially true when one lost a lover.

Of course, he never referred to my past with Mustafa in those delightful terms. As far as he was concerned Mustafa was a tumour, a strange malevolent tumour whose presence and absence killed me just the same. Mustafa was a void with a soul, one that had to be replenished or destroyed. What I romantically called a love story he referred to as both a wildly-imagined crush and a classic case of escapism from a reality I found dreary. He even had the gall to ask my parents if this Mustafa had really existed, and they confirmed that he had. What I called faithfulness to the memory of my lover he euphemized a crippling attachment to a dead man who barely had any knowledge of my feelings, and barely of my existence. (I was unduly offended by this statement and I cringed at the word crippling.) What I later called a genuine search for traces of Mustafa in the arms of other men, he told me point blank was the rebellion of a nymphomaniacal young girl.

He said that my story with the parakeet explained my early love for birds. He extracted that anecdote during a hypnosis session which he claimed offered him priceless insight into my emotional ordeal. I hated surrendering that sort of information, and refused for years to go under hypnosis again. He now begs me to do it, says that it will do wonders to my case. After my attempted suicide, my parents had believed neither me nor the doctor. They were convinced that I was mad and they died convinced of my madness.

Hoping that he'd ask me to expound, I once told him that the only true trauma was the trauma of birth, the trauma of existence. He thought that I was being funny, sulked for a moment, and said nothing. For a while, whenever we met during those days in which I roamed under the sun and sky freely, I'd get this feeling that he was seeing me more to satisfy his curiosity than anything, and as he jotted my hallucinations down in his notebook, I'd drift off to imagine my face on the cover of a bestseller, written by Dr. Fereydoon who'd dedicate the book to all the loonies of this world, and who'd send me specifically an autographed copy with the sincere note: "Thank you, Sheyda. Your madness has made a rich man out of me."

Months before ending up in jail, we used to sit to chit-chat. Unofficial and unpaid for, our sessions were no longer the tedious and mirthless hours of free association they had once been, with me lying on the couch and making stories up about a splendid childhood and toys that came to life when we were alone with the lights off and the doors shut. After so many years of therapy, our sessions were more like a day out with a friend. But now here, our interactions have changed again. I no longer have to go to his office. He comes to me. I no longer relax on his couch, rolling the whites of my eyes like slot machines until a memory makes them stop. Instead, we both sit stiffly across from one another, in a hall that smells of tears and treason.

How I long for the stink of memories heaping on soft leather! How I yearn for black cats and crucified apple trees and blue-eyed boys! How I miss your poetry, Hafez!

Back then, whenever I had mentioned being slapped or spanked, the hint of a dormant pleasure flashed in my eyes. My childhood, though not at all happy, was remembered fondly; nostalgia rang in my voice as I spoke about lullabies and porcelain angels and the slaps my mother administered to my face. My childhood suffered the blemishes of my isolation, of me being my own kind, satisfied in my solitude and observing, always observing the misery of others.

Yes, my childhood was more or less a page torn out of my family's book. Their sadness was mine. In a way I was like a dirty mirror that reflected their agonies in addition to the personalized emotional handicaps that life had gifted me. If I was crazy, it was because they had made me crazy. They were criminals and I was their scapegoat, and no God is going to save me. In this moonless world, no God is going to save me. He is asleep in His bed, peeping into the keyholes of another world. I am a sad verse in my country's past, a past I also reflect, and until my death, I'll be a verse read again and again.

"Narcissistic, but generally speaking normal," Dr. Fereydoon had announced one day, lifting an expensive pen to the dimple in his chin and slowly rubbing it. "As normal as the next person, but simply in need of a little tweaking. We are anyway, all of us, Sheyda dear, in dire need of therapy, especially in this country. I am surprised that I have any free time at all. Shocked I am that no one is trying to break into this office."

Of course, after my failed suicide, things had changed

abruptly, but only for a short while. Urged by my frantic mother, he had to intervene with my teachers and show them my medical records, revealing that I was a veteran of a persistent psycho-emotional battle and had been the recipient of therapy for many years, and that no words that fled my lips should be taken seriously, for a while at least, until I regained my previous reserve and discreetness which, as he put it, had been compromised due to "a tragic personal loss."

He had pleaded for patience and support, telling Mr. Masoodi (who in turn spoke personally to all my teachers) that every little thing helped. Every little gesture, every little opportunity of self-expression was a dot in the line of my recovery. Mr. Masoodi promised to try his best with the teachers of whom he cautioned, as a few were quite religious, but he argued that he couldn't do much about the students who were bound to have discussions about me with their parents after school.

Dr. Fereydoon lied about my sanity to save my life, my education. He jeopardized his professional integrity for my sake. It had not occurred to me that, after all those years of being nothing but his unstable patient, his actually caring about my wellbeing was a valid possibility. It hadn't occurred to me because as far as I was concerned he remained the person who lay a claim on my life. He was the professional who could wave me back to the ranks of the sane or have me dragged away in a straightjacket. He asked me why I had done it, and when I told him that it was the most logical thing to do, he shook his head and looked as if he'd regretted asking.

To tell the truth I feel very strongly now that, instead of being cured by the dear old doctor, I may have converted him to my line of thinking. Up until I ended up in prison, whenever I had spoken to him of suicide or death, he no longer argued with me. He instead looked about him like a lost man, reminisced about an Iran that no longer was and fell silent, nodding his head as if to a tune his own soul was playing. Sometimes I was sure that he thought about suicide himself. And only then did I know that I too cared about his wellbeing. We were sick of one another, but we cared. Like an arrow caring for a bow, my existence necessitated his.

My mother used to accompany me to the sessions, but after a certain age she stopped. I would be dropped off at his office in the same way and regularity which other girls and boys my age were dropped off at their music or language classes. There was no need for company; trust had been established. Money was being paid (with discounts naturally); I was old enough to take care of myself. And besides, after a failed suicide, what was there left to be feared?

Now Fereydoon, my kind and faithful doctor, was lying about my sanity, and trying to save me again.

When they had first arrested me, they had asked if I regretted doing it, regretted killing my mother. I answered them honestly saying that it should have happened sooner, because I, immoral and unhinged as many might think of me, could lie about everything except about that. They still question me. They know my answer but ask only to hear it and confirm to themselves what a monster I must be, how heartless, how devoid of mercy, of love, how full of hate and anger. They call me *Taghouti*, devil-worshipper (just as they had called the supporters of the Shah once), because only a follower of the devil, only a woman possessed, gone astray would kill her mother. They are appalled by my lack of remorse, and by my ambivalence about my own life. She deserves to die, she doesn't belong, they say about me.

Well, I think to myself, tell me something I don't know, but your God must have thought otherwise when He made me because He went through all this trouble, He thought I belonged and put me here and now you are disagreeing with His plan and want to send me back. I tell them that I had killed her and that there was nothing that could be done to change that.

I wanted to die with her, but she didn't wait. Why won't anyone believe me?

"You've cried wolf so many times," Dr. Fereydoon told me, "that now, no one believes you when you tell the truth. Why are you lying?"

When did I ever cry wolf about love?

↘ Chapter Seven

1 ↙

I HAD TRIED my hand at writing stories. As I have already mentioned, Dr. Fereydoon had been very insistent on me expressing myself. Write journals he said, write poetry. You, Sheyda, are the creative type.

What's the creative type, I wanted to ask? They dream too much, don't they? They imagine things. They gesticulate like insects fighting for territories, and are susceptible to unreasonable bouts of anger, wrecking the house one minute, and writing you a sonnet the next. They chew on their pencils and sleep with a stack of paper on their bedside, expecting inspiration to wake them, and that, they find in the morning, in sleepy handwriting. They wear berets, and stick the pointy and oily ends of wooden paintbrushes into their effeminate parted lips. They say "hum" before answering your questions, like meditating Buddhists and car engines on harsh winter days. They look at the world through rose-coloured yet thick black-framed glasses. They rub their dimpled chins when they think. They starve to death in crummy apartments with no heat or electricity. Or they gluttonously snack on lobsters and Persian caviar in chic candlelit restaurants, where the waiters' mother tongue isn't their own. And they sigh, they sigh a lot, looking at trees, following horizons. They express themselves passionately, and let their restless kinky minds drift to places. Dark, pernicious places ... The chain-smokers, the alcoholic drug-addicts! They die young, often killing themselves before life has the chance to. The right-hemisphere brained, the left-handed. The freelance lovers, the carefree! The misunderstood and crazy, the lovers of life, the secretly resentful of being alive! The creative type!

It took me 16 hours to write my first and favourite story. Two days later I walked into Dr. Fereydoon's office with my masterpiece folded neatly in the pocket of my overcoat.

Dr. Fereydoon always looked dapper. From the feet up at least, because despite the carefully-tailored suits he wore, he'd stuff his feet in nothing but slippers. The cheap, cruel and ugly plastic type which in my house were kept by the door of the bathroom! Yes, bathroom slippers, the type you could get dirty and pound cockroaches with without concerning yourself too much about damaging. He was a widower, and for years I toyed with the idea of introducing him to that real piece of work: Ms. Marjan. They would have appreciated the sex and the company. Two less lonely souls in the world. I'd have struck two very large birds with one pebble; Ms. Marjan would have been grateful to me for ending her life as a forty-six-year-old virgin, and the doctor would have possibly left me alone, finding better things to poke his nose into.

Dr. Fereydoon was middle-of-the-road when it came to religion, hearing the call to prayer, he'd excuse himself to perform ablution and pray, facing a window in front of me that overlooked a busy street. He criticized the regime in a hushed voice, whispering to me from across the table but also from behind a cupped palm, his eyes fixed to the door, trusting me yet fearing at the same time that one day I'd slip and get him into trouble.

We are a nation of paranoids. Solipsistic paranoids!

"Let's hear it." he said, clapping his hands twice for encouragement.

"No. It's too private."

"We are the only ones here."

"No, I mean to say that it's too personal. I am uncomfortable sharing it with you."

"Well, why did you bring it then?"

"Because I wrote it."

"And why did you write it?"

"Because you told me to."

"Then read it!" he said, reaching for his tea and slurping it while sitting back expectantly in his chair.

With my hand in my pocket, I started fidgeting, touching the smooth surface of the paper. "I'll give it to you, you read it yourself."

I thought about Scheherazade and how only the virgin full of stories lived to see the next day. I unfolded the paper, blew on my hands to warm them, and then placed the paper on the desk before him. "Here, read it."

The doctor removed himself from his chair and went to the open window, shut it and snapped the lock, then returned to his tea. I shuddered at the instant warmth and sat back in my place.

Black Sheep

The 20th of December, 2 pm on a boring but witch-hazel-perfumed Sunday, I was born. A healthy baby, my mother said, but just not very beautiful. I was black. Black skin, black eyes, black fleece, marked by the devil, maverick-totem, can't-be-sold-for-my-wool black! I was black.

A black lamb! A black ewe that would grow into an intelligent black sheep with no palpable benefits (my flock always reminded me). An outcast! I was black.

This is not a story about colour, but one about trust and about life: my life. My life was almost like a recurring dream, a lucid dream even. They called me Ghazal, which in Farsi means 'love verse' or 'sweet talk', it also means 'spin'. My parents never knew the meaning; they just overheard our shepherd use it and thought it sounded like a pleasant name. I learnt the meaning of it when I was two years old. I read it in a book. You chortled, I know. You didn't think that sheep could read. Well, we can, apparently.

I read in the same book that Al-Ghazali of Persia got his name from spinning; I don't suppose he spun wool, not black wool at least.

'The happiness of the drop is to die in the river,' *he once said …*

The happiness of a black sheep is to fit in with her herd. It wasn't possible, I had wasted my youth following the pretty lambs, they made stupid jokes which I forced myself to laugh at, subjected the elderly in our herd to numerous torturous lies of lurking wolves and coyotes; we would look for beehives in tree trunks and think of ways to impinge on their territory and kill them; we ran in the open fields as the bees chased us and we tripped on moss and wild flowers. We grazed with goats and chased sparrows. One could say that ours … Oh, sorry. Theirs! I meant to say that theirs was a normal childhood.

*But fitting in with them didn't work. I was too … uh. What's the word? I was just **too** much! Too much of what, I never knew, but I was too much of it nonetheless. So I instead tried fitting in with other creatures; I tried being a bird; their lives seemed so wonderful, and having the liberty to fly anywhere under the sun struck me as a most appealing luxury, to be free like that! I could be a crow; big, black with a beautiful voice and with the love for singing. But my attempt at flying off the nearby cliff left me with a broken leg and a permanent limp. I couldn't fit in with fish either; they said I splashed around too much; I couldn't keep my* head under the water for too long anyway. Actually, I did not know how to swim at all.

My owner and everyone in the flock including my parents were convinced I was trying to kill myself when they saved me from drowning in the lake.

It wasn't so bad honestly, my wool I mean. It was jet black but soft, occasionally branches, gravel and crunchy leaves would result in a tousled mess but I always made it a point to untangle it. I used to run to my mother, nuzzle up to her and ask her to make me look pretty. My mother hated touching it, it made her sad, my sister told me once that having black wool meant that no one would ever want to buy me; that I had no chance of being sold to a ... The dictionary calls them humans; homo-sapiens, people. I call them two-legged balding goats with elongated faces and misshaped leather hooves. But we, the sheep community — even though familiar with all their names — prefer to call them 'Abrahams'.

'People' is a terse description for something so strange-looking. They know so little about us, these 'people'. They don't realize for instance that we aren't so stupid and easily led as they think we are. We quite simply are very protective of each other and we are trusting. Yes, **trusting!** We follow them because we trust that they love us enough to take care of us; to feed us, protect us. They shear our wool in summer because they realize how hot it is under our thick cascading threads, these clouds of white and laces of brown and cream, our curly coats. We are helped out of them because they trust that we will replace them with others. We are trusting and grateful, not timid and stupid.

There was a story of a very brave and beautiful ram that is said to have saved a young Abraham called Isaac. This mighty ram with glowing white wool was grazing on Mount Moriah when it found two Abrahams, one young, blind-folded and lying on a wooden altar surrounded by water-thirsted branches, and the *other, a much older Abraham holding the young one by the neck and with such calmness examining a knife he clasped in his hand. The horns of the big ram were stuck in the bushes. According to the story the ram was so beautiful the sight of it distracted Abraham from killing Isaac and he instead saved the ram. Isaac was meant to live and see all that was beautiful in life, not get sacrificed by his father. Why would any father want to knife his son? Isaac saved the ram and the ram saved Isaac. The Abrahams took it home and since then Abrahams and sheep have been coexisting in peace.*

Abrahams and us, sheep, get together once a year to commemorate that legend. To mark our friendship and love for each other and to celebrate the triumph of trust, the triumph of beauty! Those who are deemed worthy get chosen every year by enthusiastic Abrahams who generously offer them a ride to visit Mount Moriah. The lucky ones get loaded up on trucks or cars and they wave goodbye to their wives, children and their siblings. They wave goodbye to the green pastures and the trees and the beehives and the sparrows, to the muddy stream that quenched their thirst and to the rocks and flowers that now bore their scents and names. They say goodbye to all that and they sing with melancholic pride as they are driven away from their homes. They left, but by choice. They only have memories now, because no one has ever made that legendary trip and returned. They knew that it was a one way ticket to Mount Moriah. One way ticket to join the ranks of all the heroes before them, to partake in the legend of the brave ram, to become part of it; to be 'the drops that die in the river' they all really wanted that. To feel validated, to feel that their lives meant something.

I was never deemed worthy; I was never picked for that because of my black wool, that only meant that I stayed long enough to see everyone I love leave me and go; my mom, my father, my siblings and cousins, one by one they all left me and assured me that one day my time too will come. My father told me once: "One day you will get picked by someone who will cut through your layers of misfortune and realize your inner beauty."

I prayed for that day to come for such a long time, I felt hollow and inadequate, I felt ugly and undesirable. The little children were scared of me. They'd only get close enough to make sure that the stones they threw hit me directly in the face before they ran crying to their parents. At one time a stone hit me so hard my nose bled; the kids thought it was funny and they laughed at me.

My only real friend was Pablo the cockroach. Pablo was an ordinary German cockroach that scurried around with his little family. He'd tell everyone that he was a Brazilian cockroach because he wanted to feel special. He hated living in the sewers and always made stories up about how beautiful his life in Brazil was, how he dreams of returning there one day and how he'll be taking his wife and kids with him. The truth is that Pablo never went to Brazil; he was born under the sink in the shepherd's kitchen. Pablo was also too old to be able to go anywhere, he loved his wife and children more than anything in the world, so many times he risked his life to feed them, scuttling along in the dark taking whatever he could find.

The Abrahams used to torture cockroaches too; they stomped on them wherever they found them; with stolid nonchalance they mauled them with anything they could find in front of them: brooms, rocks, kettles, shoes, anything! I once witnessed the brutal killing of a little cockroach with a newspaper (words can indeed kill!), the poor thing had just lost his way and was trying to return to his mother, they kept pounding the young roach until he gave up and then a child crushed him under his boot before proceeding to amputate his limbs with a stick and feed him to the cat.

Life can be so cruel. I always wondered why Abrahams treated little creatures like that. It reminded me of how we killed bees and it made me sad. Pablo always laughed and said that God *made cockroaches so ugly so Abrahams would not feel so guilty when they killed them. I sometimes really hated God, I had seen so many bad things happen and I never understood why God never did anything about it. Why did God let bad things happen?*

I always prayed to God, even though I was really never quite sure he heard me, but I still prayed because my mother always told me that God answers prayers when the time is right. God surprises us when we least expect it.

There was so much I wanted, but more than anything I wanted to feel accepted and loved despite how different I looked. So I kept praying until finally, my prayers were answered. On the 20th of December, five years after my birth, in the early hours of a crisp-flavoured morning, the sunrays pierced the dismal clouds and fell gently on my face. A little girl with fuzzy black hair and eyes as green as the pastures I played in came running to me with her daddy, wrapping her little hand around his big fingers she urged him to hurry, the sweet little girl, half-walking half-lifted pointed at me directly and said with sparkling eyes: 'This one daddy; her hair is black, like mine!'

Her father smiled as she came closer to me and ruffled my wool. I felt so special I had tears in my eyes. My owner stood there in a state of shock and relief, even he couldn't believe that someone had finally picked me, before an additional word was spoken my owner gave them a special price; this was the closest he'd ever been to getting rid of me. I didn't mind; they could take me for free for all I care. They picked me; I was special, that's all that mattered.

It's my turn to go to Mount Moriah. It was my turn to reunite with everyone I loved and those who went there before me. Finally, my turn!

We approached the little red car, I was placed in the back and as the engine of the car started and as claustrophobia settled, I was overcome by these random images of my childhood and my family, images of lying on the grass having drank too much water just staring at the sun with a swollen belly, and images of chasing butterflies in open fields. Memories of hiding my owner's fife, memories of him sleeping in the shade and snoring so loudly it scared the coyotes away. Memories of counting Abrahams whenever I suffered from insomnia! Memories of Pablo and his Amazon fiction, memories of everything. It really was like a recurring dream, a lucid dream even. I was missing those very same memories I was tired of, and I only realized all that when I saw Pablo and his wife waving goodbye to me. Pablo was crying.

"You too will be proud of me, Pablo, I promise!" I bleated as we drove off.

We arrived at our destination very quickly, much sooner than I expected. I was dragged out of the car to find that I wasn't the first sheep to have arrived there; there were many others. Two men approached, I recognized them from the legend: an elderly man and a young boy. They exchanged a few words with the man who purchased me, and gave the little girl a piece of candy. They gave me some water to drink then led me to the back. I trusted them, Abraham and Isaac; I was so honoured to meet them, finally. Finally!

In the back and on the blood stained soil I smelt the stench of death.

My mind rife with the memories of my family and those I loved. The words of my father echoed: "One day you will get picked by someone who will cut through your layers of misfortune and realize your inner beauty."

The last thing I saw was the sun reflected on a silver blade ...

And the last thing I heard ...

Was something about a most merciful God!

The doctor looked up from the paper. The wrinkles on his face looked deeper than ever.

⤳ Chapter Eight

1 ⟨

BEFORE THE DUST had even settled on my father's grave, we
learnt that, behind our backs, he'd had a second wife, an expecting second wife. He had been married to her for three years. I
was to have a half-brother, an unborn stranger who, according
to the law, on the merit of owning a penis, was entitled to twice
my share of my father's pitiful inheritance. My mother, who
had been married to my father for seventeen years, was to receive one-eighth of it, and the exact amount would be given to
the new woman who had only tolerated him for three. We were
submerged in all this dirt about my father's second life when
our lawyer read his will to me and to my trembling mother,
who sat with her hands tightly clasped around her kneecaps.

"Khanoom Porrouya, I am very sorry to be the bearer of
bad news, believe me this is the part I hate most about my job,
and there isn't much to like about being a lawyer anyway. Do
you need a glass of water? It must be so difficult for you, shock-
ing to have all this dumped on you after —"

I interrupted him, trying to discontinue any attempts at
sentimentality. He wasn't making things easier. "Can you
please just tell us exactly how much money we will walk away
with after everyone has taken their share?"

"Well, I'll need to make some calculations, but after de-
ducting the taxes and paying your father's debts," the lawyer
said, looking at his papers, "I doubt very much that there will

be anything worth squabbling over." He shifted his gaze to my mother. "Your husband, Mrs. Porrouya, was up to his neck in debt."

But that's not what my mother wanted to know.

"What's her name?" she asked, trying her best to sound calm. "His second wife?"

The lawyer fell silent, uneasily searched his papers then said: "Simin."

"Simin," she repeated to herself. "Simin."

"Fortunately," the lawyer said, "the house remains yours."

We walked out of the office, me dazed under the August sun, suffocating beneath the layers of mourning clothes. My mother walked slowly, shifting the entire weight of her body from one side to the other, stopping after every five steps to pant with stunned eyes. I held her shoulders and blew cool air on her face. She pushed me away.

"Madar, are you okay? Do you want to sit down?" I looked around for a shady spot, a park seat, anything. I saw an empty corner by a water fountain, threw my mother's arm around my shoulder, and walked with her toward it. I splashed her face with clear refreshing handfuls, unbuttoned her ropoosh and rubbed her white glistening neck with my wet hand, then held my palm for her to drink out of.

My mother blinked, as if awakened from a bad dream, her long black lashes meshed together. With her foggy eyes, she read aloud, written on the white stony fountain, the words that can be found on many thirst-quenching municipal water-fountains scattered around this city: "*Laanat bar Yazid, Rahmat bar Hussein:* Curses on Yazid, Blessings on Hussein."

Yazid was the reviled second caliph of the Ummayyads, corrupt and conveniently appointed by his father (the deviant and alcoholic Mu'awiya) as a ruler, and who in the battle of Karbala had killed Hussein, the grandson of the prophet, along with a caravan of his supporters and relatives, executing all thirsty, without allowing them a drop of water.

"Damn him," she said. "Damn him to hell."

"Yes mother, yes. Damn him to hell," I said, realizing suddenly that my mother was talking about my father. I gulped water quickly, showering curses on Yazid, and then walked us both to the shade of a tree. The grass under it was coloured in disfigured patches of wet green or lazy orange. We sat on it with folded knees, my mother with her back to the trunk and me facing her. I watched my mother weep into her hands, and when it got too painful, I looked up at the tree, at its thick and leafy branches. There, on a forked branch, I saw the tangled brown nest of a sparrow. I imagined three green hatching eggs, with three yellow breakable beaks emerging, followed by long and featherless purple necks. Like me when I was born. I felt like resting my head on my mother's lap and sleeping for days. But instead I moved to her side and held her as she cried. Despite myself I said what I thought would ring of spirituality and comfort: "God will take care of us."

My mother stopped crying. She looked at me with her black disbelieving eyes. Then she smacked me, with the back of her hand. The ring on her finger and her pink knuckles must have suffered the same amount of pain I had. My cheek burnt, my ear rang and my nose went numb, and in my mouth the bitter taste of bloodied gums made its way down to my throat. She didn't have to say anything, but I could see the words forming like sea-foam in her eyes, lapping up against the black shores of her pupils. My mother was blaming me for Rustam marrying Simin. This time too, I didn't cry because it hurt; I cried because the smack was unexpected.

We couldn't find a taxi, so we stood on the main street until a private car, a greenish Saipa, stopped, and the head of hair wobbling inside offered to give us a ride home. We climbed into the backseat, glad to be in an air-conditioned space, me still rubbing my cheek, and my mother still rolling her silver ring around her swollen finger.

The driver, a young man not older than his mid-twenties, was in a good mood. He was smoking and playing Persian pop music. He kept looking at my reflection in the rearview mirror, raising a continuous line of bushy eyebrows and smiling. I pressed my legs together, and straightened my black manteau, trying to pull it over my knees. When the manteau rejected my attempts at modesty, I finally told the driver: "Do you mind turning the music off? We are in mourning."

His happy expression flew out of the window with the stub of his unfinished cigarette. Quickly he turned the music off. "I am sorry," he said, "for your loss."

He drove us in silence, for the most part. At traffic lights he'd try to say something witty to lift the heavy mood or find something random and mundane and comment on: the heat, and the reckless drivers who drove bumper-to-bumper.

Perhaps regretting having stopped for such a miserable twosome, our driver started fidgeting, desperate to entertain himself, fumbling with whatever lay on top of the dashboard, adjusting the AC, emptying the ashtray, and with a loud click, opening the glove compartment which spilled a ridiculous avalanche of folded papers that forced him to stop his car momentarily and stuff them back in, apologizing in the meantime and offering an explanation I was too preoccupied to bother with. Finally, once we were out of the traffic jam, he felt emboldened enough to speak again, saying in the worried voice of a bad actor reading a line, and addressing out of politeness his concern to my mother: "Have you, Madam, had the chance to read about the most recent way of kidnapping women in Tehran?"

My mother shot him a look that made him stutter a clarification: "Oh, I am so sorry, it's not a pleasant subject at all, I meant to ask, I meant only to warn — "

"We haven't heard of it," I said, and watched my mother tear her pink-rimmed eyes off the driver and refocus them on the moving cars and buildings. "What is this new way of kidnapping women? Tell me, I want to know."

The man pulled his seatbelt over his torso as we passed a sweaty traffic officer, and seconds later, let the strap roll back to its place as soon as the policeman was in the rearview mirror. He sat up, with one arm on the steering wheel and the other on the knob of the stick-shift.

"The story is that the owners of some private cars remove the interior-door and window handles of their cars. They then pose as good Samaritans and offer rides, and once a lady gets into the car, they clunk the locks shut and drive the trapped victim to some secluded parts and do what they want with her."

"The filthy criminals!" I exclaimed, horrified.

"Excuse me for being graphic," he said, again addressing my mother. "Usually not one but two men would be in the vehicle. No woman can put up a fight against two men. Recently, I've read an account of a victim who said that a woman too helped these criminals, an elderly dignified looking woman, who had asked the girl to sniff a piece of perfumed cardboard she had claimed to have sprayed her latest perfume purchase on. Needless to say the girl passed out, and was found naked near some trees by children who ran crying to their parents."

I automatically reached for the cool handle of the door as he spoke, relieved to feel my fingers around it, before proceeding to the window handle and without shifting my gaze from the rearview mirror, rolling the window down, just slightly to feel a blast of hot air on my forehead.

My movements didn't go unnoticed. "It's always good to check," he said. "Better make sure before entering a car. You can't be too careful these days."

We paid him his fare, after several exchanges of taarouf, with him refusing the money, telling us what a pleasure it was to meet us, and with my mother insisting and constantly repeating what a polite enlightening young man he was. Out of breath and out of patience, she thrust the money at the front seat and we made our escape before an additional word was spoken. My mother slammed the door. I mumbled an apology and ran behind her.

2 ◖

"Come quick," aunt Bahar had said, breaking into my room, her hair in disarray. "Your mother has lost her mind!"

I was sitting on my bed with my legs folded under me, shuffling a set of playing cards. Two grinning jokers slept by my side, also musing about escaping this existence of hearts and diamonds. I looked up and asked her: "What do you mean?"

"Just come," she said, and quickly disappeared.

So I tossed the cards, put on my slippers and rushed behind her to the garden where I found my mother, scantily-dressed in a white negligee, her big breasts visible through the wide armholes. Summer was making room for an early autumn, and the strong evening wind blew my mother's sad hair on her pale gloomy face. She was standing on a parapet, towering over the empty fountain which the night before had been filled with nothing but fallen leaves and chocolate wrappers that the wind had ushered from treetops and vacant streets.

Now however, my mother was facing a growing mound of my father's clothes, his eggshell-coloured suits, blue shirts, pants, socks, even his pathetically-cheap fake-leather shoes, and was emptying on top of all that a large box of papers and photographs. The gate to our garden was wide open and a few concerned neighbours and nosy passersby, most of whom were men, were inside. I saw Mrs. Ghasemi's eyes, floating somewhere in the crowd. Everyone watched as my mother poured kerosene on everything and then shouted: "Lies, seventeen years of fucking lies."

When my aunt tried to throw my mother's audience out of the garden and shut the gate, my mother threatened to soak herself in kerosene too, and jump on top of everything. "Maman," I yelled from the patio before hurrying to her. "What are you doing? Those are my memories."

Without looking at me, she took out a red-tipped match, struck it against its box and threw it on the pile. With a loud burst, the fountain of memories erupted in flames. The blaze was so big, my mother screamed, covered her face to protect it and fell back off the parapet.

Some of the children in the crowd clapped, but most of them shrieked and ran. A couple of men I couldn't recognize were eying my mother, one of them pointed at her breasts and started laughing. An anonymous voice rose and fell: "Look at the crazy woman!" And a different voice jeered: "Great, now there are two of them!"

I felt my insides burning with my memories. Dead photographs, charred fabric, seared plastic, and lonely bits of paper were floating around me like dust and confetti. A smoke rose into the sky like a black stalk of evil leading up and high into hell.

"Get out," I yelled, standing by my mother's head, then kneeling to gather a few large stones. "Get out now, all of you. Get out of my house or I'll call the police." I threw one stone after the other at their stubborn feet and at the gate. The stones ricocheted with off the concrete and iron, and the crowd quickly disassembled. Aunt Bahar shut the gate behind them. Mrs. Ghasemi stayed.

When I returned to my mother, I found her stretched face down, her arms covering her face. "Maman, Maman," I cried frightened. As I turned her around with the help of aunt Bahar, we saw her tears streaming down her face in the hazy reddish glow of the fire. The rubbery smell of burnt fake-leather made me sick. When she opened her eyes and looked at us she said: "You give and you give, you give until there is nothing left and still, it's not good enough, nothing is ever good enough." She turned her face to Mrs. Ghasemi who had attached a hose to the lips of the water faucet, switched it on and was trying to extinguish my mother's idea of a bonfire. Bouncy droplets of water cooled my face. I removed my blouse and covered my mother's shivering body.

"He has left us with nothing, he never loved us," my mother said, her forehead glistening, shaking her head like a child with a violent fever.

Darkness slowly fell. I watched the fire consume itself, crunch on its passionate remains. I then looked at the unfortunate stone-angel balanced on a large lotus in the centre of our fountain, once a calming assertive white but now a blackened demon trying to flee the suffocation of this hell. The cup it had once held up for nightingales to drink out of was now a crumbling gray source of poison. There will always be innocent casualties, those who happen to be in the wrong place at the wrong time. I stroked my mother's face. "It's okay mommy, everything's going to be fine!"

"All I ever did was give," she said, and closed her eyes.

I felt water on my skin again. But this time it was rain. The sky took pity on us.

3 ◟

My mother had asked for no dowry when she married. Nor had she set the condition of a *mehrieh* as a precautionary measure in the case of divorce or sudden death. And as our lawyer had prophesized, there wasn't much money left of my father's inheritance worth squabbling over.

What my mother really inherited, other than the house, was my father's obnoxious smoking. She even held the cigarette between her fingers in the same confusing way he used to, indifferently yet at the same time desperately pressed to her lips which remained partially open, her teeth gleaming from between them whenever she drew her palm away, leading a flood of smoke. She loved her cigarettes in the same way the rest of the world loved oxygen.

My mother changed, in ways both exuberant and subtle. For instance, she started applying mascara to her strikingly long eyelashes, whereas before she never bothered putting anything on her eyes. "Why the sudden change?" I'd asked her, and she had said: "When God grants you beauty, emphasize it, take full advantage of it before He decides that you don't deserve it anymore. You don't want to be disinherited again, do you?"

Different shades of lipstick came to life on her lips, louder, braver colours; the kind you'd see on a parrot's tail and on the breast of a humming bird. She didn't wait for the mourning period to be over to do this; she let her hair loose and wore her makeup like a gypsy even as mourners filled our house with their loud exaggerated weeping. Some of those people hardly knew my father, yet there they were, ripping their own clothes off like peels off a rotten onion while I sat with a blank mind and a lost stare.

My mother was in a celebratory mood, and had it not been for my interference, the inconsiderate provocative Arezoo would have received two whaps on the head from grandmother Khorshid's chrome-plated cane. After the mourning period, when nana Farangis — who had been sleeping in our house — finally left us, my mother refused to cook, and for days all we had for nourishment were cereal, jam and butter, cheese and eggs, and when the days morphed into weeks and our stomachs grew sick and steadily weak from eating the same fodder, I rose to the occasion, and learnt from scratch how to make food that was readily consumable.

She slept with her makeup on, and when she woke up in the morning it would still be there, drabbed on her skin like a wet mask painted by children, from all the crying she did. Within weeks of my father's death my mother already looked ten years older.

After our money finished my mother sold our car. Then she started selling her father's carpets. Those intricately-woven magnificent hand-made pieces sustained us for a while, and even helped pay the tuition for my first year in university. But then bit by bit things started disappearing from our house, items we never used but were accustomed to having around us. Such as the old red radio, the extra rotary dial telephone we had in the guest room. Books, frames, her precious china, jewellery ...

Dr. Fereydoon had long stopped taking money from us, but I had to drop out of university anyway because I knew that my mother was buckling under all the expenses. I knew that she was reaching the end of her tether when she started eyeing her cupboard of porcelain angels. Had God and His angels been in that cupboard, she would have considered selling them too.

Uncle Dariush generously offered my mother the sum of eighty dollars a month — all he could contribute, which my mother had no choice but to gratefully accept, promising that she'd return everything with interest once she could. The money was only enough for one trip a month to Agha Ali's minimarket to secure the basics of rice, sugar, milk, bread and vegetables.

Whenever my grandmother Farangis visited us, I often heard her wishing that she had given birth to one boy at least, one son who could take care of her daughters. And whenever this happened, my outraged mother would fly across the room and shout at her: "All our problems are because of men. Look around you: all our problems!"

She'd then grab me, a big tall girl now, much taller than her and she'd shake me like she used to and say: "Never let a man, any man control your destiny like I let your father do to me. Make your own money; don't say Yes when you mean No; have bigger ambitions than making a shitty man happy, my baby."

It was during those instances that I felt my mother's overwhelming love for me, and that love terrified me more than anything in this world. She'd walk away and I'd feel the rock lodged in my stomach move. My poor mother, I'd think, as she strutted with her new confidence, her beautiful hair which hadn't seen enough of the sun shaking behind her, like a prayer rug draped over the edge of the sky. If only she knew how dirty I was, how dead I felt inside watching her suffer, how much despise I had for money and how all the love I had no one to go to with as a child had turned so sour inside of me.

She kept to herself most of the time, but after a few months she even stopped seeing her own family, refusing to let them in when for hours they stood in the sun or rain banging on the gate, violating the buzzer, begging to be let in. And she violently slammed the receiver down in their faces whenever they called. As if her humiliation was so big she didn't want even those closest to her seeing it. It was as if the knowledge of my father's second marriage was the last insult, the ultimate infliction on her pride. I stayed away from doors and phones. I saw the docile subservient mother I had known all my life disintegrate before me, and get replaced by someone I hardly knew, someone who looked fresher, stronger, and more eager. There was a new madness in her.

My mother was resurrected with Rustam's death. We were starting to look more alike, to behave in a similar fashion, and my mother, who was the same size as I but slightly shorter, even started to shamelessly borrow clothes from my closet. When aunt Bahar had heard the news of my father's betrayal, she cussed him using language I had never before heard in my life, and that's when my mother, tearing out her own hair and wildly slapping herself, entered into a screaming match with my aunt, warning her against ever speaking badly of her dead husband again, especially in front of me, before thundering out of the room and slamming a succession of doors behind her. She made it very clear that she owned the monopoly on abuse. Only she could curse the man who had done this to her.

That was the first time I had ever seen my aunt and mother quarrelling. My aunt shook with a mixture of rage and shock. After all, she had only wanted to defend her sister, give shape to the anger my mother refused to voice, and she felt betrayed by my mother's reaction. My grandmother was as mortified as I was. We both stood, looking at each other, not knowing what to do, who to run after, who to calm.

When my father died, grandma Khorshid more or less

disowned us. She saw in her son's death an opportunity to never speak to us again. She had sold her shop in Rasht, and to the disappointment of Hilla and Navid who really hated her, she had moved after her husband's death to temporarily live with Uncle Dariush in the city. Failing to adjust to the fast-paced life in Tehran with its pollution and loud disastrous traffic, she insisted that her son put her on a bus back to Rasht, refusing all his pleas to drive her there himself. It was a relief to her, being rid of us. Not once after my father's funeral did she set foot in our house, and when we visited my uncle during the holidays, she went extreme lengths to ensure that she spoke as little to us as possible.

When grandma Khorshid passed away a year later, in her sleep — stiff like a log and as smelly as a sewer rat by the time her body was discovered, uncle Dariush found, stuffed in her mattress, what equals to forty thousand dollars in cash. The old lady literally slept with her money and died with it. I've never in my life seen a love so true. She had left all her money to charity and asked that a mosque be built in the place of her house. The disbelieving grief-struck uncle Dariush who could have benefited from the money said that betrayal ran in the family.

She and my father must have had a good laugh about it in the grave.

⤳ Chapter Nine

1 ⟆

EVERYTHING WHIRLS, EVERYONE. The flies certainly do, those crazy dervishes, in an ecstasy of odours, taking only what they need from this world. They are born once, and die once, while we, the chosen, God's preferred species, die with every passing day, with every change of seasons, with the fall and rise of governments, with every sunset of lovers and friends. We break under the weighty load of failure; we are buried with our interrupted stories. We die with the death of our loved ones, we die with the death of memories. We leave without closure. That's our lot: to choke devouring each other's cadavers, living in this picturesque toilet, in this crumpling Inn. Who has it better? We, with our pretty painted faces and hidden daggers, or those decimated hideous but honest creatures, lying by the dozen at the door of my cell, in a dusty pile of legs and wings?

In exchange of a marble I gave away a secret.

Whenever, as a child, my mother sent me to Agha Ali's mini-market to buy her cheese, or a freezing string of sausages, which Agha Ali would drop into two black plastic bags for me, tying them delicately at the top into a pretty bowknot then showing me exactly how to carry them, I would pass by children my age and wonder about why none of them had ever wanted to play with me. They would be riding their bikes, or

AVA FARMEHRI

chasing each other with sticks, their happy bright voices spreading with the wavering streets, following bends that led to nowhere. Some of the young girls wore short-sleeved tops on jeans, yet covered their small heads with black or blue scarves. They carried in their skinny arms badminton racquets that were twice their size, and walked politely toward the park with their elderly sisters or loud fretful mothers, stealing quick glances at me, just to acknowledge my existence, before searching the roads for someone a bit more interesting.

The children of my neighbourhood were classified in my mind into four very distinct categories. The first was the category of scruffy boys who, without returning home after school, would drop their schoolbags on the grass of the nearby park and play soccer for the rest of the day, stopping only for drinks and to whistle at the older girls whom they knew would never send their older brothers to hit them, and who would only dismiss them as cute.

The second was the category of racquet-wielding princesses, who like young prostitutes in the making, sat on road bends crossing their legs, applying lip balm to their dolls and winding their rubber Barbie watches, or who hovered from time to time around the scruffy boys from the first category.

The third was comprised of one strange entity who for the longest time I could not distinguish as a boy or a girl, but who I discovered later was, in fact, a girl, a very pretty one too, upfront. This girl had close-cropped black hair and sauntered the streets without a scarf, wearing men's attire: rough boots, stone-washed jeans and loose and dark wide-sleeved shirts that must have belonged to her father. She hopped back and forth between the first two categories, a pigeon post of sorts, delivering news, gossip, and anonymous love notes. She blended more easily with the boys; the Morality Police never bothered her because, I am sure they wouldn't have, from afar at least, had any way of telling that she was a girl. The moment the dreadful white van of the Morality Police appeared from around corners, she always vanished like a phantasm, into thin air, only to materialize moments later when the hind wheels of the persecuting vehicle disappeared behind a different corner. Whenever the boys played soccer, she would stand as goalie, and ferociously defend the honour of her team.

I wonder now if any of the boys had ever noticed that she was a woman; that one day maybe she'd grow into one at least, or if, they had always only perceived her as a flat-chested short boy with skinny limbs and a flat feminine voice. Did they have secret crushes on her, or was she truly just one of the boys? Did they discuss other girls with her? Did they *accidentally* touch her breasts? I wonder if she grew up with a confused sexual identity. A struggle that was the price of walking freely in the streets, playing with whoever she wanted, without, like the rest of us, having to hide under mellifluous and grim mandatory garments that saw her femininity as a sin, and that decried her undeveloped breasts as a crime that led to the decay of society. I can't help but wonder about the many young girls who had dreamt of doing the same thing, cropping their hairs, scorching their plaits, and shaving their buns. Many I am certain, old and young must have had those dreams. I know I did. But my father didn't let me.

"You have nice hair," he said, "long, blonde and silky, the hair of a pretty princess trapped in a door-less tower."

The fourth and final category included the three very polite children of Mrs. Ghasemi; two very handsome boys and a girl, a year younger than I was. How lucky, I thought, the girl must feel, having not one but two men to protect her, to fight by her side when she was accused of lying or stealing things. Whenever I had seen them together, I always returned home to my mother and asked her to make me a brother or two. I thought that they were baked in ovens, like the Ginger Bread man (I promised I wouldn't eat him), or whittled from tree trunks like Pinocchio. How else were brothers made? How was I made? That night when my mother tucked me in bed, she told me, for the first time, the story of my birth, revealing to me that God set babies to sleep in warm cradles in their mommies' bellies.

"Then tell Him to send us one," I told her, "quickly, very very quickly."

The three children often played alone, avoiding strangers, chewing on the fat orange fingers of Pofak Namaki, the salted chips that tainted their mouths, tongues and fingertips with a deep sticky orange hue that required more than the power of spit to be removed. They'd finish eating, then neatly fold the red and yellow bags, and stick them into their pockets to throw later in bins. Whenever they passed by me to get to their house, they were always licking their fingers, or had streaks of brown chocolate on their chins. That's when I usually ran to Agha Ali's minimarket, and idled around long enough for him to give me something for free and send me away.

Maybe there was a fifth category: children like me, the silent spectators, who saw the world in abstract, who levitated in the margins, watching everyone from behind doors, or in peripheral vision crossing streets. Who knows how many of us were out there.

Those were the last months of a fizzling war, when my country was on the offensive. I always looked up at the sky, searched her blue eyes for trouble, secretly hoping to see an Iraqi warplane whizzing like a pregnant mosquito. I never did. I remember how disoriented I felt, how hollow and befuddled, when my mother read to my father stories in the newspaper about young Basiji boys of fourteen and fifteen, who tenaciously strapped bombs to their chests and rolled under Iraqi tanks, or who walked bravely without blinking, through minefields to clear them, wearing around their necks the plastic keys to the gates of heaven and shattering to pieces as they did.

Our old TV would spew images of an actor portraying Imam Hussein, fiercely galloping on his white horse, enacting the events of Karbala, overdramatizing, charging heroically into battle while spectators wept, and then returned home hot-blooded, flushing with revenge and pride, and sent their children to the fronts to fight for the honour of Shia's, the honour of Islam, and the scattered blood of Hussein. Those stories were what first made me doubt the sanity of a God who loved more than anything in the world "the perfumed holy scent of martyred children."

My father would cringe in disgust, ask my mother to stop reading that awful nonsense, then nod in my direction and joking with her say: "Maybe we should send this one," as I offered them both a toothy smile.

Uncle Dariush said that God purchased souls and loyalty on credit; He sold nothing but promises of sex, wine and honey that were in abundance in this life. "Why they'd want to be dead before experiencing those things is beyond me. They can have it all here, without killing anyone."

God was everywhere; there was no escaping Him in this country.

I would constantly hear Agha Ali talking to his customers, telling them about how an Arab, an Iraqi in the war, had shot his sixteen-year-old son in the arm, then realizing how young he was, stretched by his side and wept, pulling out a picture of his own fifteen-year-old and showing it to him, mumbling long sentences of Arabic that the boy couldn't understand. He then walked away, leaving by the side of the wounded baby-faced soldier, a bottle of water and a small mouldy piece of bread.

"Why?" I had asked him. "Why didn't the Arab kill your son?"

"Because he is human janum, Arab or not; a human with a good heart who knew that murder could never be justified. You could never kill a human being and remain the same."

"Ammo Ali, did your son kill anyone?"

"No, thank God. He got shot before he could."

Incredulously I said: "Thank God your son got shot?"

"No, funny girl, thank God he returned alive. Many didn't."

My memories of Mustafa's house and his family, prior to prying on him that day from the door, are very scarce. The white Paykan — which I had only seen used a couple of times by his father — was rarely parked outside. It slept in the garden every night, surrounded by trees and murmuring bushes where happy crickets sang, and happier frogs with sticky tongues feasted on them.

After his death and my attempted suicide, I had fantasies of breaking into his house, looking through his wardrobe, smelling the starched collars of his shirts, sleeping in his wide bed with his sheets between my thighs, and tending to his garden as he himself had suggested. I knew of no way of contacting his mother, and some weeks after his funeral, a large van stopped in front of his house, and emptied it clean of furniture. One by one, I saw the objects that had outlived my love, ferried away to be sold to people who didn't love him as I did.

"You should try making friends with them; just go and ask if you could all play together," my aunt Bahar, who had been visiting us with my grandmother, told me. "Never wait for others to take the first step for you."

"What if they say no?"

"Well," she said, gesturing with her hand, as if my fear of being rejected was an utter impossibility, "in that case, to hell with them, to hell with them! You don't need them. You can come back here and I'll give you my jewellery to wear."

Empowered by my aunt's words and envisioning her pretty necklace around my neck, shimmering in the coy light of the afternoon, I walked up to the girls in the park and asked if we could perhaps, hopscotch together. Their answer was very terse: a definite no.

Badminton, maybe?

No.

Can I sit with you then, quietly, just listen to you talk?

No.

Can I perch on that corner and watch you?

No.

Well, what can I do?

Just go away.

Before retreating I spotted a brown pouch of marbles on the asphalt where they had, with pink chalk, drawn a hopscotch design with numbers.

Can I see your marbles?

No.

What if I told you a secret?

Here, the girl who had been parroting the same answer for five minutes stopped and looked at the rest of the pack. After several exchanges of glances and hushed whispering, a different girl, one in dire need of a nose job, finally said to me: "It depends on the secret. Tell us your secret first, and *then* we will show you."

Sensing their excitement, I decided to capitalize on my humble success of capturing the slippery interest of nine-year-old girls. I felt so shrewd, so savvy. "It's a big secret that only three people apart from me know." I rubbed my hands to-gether, and made as if to leave. "That's four people in this whole country, this whole world. But I've changed my mind; I'll only tell if you give me a marble."

"Only three people?"

"Yes, only three, other than me!" I took a few steps in the direction of my house.

"Wait."

The first girl grabbed the pouch of marbles, walked straight up to me and instructed me to close my eyes and draw one. My palm emerged clasped around a beautiful blue sphere with a spider-webbed pattern trapped inside. I pulled the girl's ear to me (because secrets should always be whispered), felt her three golden hoops pressed to my lips, and hissed the secret knowledge I had as she giggled before turning around, and in a feeble wicked whisper, telling all her friends.

I returned back home with the precious marble in my pocket.

"So?" aunt Bahar wondered, "Did you make friends with them?"

"No," I said. "They told me to go away."

"To hell with them then. Let's go to your room, and see how good this necklace looks on you." She got up and walked ahead of me, her hair dancing with her shoulders.

I skipped behind her. The day had turned out much bet-ter than I had anticipated. When later that day, Navid asked if he could kiss me, I said yes, then slapped him, just to feel what it was like to hit somebody.

Their desire to extend a hand of friendship after I had surren-dered the one thing I was trusted with — the secret that wasn't mine to share — came as a pleasant surprise to me. It was a kind gesture to a girl who wasn't very accustomed to receiving pleasant surprises, who didn't know what to do with kindness, except to graciously accept it, without reading too much into its motives. I don't think that I've ever rejected anything — good or bad — that anyone had ever done for me, to me. It was then, during my short-lived friendship with those girls, that I experienced the true power that comes with knowledge, not just any type of knowledge, but the secret embarrassing type that people will pay to hear, or censor. They never directly asked me to play with them, but when they saw me returning home after school, they waved their short skinny arms at me and smiled with acknowledgement, and if they were a few steps ahead, they slowed their pace until we were all walking together, thus offering me for the first time in my life a small taste of that transcendental experience of being part of something bigger. They prodded me about school and my parents, and whether I had any pets or liked any of the boys. I asked them to teach me badminton, and they tried, sincerely, and failed. I looked like a giant carrying a net and heartlessly chasing and killing a butterfly.

Then one girl came up with an idea that we all thought was ingenious, adventurous, existential! I told them that, despite the tremendous amount of respect I had for the clever mind that had dreamt up such a pastime, I wanted to have nothing to do with it; I had enough experience with trouble to realize when a seemingly innocuous game had the potential of turning ugly or unexpectedly deadly. I had been caught, misunderstood, and accused of enough things despite not having yet crossed the double-digit milestone. I didn't want to add another condemning adjective to the bottom of an already long and ever-expanding list. Except that the idea sounded fun. And at the age of nine, fun was the keyword, the ideal sought in everything. We could try once, I thought, and if nothing happened, then that would be the end of it.

So we crossed the street, me leading the way, like the braggart leader of a troop of scarfed baboons with lipstick and purses. We pressed our ears and fingertips on the heart of the iron door, and when we heard no pulse of footsteps in the garden, just the usual cackling of hens on the roof and the soothing sound of the wind, brushing the green leaves of an early afternoon across the ground, we rang the buzzer, and waited. Patiently. We waited, with our open palms that tasted of powdery chalk sealing our mouths and the laughter struggling to break free. Finally an old voice came through the intercom, distant enough to be from another planet: "Who is it?"

That's when instantly and with one large roar we said it: Khanoom Ravan Ravani.

The intercom crackled, we heard breathing, loud sibilant scratchy breathing, and then she hung up. That was our cue to run.

We did that for two weeks, after school, sometimes without waiting for an answer; we'd just blurt out the name and skedaddle, hiding behind trees until we thought it was safe. The boys learnt about our game, started playing it too, except that they were boys: stupid and full of misplaced bravado. They would challenge the old lady, ask her to come down with that crazy old head of hers, walking on her chicken legs. They made fun of her hens, called her a peasant. And they would stand at the door until Hajji Khanoom's son opened the gate and sprinkled them with water, threatening to hunt them down, and hang them by their testicles.

An idiot was eventually caught, when the son ambushed him, waiting behind the door as the old lady distracted and cajoled through the intercom. The rest of the boys flashed in all directions, abandoning their captive friend at the first sight of trouble. The unlucky POW shivered like a girl on stage, and with the first few slaps confessed to everything. He gave up, a little too quickly, the names of all the boys, who in turn, gave up the names of all the girls, who in turn delivered me, the source of the Three Magic Words that drove the Hajji mad with humiliation. They served my name on a platter to be mercilessly consumed, like a dripping roasted pig, decorated with parsley and tomatoes. While death didn't particularly scare me, I envisioned a cuddlier end than hanging by the testicles, and despite not knowing then what testicles were, the ring of that sinister word frightened me enough to make me scream as I escaped. I didn't want to risk getting caught, and discovering the meaning of that word.

I tried to run, aimlessly and in circles in the park, like a poor soul fleeing a witch hunt, panting, pleading strangers with my eyes to help me. I could see Hajji Khanoom hobbling to our house with her son, his hand stretching in the modest glow of an early evening to ring the buzzer, and then both of them disappearing inside. I tried to hide, in Agha Ali's mini-market where I stayed until closing time, then in an empty joob with a cat that had sardine breath, and that like me, found the empty gutter both warm and welcoming. I watched her lick her paws lazily until a car parked next to us, and we were both forced to get out. Later, I climbed back into our garden and hid in the outhouse, where I waited with my nose clamped until our guests left.

It was late. Our garden lights were on. On each side of our gate were two bald and rounded lamps like Jack-o-Lanterns, with large elated moths dancing around, bumping loudly into them, oblivious of the purple bats spinning above it all, in a starless void of violent blue.

After they left, I waited fifteen more minutes for the anger of my parents to subside. Then I climbed the stairs, looked up at the moonless sky, and crossed myself for Good Luck as I had seen the old Armenian lady who worked in the bakery do. I removed my shoes, and made my shameful entrée to the snappy sounds of the bells on the door.

"There you are!" my father said sternly. "Come in and shut that door behind you." He called to my mother: "Arezoo, she's here."

My mother, who was carrying the phone receiver and busy dialling with furrowed brows, hung up abruptly and rushed into the hall where I stood trying to look at anything that didn't seem angry.

"Come in," my father demanded.

When I tried to save my skin by running, then talking, my father stood between me and my bedroom's door, then shushed me. My lower lip started quivering and I saw that my mother wanted to embrace me. My father stopped her by stretching a muscular arm before her, saying that I would never learn if I got my way each time I used the tears' tactic.

The world stopped spinning for one whole minute. Time had stopped for me long enough to consider that the fear I was feeling was the fear of being responsible for a transgression I had actually committed. What a realization that had been! What a true epiphany. I had played the lead role in inflicting pain and causing misery to someone, and I felt a tremendous amount of guilt, a sensation entirely foreign to me at the time, especially with regards to people who were not family. I decided to take my punishment with dignity. I approached my father, then closed my eyes and clenched my teeth, tightening my face and readying my cheeks to be slapped. I knew exactly where my mother's open palm would land, and if my father was to grab me to toss on the floor, I knew where his fingernails would sink on my shoulders. And I just waited, then waited some more.

"Hit me," I said with my eyes shut, trying to be brave. "Hit me, I deserve it."

I could hear the restless ticking of my father's watch, breath entering my mother without leaving. But it didn't happen. I waited for my mother to strike me, for my father to violently drag me to the bathroom, and lock me in the dark while I, sobbing on the cold tiles, banged the door with a helpless fist, before I wet myself, the toilet bowl and bidet behind me, like two child-swallowing ceramic monsters that found my fear amusing. But nothing! What was wrong? I opened one suspicious eye, like Hajji Khanoom's late rooster, and saw my parents trying not to laugh.

Finally, they burst into hysterics. My father, as he walked away into the kitchen, was drying actual tears from his eyes, and my mother knelt down on her knees and hugged me. "Stupid girl," she said. "Stupid, stupid girl."

I looked around me, puzzled, wondering what was going on. A soft voice inside my head was asking who had changed the rules and why. Though I too started to laugh, I laughed for a different reason: confusion, relief? That day was the day I stopped believing.

It's funny. No, excuse me, I mean to say it's tragi-comical, how the only time I didn't get punished for a legitimate misdemeanour would return to haunt me all these years later. Maybe there is a God after all, a very twisted funny one. One that I am glad I don't believe in.

Hajji Khanoom had told my parents that, if they didn't discipline me, then she would take the task into her own hands.

"What did you tell her?" I asked my father.

He grinned at my mother and lit a battered cigarette before saying: "We told her: Good luck."

Then swallowing smoke, he coughed out a blurry chuckle and started pounding his chest, tears rolling out of his eyes again. He looked so amused at the Herculean task he had challenged the old Hajji with that I couldn't help but feel happy, too. She was welcome to try where my parents had failed.

The boys never stopped calling her the name she despised. Her hate for me became so great that I could feel its pulse louder than our combined heartbeats. It grew and grew until it was the size of a storm cloud. Both of our houses slept in that cloud's shadow, under its sinister gaze.

After that day, I was never asked about why I hadn't any friends. It was to the relief of my parents and everyone that I played alone.

When I think about all that now, I wonder if she's settling an old score or just a well-meaning misinformed old lady whose eyes betrayed her. It doesn't matter, what matters is that I am here, but not for long.

2 &

My grandmother and my aunt lived alone in a two-bedroom apartment thirty minutes away by car. They visited us more than we visited them, because their place was too small, and despite my being inoculated against tight nooks, I still always grew agitated in that poorly-furnished home. When I grew agitated, I wrecked havoc in the rooms, spilling the many bottles of hand and body lotion lined in front of the mirror, mixing them with thick powder that resulted in a paste which I then applied to my face and rubbed deep, deep into my hair. I misplaced all that glittered, and challenged my disheartened family to find it again, which they never could, thanks to my creativity, but also because I myself forgot where I had hid things.

"Draw a treasure map next time," my father suggested.

At first, aunt Bahar found something pure and innocent

about my mischief, forgiving me whenever I had lost a pencil of kohl, or whenever, opening the window that overlooked the streets, I threw her slippers at the travelling heads beneath. She would, at the end of my hunting day, ask me to run down and retrieve them, but the rate of success in doing so diminished as my aiming skills developed. Many of my angry victims walked away with lonely slippers in their hands, threatening to be back for the other pair. Some walked away with both pairs, unexpected gifts for their wives and daughters. But when I replaced slippers with thick, juicy spit missiles, a man actually remained at the entrance of their building, pressing all buzzer buttons until my grandmother answered and made me go down with my mother to apologize.

Aunt Bahar would dress me up in my grandma's 60's fashion and nonchalantly add to everything I wore, regardless of aesthetic compatibility, the accessory of a straw hat from my Rashti granny's stall. She prettied me up with pink cheek powder and bright red lipstick before sending me out of the room, limping in oversized heels and instructing me to sip tea with an aroused pinkie. My father found our abuse of fashion amusing. He laughed at everything, everything but the hat, which insulted him enough to make him swear to my mother one day on our way home, that if her sister didn't stop her tasteless insinuations, her indirect stabs at his mother, that he'd never set foot in their house again. My mother told him that Bahar was too goodhearted a girl to insinuate anything and that he, as usual, read too much into things.

Grandmother Farangis was a widower. My grandfather had passed when we were still living in the North. My mother, ending three years of self-imposed exile, forced us back for his funeral. Though I remember him only from pictures, my mother filled my head with stories about his kindness, and how much I had loved him. He was very handsome, well-built and had a smooth and proud face that always made me smile at his pictures. According to my mother, he perpetually smelt of cologne, and by the time he left our house after each visit, the whole place smelt like him. He had owned a large carpet shop, which after the Revolution he quickly sold before the government could seize it by force, but only after rescuing all the carpets and piling whatever he could in both my parents' house and his own.

"Do you know why you love birds?" my aunt once asked me.

"For many reasons; first they — "

"No darling, no no no," she said, interrupting with her hands. "You love them because it's in your blood. Your grandfather loved them just as you do."

She told me how, before the Revolution, my grandfather used to rent a truck on the first day of every festival — Christmas, Norouz, Ridvan, Mehrgan, Adha, Hanukkah, Shabe Yalda, any, all ... — and drive his wife, my aunt and my mother, to the bazaar, where they'd find large cages filled with sparrows, starlings, blackbirds and nightingales, trembling from the commotion, too distracted to sing because of the many shuffling feet, frightened by little children pushing food and tiny sticks into their prisons, fluttering desperately from one side of the iron to the other, sticking their beaks out for a taste of freedom, their shifty malnourished yellow eyes waiting expectantly for the door to open, for a rough hairy hand to reach inside and grab at their necks, one by one to be sold, and their white, gray, black and purple shiny feathers exploding in a mess of colour on the bottom of the cage.

My grandfather would go through the bazaar, buying, not one or two birds, but entire squeaking cages, collecting them and with steady careful arms loading everything to the back of the truck, tying them together with a rope as thick as my mother's hair. He'd then carry his daughters, lifting them to the back as they clapped, and made them responsible for protecting the birds, before returning to the front himself and starting the engine.

He drove as far away from the city as possible, as he watched in the rearview mirror his girls laughing, with long black wind-struck locks in their eyes. The girls sat inhaling fresh spring air, potent with the colours and perfumes of blooming flowers, naming the birds and having conversations with them, telling them what the beautiful day had planned. He'd sit still with the windows of the truck rolled down, the wind untangling his gray hair, and sing in place of a broken radio as his wife held his hand, pressed it and told him what a good man he was.

He'd drive for hours, avoiding all the cars, seeking solace in hidden dirt roads, and only decelerating when the city's reflection in the mirror disappeared, and vast meadows stretched before the gates of white mountains, like the majestic gardens of a hidden land, where red tulips blushed to their tips, and white and yellow daisies burst from the soil, with their petals unfolding, extended to the sun, as if to welcome my family and their gift. Aunt Bahar said that even the birds went quiet then, intensely quiet. It was the stillness of nature, meaningful and heavy, like the melting of an ambivalent candle. Bees were suspended in the air, rubbing their precious wings together. Ladybirds dotted the earth. Oblivious hedgehogs with silver bristled flower-piercing backpacks moved on tiny legs.

My grandfather would drive into the meadows and halt his engine where the long grass and flowers started, blending like the fierce patterns on a Persian carpet. There he would park, and all of them would dismount, and help unload the truck.

One by one, the iron doors of the cages would creak, upset

with their own destinies, their base professions, and the birds would first remain still, brainwashed from fear. Not knowing what to do next, just sitting and looking at each other, waiting for that rough hand to tear them back into functioning. All cages would be open, but no bird would dare leave until my grandfather gently pulled one, and plucking its resistant feet threw it up, high into the sky. And that's when the birds, with refreshed memories, would all take flight with a loud flapping of wings, happy, thankful, exalted. And the four members of my family would stand waving to them as they pushed upwards into heaven, or toward the open gates of the horizon. Their eyes no longer yellow, but green like cypresses, red like firethorns and blue, like streams and sapphires, like berries and dreams.

And then the sky would glitter like a Persian carpet, too.

I cried the first time she told me that story. And then I begged her to repeat it again.

And again.

3 ✺

My aunt was married at the age of twenty-three, to a man she barely knew and never loved, but one whom she — as many women do — learnt to at least like enough to live with, sleep with and speak nicely of in social gatherings. I may have had something to do with who she ended up with, but I am far too modest to take full credit for ending the crisis of a woman with an unnatural aversion to marriage, or the full blame for nipping in the bud a love story that meant the total ruin of my own personal interests. What I know, and know for sure, is that she had once been very much in love. I know because I caught her.

It was during a snowy February, when along with my

grandmother she came to stay in our house while my father travelled for a week to Rasht to be with his mother. Upon my father's return, my mother had begged him to permit her family to stay until Norouz, to help with the cleaning and preparations. They had spent two months of the previous summer sleeping in our house, and my father knew that his wife had grown accustomed to their presence; her mother's joyful humming every morning in the kitchen as she soaped plates and stirred the soup, and her young sister's aimless dwelling in the empty hall, in white hot shorts and with an unread magazine, gazing up at the ceiling and fanning herself, or sitting on the edge of the fountain, dipping her slender legs inside, then stretching on an orange towel on the patio to be licked by the sun. This was the closest thing to a pool we had. My father wondered how my aunt, who was twenty-one and a restless university student at the time, would spend her free time in such cold weather.

Well, she had to be creative. Being a sun and outdoors creature, she didn't like being trapped like a butterfly in a coffee jar. So until the weather cleared, the days needed to pass, like meat on a chopping board, as quickly and painlessly as possible. We shared a room, with me offering — like the good hostess I fancied myself — my bed to my guest. The arrangement changed two days later when the cold seeping through the ground had finally made a home in my bowels. I suffered a savage diarrhoea that rendered me immobile for days. But once I recovered, I again became my aunt's guinea pig, both her midget mannequin and her solicitous confidant.

I was a pimple-faced fourteen-year-old with a smile that was too broad and a chin dimple that was too deep. My eyebrows looked like my father's chest hair, stapled upside down on my forehead, and no amount of plucking seemed to ever make a difference. My bras were stuffed with tissues, and my best friend was the same stray I had, as a frightened nine-year-old, spent a day in the gutter with. I was enamoured with a bearded stranger I had met once as a child, and love was my only conviction. I was delighted to sacrifice a bit of personal space and for a short change coexist with a female who wasn't my mother.

"Why aren't you married?" I asked her.

"Because I don't feel like it."

"Why don't you feel like it?"

"Because there are no good men left."

"And why are there no good men left?"

"Because they were all killed at the front or fled the country."

"Why did they leave or go to war if they had girlfriends?"

My aunt threw me an annoyed look then rolled her eyes. "Why why, because the sky is high!"

"Because the sky is high, because the sky is high!" I repeated. "What kind of answer is that?"

"I'll have you know that it's the most complete one."

I thought about my distant Mustafa and how much I loved him, how I longed to see him again. My heart started thumping and I suddenly wished that I was alone. "I know a man who's good but who wasn't killed."

"Oh really! Well, where is he? Let's meet him."

"He left the country, but I don't want to talk about it."

"See, I told you. But never mind, I don't care to know about him," my aunt said, in a bored drawl before yawning. She then sat up on her mattress and added with a less hostile voice: "Sheyda jan, will you be a little angel and bring that newspaper from the living room? Let's look for a husband for your poor lonely auntie."

I gave her the newspaper. "I didn't know you could find a husband in the paper!"

"You can find anything in the paper. Here look," she said, holding the last four pages in her fingers, "the personal ads section."

She opened the first page and grimaced. "Come pick one for me."

I looked at passport-sized images of men frozen in time. It shocked me how hideous some of those pictures were. "Why would anyone in their right mind send a picture of themselves looking like that for the whole country to see?"

My aunt snorted. "Who said that any of these gents is in their right mind? They were all probably high on opium when they took these."

"Well, you'd just assume that a person would choose their best picture, their best face to show to the world."

"Honey, these *are* their best pictures."

I shuddered, and then pointed to the ugliest face on the page. "This one!"

"Oh, nice pick, thanks a lot," she said with a straight face that for a second made me think that she was really angry. "That's his orgasm face." I nearly fainted with laughter, rolling my face on the pillow. "He's married too, auntie," I said, "and you, lucky woman, would have the honour of being his second wife. Oh."

She looked at me amused, imagined what it must feel like to eat the smelly fat leftovers of another woman, and then turned the page in disgust.

As I slid my index on the page and dried tears with my sleeve, she commented on my terrible taste:

"This guy likes to watch you while you sleep."

"He likes to play hide the sausage with other men in parks."

"The reflective deep type, the type that will end up eating you, and not in a good way, but in a very *very* bad way!"

"He screams suicide cult."

"Sleeps with dead bodies."

"Trucker who rapes and kills prostitutes."

"Violates himself with a wine bottle; in fact he looks like he's sitting on one in that very picture."

"Evil dictator."

"Can't live within two miles of any school."

"Well," she said, folding the newspaper and tossing it away, "that was fun. I have many mental images to dream of this evening." She picked up a metal nail file and started smoothing her nails. I collected the scattered pages of the newspaper and went through the desperate pictures again.

"Oh," she said as if she hadn't dropped the conversation at all, "don't tell your mother that I speak like this in front of you. She won't like it one bit."

4

One day, at around five in the morning, I woke to the sound of my aunt zipping up her fleece jacket. The room was still buried in the dawn-preceding gloom of a winter morning and I curled my toes with a shiver, thinking about the snow outside. I shut my eyes and listened as my aunt left the room on tiptoe. Moments later, I heard the soft jingle of bells and knew that she was in our garden. I tried to sleep, pulling the blanket over my head and breathing inside the covers to warm myself, but my curiosity made me restless, and I finally stood up with the blanket on my shoulders to get dressed. I attempted to undress but immediately abandoned the project when my cold naked arm received a blow of vicious gust. After reinserting it into the warm sleeve, I threw a manteau over my cotton pyjamas and stepped outside.

As soon as I took my first step I wanted to turn around and return to bed. The rubber slippers I had chosen to stuff my feet into were entirely wet, stiff with snow water. The sky was a reddish purple, the rich colour of fermented grapes. It was snowing, but very lightly, with most of the white granules melting mid-air. Breath was leaving me in thick drifts of mist, and beyond the patio, I could see snow dropping from treetops, quietly on the mush of muddy soil, and loudly on the roof of our car which my father had cleared just the night before.

The gate to our garden was ajar, and I walked hesitantly through the fog and through mountains of hard snow that my father had dug a path into. The nascent snow sloshed under my slippers as I tried not to slip. A frozen flower petal fell from the sky and landed near my feet. Where did it come from? I stepped on it and walked toward the entrance.

My aunt was wearing a black, snow-crusted chador and carrying a sweeper. Snow melted on her lashes. Her breathing was regular but I could see that she was shivering. She swept the pavement dexterously, and took abrupt careful glances in every direction except behind her, so that when I asked her what she was doing, she nearly collapsed with fear, robotically raising her sweeper to strike me.

"You scared me half to death," she said, trying to catch her breath, her nose releasing mist like two gentle slits on the surface of a freshly-baked inflated pita.

"What the hell are you doing here? Go back to bed," she whispered, impatiently, looking around.

"What are *you* doing here?" I asked her.

"It's none of your business. When did you get so nosy? Go. Now!"

"I am not leaving until you tell me." I pulled the blanket tighter around me and took two more steps outside.

"You idiot, get inside now. You are ruining everything."

"Tell me now and I'll go."

"Okay I'll tell you, I'll tell you, but I can't now. Just go in, and I'll tell you once I am finished."

"Promise me first."

"I promise, I promise for God's sake, I promise. Now get lost." She raised her sweeper again and made a show of hitting me.

I turned on my heels and ran. I was glad to be back inside.

Before I was comfortable in my bed again, reheating the Sheyda-sized spot I had abandoned, my aunt was back inside. I heard the soft jingle once more, her stealthy entrance on tiptoe, a shy rattle in the kitchen where she dropped the sweeper behind the door and finally, her stepping into my bedroom.

"You are a very nosy girl. Has anyone told you that before?"

"All the time." I turned a little in bed then poked only a very cold face from beneath the brown blankets. "Now tell me, why were you, like a crazy woman, sweeping the pavement at five in the morning?"

She undressed quickly, replaced her socks with a new thicker pair and slid under her blankets. "I wanted to meet al-Khizr."

"Al-who?"

"Al-Khizr, Al-Khizr!" she hissed.

"And who the hell is he, your boyfriend?"

"Oh my God, no. Don't your parents teach you anything?"

"Don't talk like that about my parents or I'll wake them up."

"Oh shut up or I'll hit you."

I could only see the whiteness of her face in the dark. "Who is he?"

"The saint, Al-Khizr the saint."

When I had heard those words, I thought that I had died and gone to heaven. My eyes glowed with flashbacks of religious stories. I tossed the blanket, invigorated by sudden warmth rising from my limbs and up through my spine and neck, until I felt that my fingertips were on fire. I sat up like a hound on standby. "A saint? We have a saint? Tell me about him."

"What do you want to know about him?"

"Who is he? Is he bearded and handsome?"

"No, silly. I mean, I don't know. I've never met him."

"Then how did you know about him?"

"I've read about him in books. Stories."

One more glimpse at heaven. Well, I thought, perhaps loving birds wasn't the only thing I had inherited from my mother's side of the family. After years of seeing doctors, I felt ... redeemed. "Recent stories?"

"No, old, very old."

I started clapping.

"Hush, keep it quiet. Do you want the whole house to wake up?"

And so, on a snowy morning, six weeks to Norouz, my aunt told me the story of Al-Khizr, the Green Man, the Immortal who had found the Fountain of Youth and drank till he could drink no more, the Wise Sage, the Beholder of Divine Truths, the Master of all Sufis who had met with Moses (yes, *the* Moses) and taught him three little but very important lessons:

1. *Things are not always what they seem.*
2. *God is infinitely Just, He is running the show and, while you may not always see it, He knows what He's doing.*
3. *The value of patience, a quality Moses didn't possess.*

This was too much, simply too much. I wanted to meet Al-Khizr, too. "Is that why you were dressed like a woman on pilgrimage?"

She fidgeted uncomfortably. "Yes, he is a religious man after all; I wanted to be on the safe side."

"You sound like me, when I was young." I moved an index finger in circular motions by the side of my temple.

She looked around, as if searching for something to throw at me. "Oh really? Well then, I am not telling you anything else."

"No, no. Please, I am sorry. You are not crazy, not at all. Tell me. What should you do to meet him?"

She sat still and smiled. "You sweep the entrance to your house for forty days before dawn. On the fortieth morning he will show up and answer anything you ask him."

"What does he look like?"

"I don't know."

"Then how will you recognize him?"

"It is said that he will come disguised ... well not disguised, but in the skin of a person you know, so that when you see him, you won't get scared."

"You saw me at five in the morning and still got scared," I reminded her.

"That would be different, because I'll be expecting it when it happens."

"Aha. Is that why you stayed here, because we had an entrance you could sweep?"

"Yes."

"How long have you been doing this?"

"For eleven days now."

"But I've never heard you before tonight."

"That's the point. You were never supposed to hear me!" She was no longer whispering now but speaking in her normal pitch.

"Well, if you don't want to get caught, try to be quieter next time. What do you want to ask him about?"

"I want to ask him if I am ever going to marry the man I love."

"The man you love?" I squirmed excitedly. "You are *in* love?"

"Hush, quiet, quiet! Of course, I am *in* love, have been for years."

"Who? Why didn't you tell me when I asked?"

"Because it's none of your business, that's why."

"But I want to know! Please, tell me about him. I won't tell."

"No."

"Please, just one thing."

"No."

"Please!"

"You are such a nagging pain. What do you want to know? Just one thing."

"Well, is he handsome? No, no. Where did you meet him?"

"Ask me something else."

"No, that is my question; you said one question and I asked. Tell me."

"Ah, but you must promise not to tell anyone, and I mean real promise, not like the one you made to my mother years ago."

"Your secret is safe with me. I promise I'll never tell anyone. You have permission to kill me if I do."

"I don't need your permission. I will kill you."

"So, where did you meet him?"

"I met him, many years ago in the house across the street."

I felt the walls shifting places and heard a bird outside let out a whistle.

"The house across the street?"

"Yes, the gray house."

I quickly lay down in bed, thinking of something to say and breathing heavily, and then sat up again. "You don't need

Al-Khizr to tell you. I can tell you myself: You'll never have him."

She looked startled and got up. "Why? What do you mean?"

I stretched, hid under the blanket and offered a muffled answer: "Because the sky is high."

She violently removed my blanket, plucking a few hairs out of my head as she did. "No, that's not how it works. Tell me, do you know anything that I don't?" She sat next to me on the bed as I rubbed my head to soothe the pain. "Tell me, I answered all your questions. This is important. What do you know? Why will I never have him?"

"Because ... he already has a girlfriend."

I saw something die in my aunt's eyes; the same thing that had died in me few years back: faith.

I told her. I told her everything, an elaborate fabricated story about how I had seen Mustafa visited daily by a beautiful woman near her age, a gentle woman with soft brown eyes who held his hand, and kissed it. I talked about their fevered rendezvous under the trees; how they saved pigeons together, and fed sparrows; how he personally washed her face and hands for her; and how he dropped for her reading pleasure love letters from the second floor window, like cherry blossoms in spring.

When she turned on her mattress, weeping silently in the dark, I didn't blink. She dried tears on her pillow, tears that were still there the next morning, and she held my hand as I lay elevated on my bed, thanking me for saving her from the webs of a charming liar and of twenty-nine more days of sweeping snow in the cold.

We just lay in the dark, dreaming, breathing and thinking about the same man. I felt no remorse. It was a question of existence, an issue of territory. All was fair in love and war and this was a war for love. It was simply, me or her.

5 🖤

Perhaps I had played a small part in my aunt's life. But so what? Many people have featured as extras in mine, leading me to this exact place, this precise predicament in which I find myself. What does it mean to hurt somebody, to break a heart? What does it mean to end a minuscule story, and how is that any different from ending a life? What does it mean when we all recover, one way or the other, in our own ways, at our own pace? Even suicide is an attempt at recovery. That's how resilient we are, if we don't like a story, not only do we turn the page, but we burn the book! What difference does it make if we heal or if we don't, when the world does, and life lets you know that that's the only thing that matters? I killed her dream in the embryo. I am the executioner of beginnings; I am the most repugnant thief; my second victim was my aunt and my crime was robbing her of her story.

I don't have to wonder why she'll never visit me in here. Why she'll never pray at my funeral. I killed her only love story, then murdered her sister. My aunt found out, eventually, a bit too late, that the brown-eyed wonder which had been spoken of with such conviction, and painted in such infinitesimal detail, was a phantasm in the mind of her little jealous niece. She realized that the only woman who had loved Mustafa more than she did was I: a disgusting delusional prepubescent liar. The next morning I checked my forehead in the mirror. It was as white as the snow outside, falling gently like jasmines being coughed up by breeze, waltzing to sad and lonely heartbeats, blanketing our whole house in a glow of purity, which we inside were unworthy of.

Do I deserve to be hanged? I was a bad idea, and I tried so many times to fix myself, to undo it. I dreamt every night of untangling my parents' knot, the one they carried in their bellies, the one that tightened around their necks; that fettered their ambitions and sewed together their broken pieces. A pretty knot, a knot they loved, that anchored them to a destiny of heads or tails and tails or heads. I tried and I failed, and now it's life's turn.

My strife is that of a whole family. We will be redeemed, my parents and I. Our salvation has been scheduled: it's in nine days' time. Our house will be washed clean. Again it will snow, but I won't be there to see it. I will be their scapegoat. Their naïve deluded Ghazal, eager to join her family.

Was it my aunt who started those rumours about Mustafa? If she ever visits me, I'll tell her how sorry I am. But if she comes to my hanging, I'll show her, I'll show her how truly sorry.

Anyone who thwarts love deserves whatever happens to them.

What I miss most is the sky, the sky at night, the sky at daytime. I haven't seen it for weeks. I miss gaping at that throbbing mess, that dusty unforgiving firmament. I miss sleeping under its dome, knowing that it's there, above me, for me to look at anytime I please, imbibing its light, feasting on its darkness, to surfeit. We are afloat in space, on a lonely blue marble waiting for a finger to knock it. That's how I started collecting marbles in the first place, when in science class we were shown a picture of the planets suspended in an unlit lantern. "Heaven's internal organs," my teacher called it. When you slid a scalpel across heaven's face, it bled stars and marbles. It gave you thunder and moonlight. It gave you galaxies, spiralling, colliding, silver and golden, bright red and fiery galaxies.

In the hot short nights of summer, we would pull our mattresses to the patio, where we'd stretch in our light pyjamas under three dim lights, airing our legs and sweaty necks,

the wind flirting with our sleeves, sliding into them and tickling our warm and full bellies. My mother would bring fresh
apples and oranges, which my father, leaning on a pillow,
would quickly peel, throwing a slice in his mouth before passing us the plate. What I wouldn't give to sink my teeth in the
sour sweetness of an orange, to just have its generous fluids
explode with that first bite, and squirt down the sides of my
mouth before I wipe them with the back of my hand, and with
a silent kiss, suck at their ripe trails and lick my hand clean.
I'd eat it whole, with its skin. An apple, an apple would do. A
crisp sour green apple with a peel so thin and sharp it fits
effortlessly between my teeth, and splits my gums.

We drank tea, sugared it with our laughter, with my father's
jokes about my sad upbringing. Tiny invisible spiders crawled
all around us; beetles hid under pots and cluttering trays;
pink dotted-brown house geckos rolled their black eyes at the
lights, dropping their tails as I tried to catch them. Indolent
slugs marked the flagstones of the patio with sticky shiny zig-
zagged tracks that I chased, and before my father could commit a salty massacre, I nudged them gently onto discarded
leaves, and placed them together on the moist grass where
they could form The Sisterhood of Rescued Slugs (TSRS). For
some mysterious reason I had the impression that all slugs
were strictly female. Maybe it's how helpless they looked as
my clinically detached father sprinkled them all with salt.
Perhaps it was the silently cruel way in which they died. I
wanted them to find solace and strength in their togetherness.

My mother sang, and I never failed to notice how, out of
my room and in front of my father, her voice always cracked.
But then, we'd turn the lights off and be swept by this beautiful darkness which reminded us of something inherent and
hideous, something dormant and vicious but very much alive
within us.

I'd watch my parents drift off to sleep: my father snoring softly, his watch catching the silver of the moon and reflecting it; my mother dreaming of miracles and normal children, sweat gleaming through the curls of her hair, and the curls plastered on her hidden temples. And then I'd look up, search the sky for our ancient Royal Guardian of heaven: the bright Vanant, the Watcher of the South. I'd think about how my ancestors glorified Ahura Mazda, the Creator of Light, how reverently they sang their Vanant Yasht, invoking protection and healing. And I'd curl up in my summer blanket, and feel bad about my desperate loss of imagination.

There we would lie until the crickets dropped their nocturnal symphonies, only for their exhausted instruments to be picked up again by the rising birds. We'd lie until the sun began its gradual and shy ascent, first from behind mountains, and then from behind clouds. There were days when we woke up in mist, and caught glimpses of a nightingale standing at the head of our fountain, drinking fresh dew out of an angel's cup. It would twist its little neck looking at us, then whistle a long melodious good morning and fly away. The mornings were always chill, cloudy, and the first thing I'd see, the minute I opened my eyes, were the red earrings of our cherry tree, or the painted nails of my wrinkled mother.

We'd hear our neighbours shutting their gates, starting their rusty engines, coughing into their fists, all with as much consideration to the sleeping world as possible. Only when the sun caressed our faces did we rise, rubbing our heavy lids, trembling in our light clothes and pulling our mattresses behind us.

"You are my nightingale!" my mother would tell me.

When I was young, I had this strange theory that there, in each of the different galaxies, existed an earth like ours. The only difference was that each earth was set in a different time period. Dinosaurs awaited extinction on one. On another Christopher Columbus was sailing toward Mundus Novus and mistaking it for India. A pious man in the Middle East had a vision of sacrificing his son; a young Joseph was being tossed down a well; and a God was being crucified. Mary Antoinette was on her way to becoming Queen without any knowledge of price and consequence. Picasso was dawdling with a paintbrush; Hemingway literally blew his brains out; and Da Vinci was in jail for blasphemy.

On a different earth somewhere, things that have yet to happen here have already come to pass. Whenever anyone suggested the possibility of time travel, I always expressed my conviction that time-travel was nothing but a hop through the galaxies. Nothing you could do there would affect what happens here, but there's a good chance that it might affect the future of that particular earth. When I looked up at the sky at night, I always felt that things were absolutely right somewhere. Things were good on one of those earths; on a planet just like ours, lives didn't need fixing. Lives were exactly what they should be in a place far away. And that thought always gave me hope. Maybe on one of those earths the car of the Archduke of Austria took the right route, Gavrilo Princip had a change of heart, re-entered the food-shop and drank himself to sleep. Mary fell in love and married a nice Austrian prince. Judas never sold his Christ.

The possibilities were endless. I wanted to go back, as far back in time as I possibly could and fix it. I'd hide in our outhouse and only behind its heavy locked door would I slit my wrists. I'd break out of my mother's womb eight months before I was due. I'd travel with pictures of caned backs, of women dressed like beekeepers and of young men hanging from trees to show to the resentful impassioned idealistic fools who took to the streets against our Monarchy. I'd slip a condom into my father's pocket. I'd beg the greedy Shah to stay. I'd carve a hole in Noah's ark. I'd tell Eve to castrate her husband. I'd whisper to Adam that pears, strawberries, and even scat tasted better than any Knowledge that grew on trees and came at such a gory price. I'd wrestle Lucifer to his knees and command: "Prostrate, Morning Star, pray to your One God, you fucking idiot!"

Who knows what else I'd do?

I would love to see the moon again. I'd shake my parents from their deathbeds, and with our cracked voices, we'd sing to Vanant.

Oh, to see a nightingale one more time.

Chapter Ten

1 ⦉

BEATRICE PROVED TO be the most fun I had with imagination. She was my complete opposite. Where I lacked in personality, in strength and confidence, she compensated and overflowed. She accentuated my impulses. If I was a lady whore, Beatrice was a whore whore. If I was wildly imaginative, delusional and romantic, Beatrice was an independent promiscuous professional, who loved fashion and loathed men, but used them to sate her insatiable appetite. If I despised religion and wanted humanity to be done with it, then Beatrice loved it. She was a full-fledged Catholic who remembered to be Christian on Sundays and for whom Jesus couldn't reappear soon enough.

If Beatrice and Sheyda were ever to meet on the street, they would rip each other's heads off, Beatrice with her long polished nails and strong toned arms, but Sheyda with her treason and treachery. Where Sheyda submitted, Beatrice rebelled; where Sheyda loved, Beatrice killed. If Beatrice received a slap on the face, she'd slap back, and if she couldn't then and there, then she'd stay up all night and plot her revenge while Sheyda slept and wet herself dreaming about dying. Beatrice had her heart rolled up in armour and she made me feel safe.

"Beatrice, call me Beatrice!" I demanded of my mother. "From now on, that's my new name." Had my father been alive he would have loved the name, and would have insisted that we legally change the original picked for me at birth. Sheyda:

a name my mother had chosen. "Lovesick, so that love will be her sole drive, so that love will be her only sustenance." In that respect I have been a success; I've satisfied the ideal my mother had for me.

Beatrice offered me an outlet to metamorphose into who I wanted to be, away from Iran and away from my parents, away from my past of false convictions, lies and theft. It was true what my mother had taught me: that imagination could take me anywhere. It could drop me anywhere too if it pleased. I could be anybody; I could be as sane as one person, as cultivated as another. I could be as brooding or vulgar as a villager with no training but in the arts of milking cows and beheading chickens. I could transform into a business woman, a classy psychologist. But I was Beatrice, Beatrice the Italian jezebel! How liberating it felt. How freeing! For the first time in my life I had been in a position of power, in a position of dictating my own destiny, asserting my own will, dancing to my own tune and not to the shady fatalistic euphony of the stars, with its deafening melodies that only madmen heard.

The Chinese were the truest visionaries, they had offered me precious peeks into a liberating heaven far more enthralling and real than any God could offer. Entry into that heaven rested with my new knowledge that the truest form of freedom came from within; one had to scratch a match and throw it hissing inwards. The dry embers had to be ignited and the tiny glint fed until its fires spread and converted everything to ash. And this freedom, this commanding presence, made it clear, that whatever price, whatever ransom it demanded for letting my captive soul free, for setting my passions alight, then that ransom had to be paid.

Beatrice slowly stripped herself out of my shackles. She wanted to be free of love and attachment and loyalty and obligation, while Sheyda's ambition was a freedom of God and parents and thoughts. And between the two I learnt that my mind was as alive and imprisoned as my soul. My mind was as inhibited as my body. But once it had tasted that nectar of freedom, which like three drops of magic potion healed my wounds, it soared higher and higher until I could see it no more, but could only feel the nylon thread sinking painfully into my fingers and the vigorous spool pulling the rest of me, up and far away from here.

Together with Beatrice our one heart and one body broke taboos. The freedom we experienced together was the true freedom that God didn't want any man to have, and men didn't want women to understand. I was the only one I had to answer to; my morality was the one morality I had to consult. And then I realized that nothing was more frightening than this freedom. Not knowing what to do with it, how to channel it ethically and in peace.

After months of practicing, I learnt to flip personalities with noted ease. Within seconds Sheyda would become Beatrice or Beatrice would switch to Sheyda. There usually had to be something to trigger it, a sticky situation, but sometimes I'd simply alter posture, voice and behaviour at the request of my amused aunt Bahar who insisted that Beatrice's disposition was much nicer than Sheyda's, and who said repeatedly that she could see herself going out shopping, picking out clothes and being picked up by men in the company of this flirtatiously delightful alter ego.

Whenever my mother angered me it was Beatrice who responded, who stood up for me in the way that no one in my life had. It was Beatrice who cussed unapologetically, who haggled with no shame, and who winked at men and slipped her jumbled phone number between their fingers, then giggled about her mischief on her way home. It was Beatrice who killed, beautiful, sane and elusive Beatrice who abandoned me as soon as I was captured. Beatrice committed the crime, but Sheyda took the fall.

It's always good to have someone to blame.

She was always lurking inside, waiting for the right moment to make her presence known. I don't know how many other Beatrices there are inside of me, how many more Marias and Janes, Shirins and Taranehs, Delilahs and Anahitas ... I don't know and I don't know anyone who does.

Every repressed desire in me has a personality, a life of its own. If I let it, it will have a face and a voice. It will have dreams and ambitions. It will want to break free, break me and break out of me. All of them have wings, snipped wings. If I let them, they will carve out of Sheyda, outgrow her parasite cover and leave her behind, like a snake shedding its skin when a riper prettier one is formed beneath.

I never had a chance to develop that theory. Now it seems abundant, even Sheyda is abundant, a luxury on display. A terror, a criminal with a blotched past who will be hanged soon.

2 ◜

On a Thursday afternoon several months ago, I was returning home after having spent the morning in the arms of a man who kept kissing my feet and telling me that I was the most beautiful girl he'd ever seen. *Mustafa!* I had thought when I had first seen him. He was a younger almost-replica of my Mustafa. His name was Mohsen and he said that he loved me. He was the first man to ever say those words to me. And in my clumsiness I said: "Mustafa, I love you, too."

He blinked in the almost darkness of the curtained room, dust motes spun in the white pillar of light that had found its way through a slit in the fabric. "What did you just say? Who?"

"*Mohsene ma*," I corrected myself quickly, trying not to look appalled by my mistake. "My Mohsen, my benefactor, I love you." I spoke the honeyed words and watched his features acquire the gentlest expression, one such as I've never seen on a man's face before. Not even on Mustafa's.

When I think about it now, I feel that perhaps I was sweet-talked into expressing my love to him. I was triggered by the many verses this lover had penned for me. "I am in love, I am desperately in love," he had sighed earlier that day. "No one knows of your misery, heart. No one knows!" And then he urgently stuffed a piece of paper in my palm, with lines that contained touching poetic hallucinations:

> *The sea was a day old, and the moon two. But*
> *my love for you, oh, my love for you, my love you ...*
> *I am a tear in your eye, a cloud in your sky, a petal*
> *in your flower, a cobblestone on your path, a tree*
> *on your promenade ... No freedom without you,*
> *oh my love for you ...*

I felt such grief reading those words and looking at his flushed passionate face that I simply had to snowball those three magic words back into his ears.

"Say them again, oh please, Sheyda repeat them." he begged feverishly.

I never did.

When I asked him about how he knew that he loved me, he put his fingers through my hair, and gave me the most childish answer. "I know because, if you were to die, I'll be very sad. I'll grieve for you, I'll miss you. I will — God forbid it."

What a startling answer! It shook my very foundations

like a raccoon rattling a tree, not to uproot her out of existence, but to see her distress as her fruits and branches dropped. I was glad that he didn't redirect the same question back at me because I wouldn't have known what to say, and whatever answer I would have offered wouldn't have been the truth. I contemplated his words as I walked the streets back home. And because I couldn't think and walk at the same time, I decided to wave a private car and pamper my feet further.

When a hideous orange vehicle stopped, I searched the driver's face for mean wrinkles around his mouth or any signs of malice in his eyes, and then checked to see if the handles of the car were there. Finding everything in the right order I climbed in, and despite the windy afternoon I rolled down the window. The russet leaves and sad scents of autumn carried with them the promise of rain, and I impatiently gazed up at the gray clouds and watched them sweeping and thickening into a mountain with no summit.

A shiny cross hung from a red string on the neck of the rearview mirror. Out of habit or out of genuine respect and tolerance, I am not sure, but the driver, who was listening to the news broadcast on the radio being read by a man with a robotic but arrogant voice, turned it off upon hearing the call to prayer. As soon as that ended, he switched the radio back on and this time we both listened to classical Persian music chasing the rueful voice of the muezzin away. The sharp cries of the santour's strings being repeatedly hammered made me want to break out into tears.

Where was this life taking me? And why wasn't it going fast enough? I wanted to say something to the driver, whose broad shoulders and fat back occupied a seat and half, and whose nape was covered with the same grayish tangled hair that grew on his head. I wanted to say something about how magical life was sometimes; the rare moments of utter resplendence it offered when nature played her role and mastered it to such perfection that she deserved a standing ovation. I wanted to say something about how beauty and ideals were once my religion, and how nature was my God; a God that gave back to me, that added to my wellbeing, that elevated and transcended. I worshiped her with my eyes and senses. And if and when she unleashed her anger, she did so intrinsically, spontaneously.

Yes, Nature did so by way of her nature. Not by a driving force of evil, not by a will or a mind of her own. She just expressed herself the only way she knew how, the only way she could. Even in her destruction there was beauty and her beauty was forever the result of chaos. I wanted to say that it was always people who ruined beauty for me. But there were no words for this music; there was only love. And I thought about my mother, and about my father and aunt Bahar and Mustafa, and had that car been mine, I would have parked it somewhere under the shadow of the great Damavand, with its snowy dominant peak rising above Iran like a sentinel.

Who was it protecting? I don't know! Was it protecting us from the world or saving the world from us? I would have then stretched in the backseat and slept listening to my agonies being plucked out of my soul like the tunes out of the wooden cavity of that instrument.

But then another young man waved for the driver. The driver stopped and let him into the passenger seat, turning the music off abruptly. They started a conversation about their favourite brand of cigarette, which soon developed into a heated argument about the best folk musician in Iran. I was still enraptured with the music the man had stifled with a click. Preoccupied, I watched faces and shapes take form in clouds, then melt and blend into each other like ashes and dirt in a cemetery, forming something bigger and grander, ranges of unclaimed territories waiting for birds with strong enough wings to fly high enough and own them. There in the clouds' summit the Phoenix reigned as king, but most birds were too tired to travel the distance.

The driver dropped this passenger off, and when we were alone again he cleared his throat to make it known that he wished to say something to me. I drew my eyes from the magic of the clouds to look at his curious gaze in the mirror. Two sets of brown eyes locked, and I smiled because he reminded me of my father. His strong jaw and fierce dark eyes under the scruffy eyebrows and unstitched sun-kissed wrinkles made him look like he had suffered, manually suffered in his life. He smiled back at me and that saddened me more. I had wished then that he'd replace his gaze of fatherly affection with something more unnerving, something more tangible and less tolerant. I wanted him to turn the music on again. But he didn't stop smiling; he didn't switch the radio back on. He just drove humming to a song I couldn't recognize, one in his head. Maybe he was some girl's bird-freeing grandfather.

"You look like my eldest daughter." he said, closing the window so that I could hear him.

"How?" I asked. "In what way?"

"In every way: The dark eyes, the hair, the tiny nose and dimpled cheeks."

"She must be very pretty in that case." I said with a bumptious chuckle, momentarily forgetting my sadness.

"Ha, yes," he said laughing. "Very beautiful, but all of us Armenians are pretty; we can't help it, can we?"

"Oh, Armenians are definitely gorgeous," I said, "but who said that I was Armenian?"

The proud and ridiculous grin on his face disappeared and reappeared in a moment. "Really? You could have fooled me, Khanoom. But you just didn't strike me as Aryan, your —"

"Hair is not dark enough? My eyes are too shallow?"

"No no no, not at all what I meant." he said. But when he didn't know what to add, he fell silent. He scratched his arm, and then sank into thought, guilt tickling his nose. I broke the silence by saying: "I don't look Aryan because I am not."

He glanced up and his eyes glowed in the mirror. *"Aha,* Khanoom, see I knew it!" he said with satisfaction. "Well then, where are you originally from?"

Beatrice and her confidence took over. "I am Italian by origin, my parents are I mean. But I was born in Tehran, grew up here, never left."

"Bah bah," he exclaimed, "Italy! Beautiful country, beautiful people; oh the art, the civilization, the football team! I've never met any Italians in this country. *Vali ghorbone Italia beram mann!*"

"Merci, Agha, merci." I laughed amused and relished the moment. "That's true; the world has a lot to thank us for." I shook my head humbly. And before he could ask me about my name I volunteered the information: "My name is Beatrice."

"Bah bah bah," he said, "Khanoom Beatrice, pleasure to meet you. And do you speak Italian?"

This was, oddly enough, the question that no one had ever thought of asking me before. I had no answer ready, but getting carried away, I offered one without putting as much thought into it as I should have. "Oh, but of course! Fluently, Agha. It would be a shame to have Italian parents and not learn that brilliant language!"

"Affarin behet, well-done, that's what I always told my children who constantly complained about Armenian being difficult. But now they are all grown-up and speak at least four languages each."

"Four? *Mashallah!* And how many languages do you speak, Sir?"

I didn't have time to regret asking the question because he fired his answer very quickly.

"I speak six: Armenian, Farsi, Arabic, Kurdish, French and Italian!"

My face felt very hot suddenly. I could feel lines of perspiration forming on my forehead, behind my ears and under my eyes.

"Italian?" I asked, rhetorically, a quiver in my voice. "Oh Sir, a true polyglot you are!"

He stopped the car for another passenger, the door handle clicked, and a chubby but pretty woman in her mid-thirties got in and sat next to me. I hoped that this intrusion would end our conversation, but to my disappointment he quickly picked it up.

Before I knew it and giving me no time to psychologically or emotionally prepare myself, the man was speaking to me in Italian faster than I had heard any human being speak in my life.

"Piacere di conoscerla, signorina. Mi chiamo Antoin Spadavakian. Bella ragazza! But I have to ask: Perché sono i tuoi genitori che vivono qui?"

"Oh," the woman next to me said, moved by his smooth titillating sentences, "what a pretty language! Is this Italian or Spanish you are speaking?"

"Italiano," the man said. "Parliamo Italiano."

I shook my head at her and tried my best to smile without vomiting.

I rummaged my handbag in search of a napkin, an invisibility cloak, a shotgun, or anything that could save me from my embarrassment. My hands were beginning to sweat rivers and were leaving wet marks on the black leather of my bag. The woman next to me seemed just as excited to hear me babble back in that beautiful but impossible to pick up in five minutes language. That was the moment when I wished that I had purchased that tiny green *Learn Italian in a Week* book that I had spotted months ago behind the glass of a street kiosk. I tried to quickly think of a list of the Italian words I knew ... *Pepperoni, Ciao, Pizza, Dolce, Pasta, Mafia, Michael Angelo, Vita, Mozzarella, Pisa, Vespucci Amerigo, Venice, Si, Spaghetti, Bravo, Dio* ...

I grabbed the pointy end of my scarf and dried my face with it. Finally I exclaimed with a laughter so queasy I nearly threw up just hearing it travelling to my ears: "Si, si ... Mamma Mia, Mamma Mia." And under my breath I thanked heaven and hell and whoever whatever was responsible for the gift of ABBA.

"Di che parte dell'Italia sei?"

"Di che ... Di — " I stuttered.

"Di che regione, Nord, Ovest — "

"Si si ... di, di — "

"Di Nord?"

"Si. Di Nord." I shook my head and averted my eyes. What in hell's name was this man saying? And what nonsense was I telling him? The woman next to me snorted, loosened her headscarf, unwrapped a noisy piece of caramel toffee and threw it in her mouth.

He seemed all too happy about catching me in a lie that he no longer cared for an answer. He was amused by his cleverness, excited by his fluency. He kept speaking in Italian in such speed that I felt his words were what fuelled the car, and I was about to suffocate. I felt like dying, and it wasn't the smooth and clean kind of death that I had always imagined mine to be; a death severe in its finality, like a blade sharpening itself on tender liver. It was the anticipation of pain and suffering, this precise suffering that scared me to the point of tears. I would die slowly and my lover would miss me.

"Stop this car," I said in Farsi "Please stop it."

He wasn't listening. The woman chewing her toffee was

laughing out loud, an opened white plastic bag of candy placed on her heavy knees. Candy my father used to bring home for me from his factory.

"Signorina Beatrice," he finally said, "dove andare bugiardi?"

"Ha?" I wondered, breathing heavily and sticking my head out of the window for oxygen. We locked eyes in the mirror again and I wondered where his paternal affectionate eyes had gone.

"Chi dice le bugie, dove va?" he asked, smiling slyly before translating: "Where do liars go?"

I started banging on the door with my whole body, the woman next to me sat back in fear as I pounded harder and harder. "Agha," she said bundling the plastic bag and hastily putting it under her arm. "Agha, let this lady out of the car, and let me out, too."

"I get motion sickness in cars." I said, trying to justify my behaviour. "Open this door, I want out. Open it or I will jump."

"Vey," he yelled. "Okay, I will I will. I can't park here but I am stopping at the end of this street, you can both get out."

He stepped on the gas and kept shooting worried glances at me in the mirror, "Are you going to get sick? Don't throw up in my car! I was just joking with you, akhee." He quickly made for an empty space in a corner.

The sweet smell of chewed caramel toffee was in my nose. I thought about Dante Alighieri and for a moment my fear and ignorance subsided.

"Inferno," I said, with my undigested breakfast and my stomach-acids rising back into my throat. "Inferno."

"What?" he asked.

"That's where liars go." I opened the door and as the car came to a slow halt, I retched a greenish watery lump of something I had no recollection of ever eating.

⤳ Chapter Eleven

1 ⟜

I SPENT MY life feeling like a curse and a blessing; like an evil-eye amulet that people hung on their doors, between their children's eyes. I was a blue stone, tied loosely on the mirrors of speeding cars, and with every application of brakes I swung and danced with rosaries and the ancient symbols of Farvahars, shimmering stars of David, silver crosses and Qur'ans, tiny and split-open. By simply being, I was a charm for my mother who wore me around her wrist, a charm that deflected envy because I was on no one's wish-list for the perfect daughter, mother or wife. No neighbourhood women enquired about my cooking skills; no old ladies eyed me admiringly after school, or asked my mother if I had already menstruated. My father never had to concern himself with refurnishing my marital house. There would be no dowry to accept. It was no wonder that he had left us nothing.

I was never sure of the reason behind this. Was it my mother's pre-wedding pregnancy? Or was it my reputation as a manic suicidal who would possibly set her husband's attic on fire? Was it the same reason no children wanted to play with me? It didn't matter. I had rid myself of my hymen at a very young age, and no Iranian man in his right mind would marry a girl who'd been tampered with. Hymen was equated with virginity and I had no intention of having one of those repugnant and insulting five-minute hymen reconstruction surgeries performed on me. And even if I did, I couldn't afford one.

So when my affair with Mr. Masoodi began, virginity was the last thing on my mind. It had started in the same way it would with all the other men: I seduced him. It was very uncommon to have a male principal — and a handsome one at that — for an all-girls school at the time, and opportunities being such scarce commodities in my life, I strongly felt that, when an unlikely and pleasant one presented itself so conveniently, one was morally obliged to take full advantage of it.

And so I did.

After my attempted suicide, my visits to his office were irregular. I was told, with my mother present, to drop by anytime I felt the need to talk, to express my concerns or to receive feedback. I only did when my progress in school was seriously stymied, or when any of my disgruntled teachers sent me there to be told off. He never told me off. Always spoke softly. At first I envied his wife, and when I had learnt that he was a forty-three-year-old bachelor, I envied his lovers.

During those visits we discussed nothing but my plummeting grades; not once did we cross the line of decorum. "How is your mother doing?" he always asked me, never wondering about my father. Only when we became intimate did he reveal that it was out of guilt, guilt for harbouring indecent feelings for me, that he never mentioned Rustam, who would have surely been outraged enough to riddle Mr. Masoodi's body with bullets, and then thrown the bloody squelchy mess next door to be pecked by omnivorous hens.

Ironically, my father's funeral was where we had met out of school for the first time, and it was there and only then that I had realized how very handsome this man was. His broad face, masculine and clean-shaven, his inquisitive black eyes, always peering with a clever sparkle from behind large silver-

rimmed spectacles, a strong waist and strong shoulders that
I had elaborate dreams of straddling. Even his hair, dust-co-
loured and with a receding hairline, gave him this air of experience and authority which I craved, and felt the immediate
need to quite literally tap into.

I wanted to see his head from all its different angles. I
wanted to breathe on his neck, lick the tips of his beautiful
teeth, count the moles on his back, search his body for childhood scars and warm his ears with my unexploited filth. The
second meeting took place six months later at aunt Bahar's
wedding— the only time after my father's death when I saw
a smile on everyone's faces, everyone except my aunt — and
that was where I shamelessly flirted with him. By the time of
the wedding, my mother had developed a soft spot for the man
who was taking her unstable daughter's side, and when she
had suggested inviting him, asking me personally to drop off
the invitation next day in school, I felt a violent throb in my
whole body that I almost fainted with excitement. And with
wandering fingers I shuddered that night at the thought of
his black eyes.

I spent days shopping for the perfect dress. He was going
to see me in that wedding without a headscarf, without the
pale long-sleeved school uniform that made us all look like
nuns, and I wanted to make a lasting impression. When the
day had finally arrived he hardly recognized me, just smiled
from a distance when my mother pointed me out to him in
the crowd, and when I went to say hello, he put his flat palm
on his chest, in the way that religious men do, politely refusing
to shake my hand.

Fine, I thought. If he wants to play that game, I'll play it
with him. I avoided looking at him all night, but made sure
that he saw me dancing with uncle Dariush, Navid and his
now grown-up friends, clapping softly, tossing my blonde hair

and with an absent-minded gaze, removing it from my face with a flick of my finger. Even Dr. Fereydoon was present, and complimented me by erupting upon seeing me: "But you look, you look so pretty!! Oh Sheyda," he said, holding his hand with my wrist in it above my head and watching me twirl in my sky-blue dress, "if I had a son your age, you'd be celebrating your own wedding in a month!" I blushed and thanked him, and felt very happy when I noticed Mr. Masoodi fidgeting upon hearing the eagerness in the doctor's voice.

I wrapped my lips delicately around morsels of food, eating everything with a fork, extracting it slowly, clean, out of my mouth and then chewing like I had all the time in the world. Whenever he stood, I made it a point to hover behind or next to him, biting my lips, chatting shyly to elderly ignorant women or to boys who were trying to impress me. I'd let my elbow bump into his, the soft fabric of his suit jacket would linger gently against the naked skin of my shoulder, and I'd feel us both simmering in a pot over an impatient flame that wanted us to be alone, alone behind closed doors. I shot down any attempts that he made to try and approach me, looking away in disinterest, or hurrying to take pictures with people I had no desire of creating memories with.

I retrieved a tiny bottle of perfume from my purse, dabbed some on my finger and ran it behind my ears and in the hollow of my long neck. Only at the end of the night, when he approached us to excuse himself and take leave, did I squeeze his forearm, leaning close enough for him to pick up my scent before whispering: "Thank you for coming, Mr. Masoodi. It was nice, so nice seeing you tonight."

All he said to me after a moment of dizziness was that I smelt like a meadow in springtime.

The only other person I could think of after the wedding was my aunt Bahar. I thought about how she had probably walked into a cold hotel room, slipped out of her pretty wedding gown and slept with a stranger she didn't love, because the one she had loved was dead.

The next morning when I had visited Mr. Masoodi in his office, for no reason at all but my desire to see him, he had a massive erection which he first tried to conceal under his desk, and then — when he stood up — under a blue folder. He wore a new ironed suit, and all the girls that day, most of whom already had desperate crushes on him, tattled about how unusually well-dressed he was. I went home without telling them that I had kissed the neck of the man they were talking about. I had also touched his thighs and received a lustful wet kiss on my mouth.

I told him that I wasn't a virgin, and thus absolved him from the pressure and pleasure of being the one to deflower me. Initially, his motives toward me were very clear: I was a fantasy, but so was he. He was never going to marry me, nor did I want him to, and neither one of us wanted a scandal. Later I realized that, when he had mentioned the word 'feelings', he had meant feelings that transcended lust. He never gave utterance to how he felt, he simply noted that they were there, those confused, delicious, taboo and illegal emotions. "I feel ... This is not ... I want ...," he'd say, "You are ... Sheyda I ..." But he never finished any of his sentences.

Three weeks before my eighteenth birthday, I lost my virginity.

When we first made love, he had wondered why the experience was so painful for me, considering all the lies I had told him; that he was my third man and that I had been religiously masturbating all my life.

When I started staying out late after school, my mother's sensitive nose detected something. "Where are you going? We never have lunch together anymore." She knew there was a boy, constantly interrogated me, hoping for a name. Whenever she tried to admonish me or extract a solid explanation, I made up stories about being depressed and doing my home-work in a park behind school. I also sometimes threatened to kill myself and that's when she simply developed the tactic of asking me to pick something up for lunch on my way back home, to make sure that I was home after school. My forty-five minutes of coitus with Mr. Masoodi suffered slightly at first, but then with practice, we finally got used to (and even learnt to enjoy) the twenty short minutes we spent together exchang-ing breath and saliva.

Regardless, he was the last man in the world my mother would have ever suspected.

"He's such a good man," my mother kept saying about him, "so caring and thoughtful. He chose to stand with us against many people. Very few men like him nowadays. How grateful Rustam would have been to him, how grateful."

Those words were an echo of a statement she had once made about Mustafa. I realized then how truly naïve my mother was about men. Each time I was in Mr. Masoodi's arms I thought about her. Yes, Maman, I'd think to myself, Mr. Masoodi is a caring lover. He is a very thoughtful man. And Rustam would have been grateful.

I remember how Mr. Masoodi, lying on his back, had once asked me: "Why are birds always surrounding you?"

"Pity," I said. "They feel sorry for me."

"Why would birds feel sorry for you?"

"Because they can fly, and I can't."

I then sat on top of him, leaned forward so that the soft ends of my hair tickled his shoulders and danced in the can-dlelight. "Close your eyes," I said before embarking on a mis-sion to kiss every inch of his face. I kissed his shut lids, bit the tip of his nose, pressed my lips tightly on the soft skin of his neck and ran my finger on his lower lip. "One day soon," I whispered, "we will all fly."

He moaned, snatched my palm quickly, and pressing it to his face, started to hungrily kiss it as I playfully tried to release it from his grasp.

"I have never seen you cry, do you realize that?"

"I have a sponge behind my eyes," I said, smiling. "I do cry, but on the inside. Here, feel this." I brought his finger to the edge of my eye which was wet with invisible tears. "I am crying now. I am crying all the time, but no one can see my tears. Even I got used to them."

I put his damp salty finger in my mouth and slowly sucked on my own sorrow. "Some pain is too great, some pain is ... Ah, but I am crying now. Always crying."

I slept on his heartbeat.

2

After dropping out of university, I started working in a bookshop called *Gulshan-i Raz* (Rose Garden of Secrets), the same one I had found Mustafa's books in. The owner, Agha Amiri, was a generous cultivated man. When I had asked him if he would hire me, he said: "A girl must get her education somewhere. If a bright young lady like you doesn't want to go to university, then she belongs here among books! All I ask is that you be punctual and, well, don't socialize with the customers. You are a pretty girl and we want them visiting this place for the right reasons."

It was a part-time job because he himself couldn't afford to employ me on a full-time basis. Regardless of the money, I worked extra hours. He had to sweep me out at the end of each day with the evasive dust, with the last of his talkative customers, with the cozy warm smell of mint tea, and with the fragile ants that had built an empire in the walls and floors of his threshold.

Gulshan-i Raz was sandwiched between a florist and a jewellery store, and though no one had ever rushed in with an emergency purchase for a Dostoevsky or a Milton, Agha Amiri made his books available to the public at eight o'clock sharp. He always walked into the bookshop with a fragrant white rose in his hand, which he offered to me along with the greeting: "Sobhet b kheyr khoshgelam!" to which I would re-spond with the same: "And a good morning to you, too!"

On his way out at the end of the day, he'd ogle the sparkly jewellery, the perfect rounded pearls that lamented their frac-tured mothers, and the expensive Indian bangles and Persian necklaces that belonged on long elegant necks and freed wrists, and then he'd ask me to pick something out for his wife while he caressed the emptiness of his pocket. "You have great taste, expensive taste. When I have money, I'll come back and buy it for her," he always said, and with a diplomatic smile drove us both away from the blinding unaffordable glitter.

We'd sit together each morning, sipping our tea on a square table out of cheap blue-rimmed cups, and he'd tell me about his family, how his wife was pressing him to book a vacation to Kish Island in the summer, how his teenage son begged him for a scooter, and how their depressed pet terrier Tofang (Gun), after being snuck out of the house and into the car one night and driven around the city, then for months being de-prived of the mere sight of a park, kept chewing Agha Amiri's shoes and peeing on the carpets.

"Oh you should have seen how happy he was!" he said. "He poked his fluffy brown body out of the window and opened his mouth to the night, his long pink tongue dripping froth and saliva on the empty gray streets. I did it once and now each time he hears the car keys he starts wagging his tail like an out of control windscreen wiper, and then alternates between a loud bark and a miserable pleading yelp! What can I do if it's illegal to take dogs for drives in the car? The police will arrest me! And I can't walk him in the park without crazy women complaining that a dog is a *najis,* dirty creature, and shouldn't be anywhere near their kids."

I gulped my tea and laughed at his words. "Everything suffers in this country. Humans, animals, ants and angels, we are all equal here, locked up more or less, we all suffer."

I never told him about my past; never mentioned suicide, Mustafa or my father. I never mentioned my whereabouts to my mother, just told her that I had found a job and handed her the precious money at the end of each month. When any of my boyfriends entered the bookshop and chatted with me in front of the clients, or stopped outside across the street, waiting for my workday to end, Agha Amiri simply tsk-tsked without saying a word. After a few times of hearing him express his tacit distaste at my behaviour, I issued an order to all my lovers to never visit me at work. I didn't want to be seen with any of them anyway, and frankly, I was more afraid that they'd run into each other.

I'd sit behind the register on a high stool, crossing my legs and hunching over books, careful to not leave any imprints of licked fingers, paper-cut-blood or deep indents on their crisp pages, touching them as delicately as I touched my lovers and myself, and then devouring the words and sentences with my eyes, sweetening my tea with iambic pentameters, driving the music and the realities and pain of other countries into my malnourished belly, memorizing the desperate lines, sighing, frowning, laughing.

Pushkin shattered me to pieces. Tagore was an impressive disappointment; how much I would have loved him, had he only chosen the objects of his love more carefully! I read about the Qajar dynasty which had sold my country, one concession at a time, to pasty snaggle-toothed monsters with insatiable appetites for power and oil. I fed the famished in Ireland; rice, nan, steaks and healthy plump potatoes, thick soup that they drank out of my hands, and when catholic children were shot with their mothers, I sang hymns at their graves, and sprinkled white flowers on the red dirt saying: "Fly my birds, fly my sparrows; never will you know hunger again."

The fairies of Yeats stole me into their magic realms; they fed me berries and we leapt and chased and danced in the silver of the moonlight, and when it was time for me to return I cried. I dreamt about The Lotus Eaters and wondered if any narcotic plant would be strong enough to make me forget about home and my mother.

I wept for the fate of Mohammad Mosaddegh, this country's only hero and the only man who put Iran before himself. I admired the secularism of Ataturk, and the revolt of the Turks. I hung around the neck of Christ the Redeemer, and he fluttered with his spread arms and lifted me above a landscape of fresh green, sparkly white and blue and a happy kind nation of samba dancers. People prayed in his gigantic silhouette, but only I flew away, blowing kisses like a diva to her fans. I slept in the faraway temples of India, with yellow-garlanded priests in thick orange robes swinging incense under my nose, marking my forehead with a tilak of red turmeric and sandal paste, and blessing me in an ancient tongue beneath multiple-faced four-armed green and blue Gods with beautiful faces and kohled eyes, while fearless rats tickled our feet and holy triumphant cows wandered the streets.

Books sang praises to past religious heroes; others vilified our dead monarch who had fled to his exile carrying a handful of Iranian soil in a box, and who had died with a broken heart like a drowned sailor in his sleep dreaming of a familiar shore. I turned page after page, imagining that fantasy that was America; that distant land of Stars and Stripes, or as far as we were concerned, Bullets and Skulls. I wondered if the lips of those blonde cowboys tasted better; I wondered if I would sleep more calmly in the bulk of their arms, and I cursed with a loud voice which Agha Amiri echoed, those slimy two-faced British who with their greed inflicted grief and misery on half of the world.

"I've never seen anyone read so much, it's bad for your eyes," Agh Amiri would tell me. "Go home. Go home to your family."

One day Agha Amiri walked up to me and pointed at a couple who were standing with their backs to us, browsing the hard-wood shelves and struggling to restrain their laughter, and asked me to help them while he made a quick phone call. I looked up from my book, took a few steps in their direction and then froze once I saw the side profile of the woman's face. I hid behind my scarf and quickly motioned to Agha Amiri, who approached me with a concerned look. "What's wrong? Who are you hiding from?"

"From them," I said, "those two."

"Why, I don't understand, who are they?"

"That's my mother."

"Oh, about time I met her. Please introduce me!"

"Agha please, I don't want her to see me here. She doesn't know that I am working for you."

He followed me as I retreated behind a shelf and ducked, pretending to tie the laces of my tennis shoes. "And what will happen if she finds out? Will she mind?"

"No," I said, lying with a muffled voice, focusing on the floor. "It's just that I haven't told her yet, and she might get upset. Please you help them; I'll make that phone call for you."

Agha Amiri shook his head as he looked at them again. "And the man, is that your father?"

I glanced stealthily at the skinny man with neat hair who looked comical with a shirt two sizes too big. "Yes," I said, and rubbed my forehead, "that's my father."

ᔰ Chapter Twelve

1 ᔰ

"OH SAVAGE LIFE, oh impermanent beauty, help me, help me! I want to feel again, emotionally feel." That was a nurtured thought in prison, a mantra I repeated sacredly and with rigour. At times, when I slept on my bed looking at the ceiling, I imagined the thick and heavy upturned playground for empty stares and spiders, slowly pressing down on me, stomping me like a galloping hoof drumming on the head of a defeated cavalier, like a slow but smooth elevator squeezing all the air out of my cell, speeding with my breathing and the circulation of blood in my system, the pink moles on its pale skin enlarging the closer it got to the whites of my eyes, and the painted bumpy wrinkles bursting like soap bubbles on my lashes. It would descend, getting closer still until it crushed me and my dusty bed into the cold ground.

I was disciplined through extremes and opposites, simply because life had disciplined me. Not my father, not my mother, but life: vindictive and breath-taking life. The bait of moderation is always dangled inches from our faces, never too closely, but far enough to make us want to cross lifetimes with the hope of reaching it, and dying, with a blurred vision of its taste. Middle-of-the-road; that delectable balance. Off white; that boring shade! Life is extreme, like me, like my mother.

I grew very silent in my solitary cell. Often, when my head was bashed against the walls by the warden for not saying

Thank You or Sorry, or for not answering quickly enough co-
herently enough when asked questions, my lips moved but I
didn't hear myself. Not a single moan escaped me. I didn't
know if I had lost all sensation to pain, if anger had simply
abandoned me, or if my voice had packed up and left. I went
from being talkative, from having debates with Beatrice, from
reciting poetry to the shadows of my dead loved ones, loudly
after midnight, quietly in my sleep, to a world of utter silence.
I retreated into that void that had at first so frightened me.

I never heard a squeak, a desperate yelp, or a small voice,
nothing! Life outside of me was muted, the commotion of the
world ceased. But inside a volcano was erupting, cymbals were
being clashed; drums were celebrating a human sacrifice and
a cannibalistic feast; thunder split the heavens in half; the
oceans heaved with my sorrow; and blood spun as my sanity
spilled. I'd lie in my bed imagining tortured spirits emerging
from the walls. They'd sit by my bedside telling me their stories as I drew my feet to my chest in fear. I'd stick my fingers
in my ears and sing to myself songs that I couldn't hear. I'd
sing until a sleepy guard peered in from the trap at the top of
the door, and with cracked angry lips threatened to slap me.

After a week of solitary confinement, my voice returned. I
could hear myself laughing again, looking at the walls, waiting for the demons to claim me, lining under my bed my trea-
sured collection of dry nails; a collection which I, after closer
inspection, discovered to also contain the broken teeth of my
previous cellmates. I thumped them all like beads, arranged
them on my bed, and then rearranged them again until I fell
asleep.

Some nails weren't mine, were too big for my fingers, were
too blue for my hands, but I kept them anyway. With their
assistance I started counting the days I had left. They were

my dirty calendar. It was something of a game to me. I needed to keep busy. I'd think to myself: why is it always dark in here? Where is the sun? Where is uncle Dariush with that watch and picture? When one of the guards came carrying the disgusting breakfast of tepid tea and bread, I asked her: "Where is it, the sun?" As if she and the sun were on speaking terms, and if she had felt like it, she could have arrested it and brought it into the cell to have a quick chat with me, or maybe, she could have taken me outside to see it.

I knew that, beyond the walls, siren-voiced mothers and proud vacant fathers were brought to their knees by the weight of their sadness, crushing the buds of pink flowers, burning candles and crying at the gates of the prison. They called out the names of their children, and their voices clambered the walls but then terrified at the horrors of the place, lost their balance and fell, never to stand up again.

Their children were made deaf by all the beatings to their heads, by all the fake-hangings which the interrogators found funny. They were led out in the dark to be silently shot in the courtyard as they rubbed out of their sleep-deprived eyes dreams of soft beds, and fantasies of warm clothes, bubble baths and hot home-cooked meals that smelt of their mothers' fingers.

My sole concern was that they'd hang me indoors, in the prison's hall. That they'd line me up on a high plank in a dark room, along with the other crazy women who no longer cared whether they lived or died. Men or women, they all just wanted out; standing on their feet, or lifeless in dirty old sacks, with man-made holes in their skulls or rickety loose necks. I wanted to be hanged outdoors in the open air, under the clear blue sky. I wanted the sun to watch me approaching her, climbing her rays like a yellow stairway until I could pluck her light and weave baskets, like my traitor grandmother had done.

I sometimes imagined being a famous political prisoner. Humanitarian organizations worldwide would be reviled by my government's contempt for freedom and its lack of respect for everything with a soul. Faraway countries would be offering me asylum, throwing their red and black passports at me. The international community would attempt an intervention; it would taunt my country, pressurize it. My happy hardened face would be pasted on the pages of international newspapers, and under it, captions and paragraphs of disgust and sympathy would be printed in foreign languages. Aunt Bahar would cut out scraps and keep them for me to read on the day of my return home. My hallucinating eyes would scream my name through my images: Sheyda, Sheyda; *the Lovesick*!

And if I was to be released, after hefty bribes were paid to mustachioed criminals who lurked freely in the same building, wearing their official uniforms and leather boots, then eager journalists would wait for me outside the gates to capture what the absence of walls did to my face; to hear me violently cough holding my throat, inhaling the fresh chilly breath of a March morning. I'd raise my fingers up in a proud V, and I'd chant: "Victory is ours" while a crowd of Iranians cheered and clapped. Cameras would be clicked furiously, and I'd squint at the white flash lights, and with a broad grin of equal brilliance, try to deflect their flattering assault.

"Grazie, grazie a tutti!" Beatrice would say, but Sheyda would smile; that contended haughty half-smile of heroes and war-criminals. Journalists would throw their questions at me while I blinked admiring their determination to make headlines, to document my first words as I defeated the turbulence and landed on safety. They'd fumble with their devices, tripping over the many wires and sticking microphones in my face to film that triumphant moment. "What do you feel after being away for so many years and finally being out?" And they'd look at me with hopes of a poignant answer, anticipating passionate wisdom to shatter my lips in a torrent of words, but I'd just look ahead blankly and utter only one: "Nothing."

Absolutely nothing!

2 ⦉

Five days before my execution, the guard opened the door and told me that I had visitors. She nonchalantly tossed me a black chador which I wrapped around my body. I was then led through a passageway of clanking cells, and up a narrow dark staircase that echoed our footsteps. The stale foul stench of un-flushed toilets also walked with us. At the door to the hall, a rough hairy guard called out my name, then with a red pen, put a tick next to it on his folder. In the public visitation area, I saw uncle Dariush, Dr. Fereydoon and my grandmother, all with their eyes fixed on the door from which I emerged. My eyes wandered the stuffy crowded hall in search of Navid or any other familiar face, and when I couldn't find any, I sat down across the table from my visitors.

My grandmother was weeping silently as she pressed my palm into hers. With an embroidered napkin, she dabbed at the tears that seemed to be running from a hidden spring. Uncle Dariush kept cursing under his breath, moodily looking sideways. When he caught my eyes, the harshness in him dissolved, and he smiled tenderly. Dr. Fereydoon's eyes drooped, but he too tried to smile when he saw me.

"Here to say goodbye?" I asked, trying to be a sport about dying. My grandmother broke into a muffled cry.

"Sheyda jan, in harfa cheye?!" uncle Dariush chided in a

sad drawl, as he held my grandma's shoulders and tried to calm her. "How can you say such a thing?"

"I've been here for nearly two months, and only now she visits me, uncle. What am I supposed to say?"

A moment passed and no one answered. Uncle Dariush started coughing.

"Your grandmother is sick," he said after his painful coughing fit ended. "And she isn't done mourning her daughter."

"Fair enough, but where is your wife? Is she still out of town? Where is Navid? Where is aunt Bahar?" I asked with indifference.

"They will come; they wanted to come today, but —"

"Never mind, dear uncle."

I felt restless, agoraphobic. My legs, as if with a mind of their own, kept crossing and uncrossing under the table. I was agitated and wanted to return to my cell. I removed my hand from my granny's clasp and stood up to leave, shoving the table and hearing the metal legs of the chair creak behind me and fall back.

Dr. Fereydoon rose from his chair and grabbed me from my sleeves. "Please sit down." he begged as I looked around the room with dazed eyes and tried to break free. "Please."

A guard shouted from the back of the hall and told us to keep quiet.

"The old lady changed her story. She changed her story," Dr. Fereydoon said excitedly.

"What old lady?" I asked, allowing him to pull the chair back up and seat me down again.

"Hajji Khanoom," my grandmother said. I realized then that it had been weeks since I had last heard my granny's voice.

"What story?"

"*The* story. She visited your grandmother's house yesterday and told her everything. The truth! When she had heard about your verdict, she felt terrible. She said that she will come here herself and change her testimony."

"She's lying," I said. "She's just a crazy old woman with a conscience and a weak heart!"

"No," said my grandmother. "She swore to it on the Qur'an."

I let out an offensive chuckle. "She swore on the Qur'an?"

"She might have been a miserable hag all her life, but she never lied. I am her friend."

"You were."

Dr. Fereydoon tightened his grip on my wrist and spoke through pursed lips. I wore his fingers like the watch I had wanted. "Stop this sickening lying. You did not kill your mother." I watched a glossy line of sweat form on his forehead; it stretched all the way to the corners of his temples. I wanted to take my grandmother's napkin and dry it for him.

I looked back into his eyes. "I did, doctor, I did. Believe you me."

Uncle Dariush slammed the table with his fist, finally yielding to one of the many emotions that inhabited his face. "You did not!" Spit flew out of his mouth and dripped on his gray stubble.

"I did. I killed my mother just like I had killed the old lady's rooster," I said with a jeer.

My grandmother stopped crying. "You never killed anything; you never killed anyone. You are my child, my little Sheyda who loves birds."

"I did."

"Impossible."

"Possible."

"Why?" my uncle asked. "Why, why? That's all we want to know!"

"Because the sky is high, because the sky is so high!"

"Answer!!"

"My Trinity is dead."

"Okay, that's okay. That's okay. We love you, we forgive you. We just want you back home," he said.

I gazed at all three. "I love you, you and you," I said. "But I don't want anyone's sympathy. I deserve whatever happens." I wanted to get up and kiss them all for the last time. But I couldn't stand; I felt paralyzed by their voices.

"Did anyone hurt you?" my grandmother asked in a voice that echoed the misery and concern of every mother present. "Did they do to you what they do to the other women? Has any man—"

"No. Apart from a few slaps and punches here and there, they've been good to me. It's not so bad, really. You get used to it. You can get used to anything. Humanity is so resilient; we can survive on so little ... We can, oh grandmother, no, no, no man has touched me."

"Those bastards!" Dr. Fereydoon said, and the line of sweat forked into two trails on his temple. One glistening trail led into his hair, disappeared behind his ear, and the other slowly travelled down his red cheek.

"If anyone lays a hand on you, touches a hair on your head, I will kill them myself," my uncle said.

"I know you will." I took my grandmother's hands and ran her gravelly fingers on my face. "You carried me when I was born."

I looked at uncle Dariush and said: "You never got me that picture; you never brought me a watch. Now I have five days left."

"I brought them with me today. Aunt Bahar found a picture she thought you'd appreciate. She had rescued it from your mother, but the guard outside stripped me off them along with my lighter and cigarettes. He said that they'll give them to you later today, once you are back in your cell; if not the watch, then only the picture. Apparently, watches are against regulation."

"Well, I need to go now. I am tired and want to be alone."

"We sat for hours in the waiting hall," uncle Dariush said. "Spend a few more minutes with us."

"But you are not saying anything, uncle."

"What can I say? What can anyone say? You are my brother's little girl. I will protect you like I would my own son."

"Say hello to aunt Hilla and Navid," I said. "I will miss them." I was amused by my use of the future tense, as if I was simply travelling to a new country to which my dear mortal relatives had no access. "I miss them now, but I will miss them more when I am gone." I don't know why, but after saying that, even I found the casualness with which I spoke frightening. I then looked at my grandmother and told her: "Kiss aunt Bahar on the forehead and tell her it's from me."

"They will visit you tomorrow," uncle Dariush aid. "All three will be here. We will visit you every day."

"Thank you, but don't force them. There is no need. This is a sad place."

"They will be here. We will all be here tomorrow," he insisted. He tried to stand up but collapsed back onto the chair with his hand on his heart.

Dr. Fereydoon immediately stood and grabbed him. I had no sensation waist-down. Without attempting to move I said: "Oh uncle, no. Please, it's okay. Don't be afraid, don't worry about me."

I glanced at my weak trembling grandmother who appeared to not have slept or eaten in weeks. She was bony and in a matter of seconds was seized by an uncontrollable shiver. I wanted to leave so her shivering would stop. I breathed with difficulty as I watched the other prisoners conversing in mumbles and whispers with their families. Laughing and crying at the same time, in a farcical display of extremes. My leg jerked under the table and I too started to shake. I rubbed my elbows.

"I am talking with the person in charge of your case, I have spoken to your lawyer and I will go to the judge himself if I have to," Dr. Fereydoon said. "I'll beg every mullah; I'll kiss every hand and forehead; I'll pay off every guard. We will get you out of here. But please, please, stop your lying." The trail of sweat finally reached the edge of his mouth, tickled his lips. With little thought and with the back of his hand, he wiped the shiny line off his cheek first, then off his forehead. The captured sweat was now on his thumb and index finger. It would continue its journey, but I was going to die.

"I killed her," I said as I stood up on unreliable legs and walked away. "Believe you me, believe you me."

"Stop, just stop your lying!" the doctor shouted after me and began to cry.

3 ☾

It was a Tuesday.

My mother died on a Tuesday.

It had snowed all night. I had awoken at five in the morning, listening to the snow silently pile, melting gently on my defensive window. Try as I might, my mind refused to retreat into that tasty haze of dreams. So I stayed in the quiet presence of morning shadows, watching the reddening hues of dawn through the cream delicate drapes. At six I got out of bed, dressed and sat in the living room with a blanket hugging my shoulders. With my head pressed on a pillow, I watched the red hues being slowly replaced by that decisive grayish white of daytime. The scents of an empty house brushed under my nose. I listened closely to detect my mother's movements on her bed but heard nothing.

It was seven o'clock when I stepped out into the garden. There, I shovelled a large icy patch of snow, and on the frozen grass and wet mud beneath it, I sprinkled bread crumbs for the desperate birds. From treetops they watched me with the innocence of their little black eyes. And as soon as I finished and turned toward the door, they flitted their brown and gray wings and dove toward the food. I opened the garden's gate and quietly left.

I departed, with an inexplicably queasy stomach and without breakfast. And in flat rubbery boots and under many layers of wool and cotton, I walked the distance to work. I jumped over gutters runny with snow water. I passed through slush piles of white snow blackened by soot-like tire tracks. Cold meowing cats disappeared under cars. They sought warmth inside the engines and nothing was visible but their dancing tails.

Five minutes into my walk, I spotted the birds following me. I smiled at their gratitude.

In the bookshop, I sat through four hours of nothing but reading, slumping into my chair, and coughing into a tissue.

"You look pale," Agha Amiri said, pushing a cup of tea in front of me. "What's wrong?"

I tried to look up from Ferdowsi's epic. "I am okay, a bit cold."

"You should go home and sleep; things are slow today."

"No. If I go home I'll end up feeling worse. Here I have things to distract me."

"But you are making all our invisible customers sick," he said, jokingly.

I laughed, but my laughter quickly turned into a deep excruciating cough. I pounded my chest with my fist to get the cough out.

"That does it. Shut that book now and go home right away.

As your boss I am ordering you. Go home to your mother and let her take care of you."

"No," I grunted.

"It's not up to you. Go home, have some soup, and only come back when you are one-hundred-percent better. Go home to your mother, with you here and your father at work, she must be very lonely." He then dug into the side pockets of his pants, releasing receipts, a toothpick, a blue paper clip and finally some money. "Here," he said, stuffing the cash into my hands. "Take a taxi back home; it's too cold for a stroll."

I was too weak to argue. I stood up, wore my trench coat over my ropoosh, waved to my boss with my dirty tissue and left the warmth of the bookshop back into the biting cold. I walked to the main road, stood long enough for my running nose and my ears to get so stiff with pain that I felt like breaking them off and tossing them. A few taxis honked for me, but I ignored them. I looked at the birds and followed them back home on foot.

Agha Amiri was wrong. My mother had company.

When I had pressed the buzzer, five minutes passed before my mother's confused voice came through the intercom. When she realized it was me, she sounded very displeased, and for a few moments proceeded to berate me for returning home early. Finally, she hung up without buzzing the door open. When I rang again she mumbled something about needing some time. Five minutes later the gate to our house opened from the inside, and a grinning mullah with a turban and a brown open robe stepped out, offering me a religious man's salutation. His breath smelt minty. Taken aback, I returned his greeting with more humility than I had intended, and then looked away from his lustreless smile. I entered my house quickly and slammed the gate behind him.

Enraged, I sprinted up the stairs, taking all three steps with one large stride and walked into the house with my boots on. "Maman," I called, "Maman, where are you?"

The TV in the living room was on; the pictures it emitted of a woman playing with children were of poor quality, with the signal constantly dropping. I pushed the red button on the remote control and the show went away.

"Maman?"

I heard nothing but the emptiness of my voice. I looked in her bedroom and noticed the wrinkled hastily arranged blankets and soft pillows dented with head impressions. I caught the confined whiff of sweat and nudity. He wasn't even the same man I had seen her with in the bookshop. How many were there?

"Maman," I shouted angrily, "answer me." I pushed the door of the bathroom open, paced back and forth between the living room and the hall, nervously turning light switches on and off and looking at my sad reflection in the mirror. And then I finally entered the kitchen following a frigid air draft that flowed from a mysterious place. I noticed a blue steel ladder connecting the floor to the open roof window.

Carefully and at the mercy of the blowing wind, I climbed. First my head protruded out of the square opening of the window, and then the rest of my body followed. The ladder wobbled under my weight as I balanced on the last rung, and burying my red knuckles and elbows in snow, I pulled myself up.

In the nineteen years I had lived in that house, not once had I been up to the roof. And as if the sky had been waiting for me to appear, it started to melodramatically snow. I looked up at the snowflakes twirling with a soothing sparkle on their journey down, and then I chased with a downward gaze, like an enamoured God, their muted landing on the earth in our garden, on yellow shivering flowers, on a cherry tree with hidden treasures, on the cars hibernating in the streets, on faithful birds and on the hungry tongue of our empty driveway. From above, I could see into our neighbours' gardens. Even Mustafa's garden was clear from where I stood.

Oh, I thought, if only I had known about this place when I was young! Everything looked so peaceful, so untouched, as if a big bag of flour had been spilled off the sky's counter and was covering everything with a white mess. For a moment I forgot what I was there for. I tore a soft lump of snow from beneath me and passed it on my flushed forehead. My anger melted.

"Maman!" I said again, my voice softened by the snow.

I saw my mother behind the large black saucer of the satellite, carrying a heavy rake and, to the best of her ability, trying to scrape the snow off without falling. She wore nothing to cover her head, and her once beautiful black curls now looked wispy and gray, like the ash of a consumed cigarette. Red lipstick was smeared on her mouth, and black kohled tears trailed from her eyes. Her nostrils were as red as my knuckles, and when she breathed, the mist from her panting mouth was abundant. She wore a creased white overcoat and blended beautifully with the background. I swished toward her, leaving my footsteps in the snow.

"What are you doing?"

"I am taking care of you."

I grabbed the handle of the rake. "Let me help."

She struggled on the snow, almost losing her balance, and then snatched it back with such violence I nearly fell, and said: "No. Leave it."

"Fine!" I said, frightened by her sudden aggression and stepping back. "I was just trying to help!"

"The channels are not working. Everything is blurred and imperfect."

"Mother, it's okay. I understand."

"The signals have all dropped. It's so boring, so boring without all those foreign channels."

"Mother, it's okay," I repeated. "I understand. You are angry and lonely. But, why bring an ugly bear to our vineyard, a pig to your orchard?"

My mother threw her head back and surrendered to a joyful childish laughter. "A pig to my orchard? They pay very generously these pigs, and this one was doubly religious; they pay more when they feel guilty."

I just stood in silence, not knowing what to say.

"Sheyda?"

I looked up at the precipitating snow, and deep into the watery eyes of the sky. Where were God's angels?

"Sheyda, Sheyda?" my mother called. "I am tired, baby ..."

I watched snowflakes floating angrily in accompaniment to the wind's passionate music.

"... of this life, I am alone."

I was entranced by their performance. Completely entranced!

"Sheyda! Can you hear me?" she asked.

Without removing my eyes from the dancing of the flakes I said: "Yes, mommy, loud and clear." I then followed the sparkly silver motes into my mother's hair.

"See this body?" she said unbuttoning her overcoat. "Hey! Look at me."

I moved my eyes from her hair to her distraught face.

"Yes."

"It has been ravaged by twenty-nine men who never loved it. See?"

She then took three steps to the back without taking her eyes off me, and then stood on the edge of the roof. "See?" Her house-slippers were flattened and soaked like a worn sponge.

"Mother," I said. "You are brave."

She smiled. "I wish I never bore you."

"I know. I also wish ...," I said, on the verge of crying. "I broke you to a million pieces."

"I would have never married. I would have left Iran, would have gone to America."

"You would have met your old English teacher, Mr. Carl."

"Yes," she said, happily.

"You would have dressed as you pleased. Like those women on TV."

"Yes."

"You would have found a job, and maybe married a man who loved you."

"Maybe!"

"You are beautiful, mommy."

Her smile broadened. "I used to be."

"Mother!" I said again, and then asked her a question with my eyes. She offered the affirmative with her own.

"Wait."

But she didn't. She just stretched her arms theatrically, and without taking her eyes off me, let herself go, trembling with the joy of a released snowflake and falling serenely into our garden. I heard the soft rustling of her white overcoat, like the wind caught in a Mediterranean sail. I knew that she fell on the rails because I heard her spine snap. I calmly took two silent steps toward the edge, and looked down, but before I could do anything, before I could jump, I heard a piercing agonized shriek, and when I turned toward the noise, I saw Hajji Khanoom wearing her blue flowery chador, standing pale on the roof of her house, her two palms holding her terrified face and the deep abyss of a frightened old mouth. Her hens gathered around her sedately pecking at the seeds that spilled out of the bowl she had dropped on the snow.

I smiled at their indifference, the world's indifference. But what saddened me was that the world was as indifferent to my mother as it was to me. And when I bent over the edge to look at my mom, she stretched with her back bent like a rainbow, like a gymnast stuck in an impossible pose, the rail having split her in half. My mother let out one misty sigh that travelled upwards against the snowy current. I touched it with pale fingers and felt her life leaving her, dissolving in my palm. The green long barbed leaves of plants living in pots crawled to touch her hand, to comb her hair and check for pulse. There was none.

Her eyes were open. But she wasn't looking at me. She looked past me and past the roof and past the seven heavens and past God. I wanted to fall into her eyes and drown. My mother's eyes which were black and haunted, like abandoned dark wells, slowly shut, forever concealing the precious whites inside them. Blood, red like her nail-polish, bubbled out of her mouth, dripped onto the caked-with-snow rails that held her, and transfused into dark and sweet sherbet.

"Khuda Ya," the old woman screamed. "Ya Ali, Ya Hussein."

The hens started cackling at the distress of their owner; they ran on scrawny legs, fluttered from one corner to the other, shedding colourful feathers and seeking shelter from her voice.

"Khuda Ya. Ya Hussein."

She then started calling out the names of entities that could actually help her: Her son's, her daughter's.

I smiled at that, too. Glanced quickly at everything around me, said a silent goodbye to the world, to Mustafa's house, to the dead black angel of our fountain, to our cherry tree, to the birds that perched and watched me and my life unfold like the most offensive human drama. "Humanity is disgusting," I told them. "Watch something else or turn off your TV and do something better with your lives."

I then closed my eyes, spread my wings, and jumped into my mother's gaze.

"Not a single broken bone in your body," the nurse who stood by my bed in the hospital said. "You are a walking miracle. God was looking over you! It was as if the angels in heaven had carried you on their wings."

Two hours later the police arrested me. Hajji Khanoom had told them that I had pushed and killed my mother.

When they asked me, I said yes.

⤳ Chapter Thirteen

TWO HOURS AFTER returning to my cell, a guard came over, opened the bottom trap of the door from which food trays were pushed in, and inserted a watch with a leather strap and a square picture. "Here," was all she said before shutting the trap again and hovering away like a bored ghost.

I got off my bed and removed them from the floor. I sat on my knees and looked at the picture. It was one of my father, mother, and a handsome young man, with sharp black eyes, carrying a water hose and smiling to the camera. Flowers wishing to be immortalized stuck their green tender necks and bright and colourful hairdos into the bottom of the picture, and the elbow of the deceased stone angel in our garden protruded from one side, but above my Holy Trinity and behind it, stretched a blue horizon with two white clouds hanging low like flurried sails headed south. I ran my fingers on the happy faces then pressed the picture to my heart. See you all very soon, I thought.

The watch was aunt Bahar's. When I was younger I had begged her to give it to me. She promised that one day she would. But then we grew older and forgot about it. The arms pointed at twenty-minutes past five. I wore it on my wrist and went back to bed. I hid the picture in my bra, and fell asleep listening to the nervous tick-tock of the watch. If we were buried together, then it would serve as a reminder to the maggots that time ticked even when we were gone.

I woke up to the metallic noise of the door being unlocked. The room was in entire darkness, and a guard shone a flashlight in my eyes and yelled at me to stand up and get ready.

"Get ready for what?"

"Just get dressed."

She threw me a pair of shoes. I blindly wore a second pair of socks. I felt for the picture in my heart and fingered the watch. "I am dressed," I said.

"Wear this chador," she ordered and offered me the same one I had used earlier.

I squinted at my watch, trying to check the time in the dark, following the evasive light in the guard's hand. How long have I slept? What day was this?

"What time is it? Where are you taking me?"

"It is now *exactly* midnight. Time to say goodbye!"

I can't remember where she took me from there. All I know is that we got into a room and that a door closed behind me. I remember ugly faces and the butt of a gun violently ramming the back of my head.

When I came to hours later, I found myself lying in a cold room, next to a pool of my own vomit. I found one tooth in the yellowish mixture of soup, bread and tea, and after tonguing the gap in my mouth, realized that it was mine. I remembered swallowing it, but had no recollection of vomiting it out again.

Before I had time to make sense of anything, a man who appeared to be very upset with me for some reason entered the room, then roughly pulled me back up on my feet. "Come," he barked and pushed me in front of him. "Wear your chador properly."

My whole body ached, my wrists were blue and the glass screen of my watch was shattered, but my arms, defiant, kept moving. When I walked, I dragged my leg behind me, and when I was out of the room, I saw a queue made up of four men and three women waiting to be led somewhere. We were then all blindfolded, cuffed and guided out, through halls, up and down stairs. My feet were giving way under me, but someone kept poking my shoulder from behind with a baton or a gun, I can't be sure. I heard the angry man command a guard to open the gates, and once he did, I felt a violent cold wind gust and frisk me head to toe. I trembled happily: we were outside.

The whole universe was asleep, except us. At first I heard a car drive off quickly, but then, all I could hear was the agitated footsteps of men shuffling about, and soldiers expectantly, impatiently caressing the triggers of their guns and rifles. There were ambiguous ticks and sounds that came from beneath our legs, insects scuttling about, running for their lives, dewdrops colliding with stones, and grass pushing forth from the soil.

When our blindfolds were removed, we were instructed to climb into a white van that awaited us on the road. I sat with the three women, not knowing where the men had disappeared.

I settled sideways into a comfortable leather upholstered seat. One girl sat next to me and the other two sat facing us. When my eyes had finally adjusted to the darkness, I recognized the green eyes of the young girl in my old cell. I almost told her how good it was to see her again, but before I could say anything, a woman guard wearing a black chador got into the van with us and slammed the door behind her. I smiled at the young girl, but when she saw the gap in my mouth she rocked with revulsion and looked away.

The three women were in a terrible state, but from the terrified look on their faces, I realized that I wasn't in a better condition myself. Images started returning to me. I had a choice between believing that I was being driven to my death with the thick dirty semen of three different rapists inside of me, trickling on my inner thighs, or between dismissing everything that had happened to me that night and regarding it all as the remnants of a bad dream.

I chose the latter.

"Where are we going?" I asked the guard who sat to my right.

The prisoner sitting on my other side said: "On a picnic!" She then laughed and added: "Where do you think?"

The guard said nothing.

The green-eyed girl looked composed, and fixed her eyes on a point between me and the guard.

"I have four more days to live," I said. I was talking with a lisp and found my voice shattered and funny.

"What difference will four more days make?" the guard asked.

"My family wanted to say goodbye to me."

"Well, I guess they are going to have to do without goodbyes. But don't worry, they'll find out about this tomorrow."

The woman sitting furthest away broke in a despairing wail.

The guard ignored her and asked me: "Do you want me to deliver a message to your family?"

I thought about her offer for a moment and then said no.

I looked back at the green-eyed girl. "Hey Sabzi," I called out to her, "what's your real name?"

"Asal" she said then closed her eyes and tried to sleep.

Honey. Her name was Honey.

We were being driven fast to our death. I could see the sun slowly burning candles behind the horizon. One by one, the corners of the sky began to light up, like the walls of an ancient dark cathedral. The call to prayer broke from all directions, chased nighttime from every crevice, calling the devoted, the sincere and hypocritical alike to their morning prayers, reminding them of their duty to God. But all I could concern myself with were the birds. I swear for the hundredth time that they recognize me. They must have spotted me out of the gates, then travelled the skies to inform one another that a ceremony for one of their own was about to take place. It was euphoric: sparrows, pigeons, and even ravens dove into the waves of blue, chasing our car.

"Look," I said to the women. "Look at the birds outside. Look at them claiming the sky. They are following us."

"Strange!" the guard exclaimed as she lowered her head to gaze out of the window. None of the other women bothered.

"It's going to be a public hanging," the chatty prisoner who seemed to be in a genuinely good mood said. "We are lucky. They want to show the rest of the city what happens to criminals. They want to put the fear of God into them."

I giggled at the word Lucky. "What's your crime?" I asked.

"I killed my husband. He had been sleeping with my friend throughout our marriage, and when I had asked him for a divorce, he refused to give it to me. They arrested me before I could finish off my friend. What about you?"

"I killed at least four people and a rooster."

She snorted. "A rooster? Okay, I don't want to know about that, but at least four people?"

"Yes, at least! I was also accused of apostasy a few hours ago."

"How so?!"

"I told a man who was beating me: 'Curse your God, I renounce him!'"

"That explains your teeth," she said.

At that moment, I remember wishing that my arms weren't

tied behind me, so that I could have swayed with mirth. I wished that I could have, for the last time, burst with a good wholesome laugh that would have cleansed me and my body from any feelings of nostalgia.

"What about her?" I asked, tilting my neck in the direction of the sobbing woman. Her eyes were swollen. She wanted to dry her face, but failing to reach her elbow or shoulder, finally rubbed it on the back of the front seat and looked away.

"Oh her!" my companion said sarcastically. "She committed the ultimate unforgivable sin!"

"And what's that?"

"She was born a Kurd, and is a Bahai." She laughed. "Can you imagine? They must have felt like they had hit the jackpot when they found her."

I tongued the gap in my mouth and sniggered, then looked at the wailing woman and said with an exaggerated lisp: "Don't cry thithter, oh thithter, don't cry, be thtrong, it will all be over thoon."

Even the guard found me funny.

The van stopped in the middle of a vast empty stretch of land and space. There were small hills of white sand and gravel, and large piles of bricks stacked like Lego pieces. It seemed like a construction area.

When the door of the van opened, I was the last one to get out. I felt like one of those hesitant birds my grandfather had freed in the wilderness, afraid to step out of my comfort zone. The guard finally grabbed me from my arm and dragged me out. "Hurry," she said. "I still have a long day ahead of me." How insensitive, I thought, that she should mention the long day awaiting her to prisoners who were going to die.

"I will see my babies soon," the green-eyed girl said and

finally smiled. When she turned around to stand in front of me, I realized that she had wet herself.

We formed a straight line and walked with the guard behind us. She delivered us like care-packages to a young soldier, and then without saying a word, returned to the van.

"Are they going to give us water to drink? I am thirsty."

"Water? Sure! And wine, and honey sandwiches on fresh taftoun."

"Where are the crowds?"

"They will come, don't worry. They'll finish their prayers first and then come. You'll get your five minutes of fame."

"You are funny," I told the woman. "I wish we had gone to the same cell together."

"The same hell, you mean?"

"We were in the same hell!"

In the distance, I saw the black spine of a crane in front of the white peak of a mountain. Its single arm was yellow. Then I saw three more, all placed in the backs of pickup trucks like overgrown praying mantises. I watched the birds fly, circling the first heaven, and then gently landing on trees to watch us being freed from our cages. They were here before anyone. They wanted us to fly together.

Behind me, I heard the Bahai woman reciting a prayer: "*O God! Keep me steadfast and make me firm and staunch. Protect me from violent tests, and preserve and shelter me in the strongly fortified fortress of Thy Covenant and Testament. Thou art the Powerful. Thou art the Seeing. Thou art the Hearing.*" I waited for her to finish, but on and on she chanted with a frantic frightful voice like an incantation of sorrow: "*O Thou the Compassionate God. Bestow upon me a heart which, like unto glass, may be illumined with the light of Thy love, and confer upon me thoughts which may change this world into a rose garden*

through the outpourings of heavenly grace. Thou art the Com-
passionate, the Merciful. Thou—"

"Stop please," I begged her. "I can't hear any more. Pray silently or be quiet. I can't listen to this."

My stomach rattled, and bitter vomit rose to my throat. Standing up, I emptied my mouth on the dirt by my feet. My shoes were soiled. They were my old shoes. I was happy to see something familiar. I fell to the ground, bent on my knees with my hands tied behind me, and on a plastic bag of *Tofak* chips and between the few butts of extinguished cigarettes, I spotted another tooth.

"Get up," the soldier said. "Time to go."

People started gathering, parking their cars around the site. There was a flood of heads, all gathered behind the iron fencing, looking pensively with murky eyes, standing on tiptoes with their mouths open and their curiosity piqued, just like I used to when I was a young spy, a Bond girl. Bit by bit the crowd grew, and I started to search the eyes and faces. They all looked like they could have been my neighbours, my distant relatives, my lovers and brothers and sisters, my unborn babies. Some of them brought cameras.

The four men were to go first. Their driver had raced ours to this place. They stood on the backs of the trucks. The first two were too young, and the remaining two, too old. I saw two masked hangmen with strong arms slip blue and yellow nooses over the red-rimmed eyes and frightened necks.

Tanned men in green uniforms stood between us and the masses, some wore military caps, and others protected their heads with hard green helmets. Some men had small beards, and others owned proud moustaches. They carried their batons in their hands and wore their guns in belts around their waists. A few ambled with machineguns, casually puffing away at their cigarettes.

The sinners were blindfolded. I couldn't see their eyes anymore. Only then did I get scared.

When my turn comes, I will refuse to be blindfolded; I will look the hangmen in the eyes as they slip a noose over my head, as they relax it around my neck, like the tie of a groom on his wedding day. They will miss me when I am gone, in the same way the full moon is missed on the blackest night. I am no nightingale, mother; I am no sparrow, Rustam jan. Mustafa where are you? Come and listen: Sheyda is a Firebird, the wise Simurgh. I am the Phoenix, these snakes' worst nightmare. My feathers are torches to the underworld. Three Times Over I have witnessed ruin, and now, plunging into fire I'll witness my own. Three Times Over has my world been destroyed, and Three Times Over I have outlived it. I am immortal, a reflection of you, oh confused wandering birds, people of my country. From my ashes, from my scorched orange feathers, from the rainbow in my tail, I will rise in a nothing far away from this rubble. My strong wings will carry me away from your God and my only song will then be that very thing I never had ...

The whole area rang with the aftermath of the call to prayer. There were solemn echoes of anger and tears. Then suddenly religious testaments of faith bellowed to fill in the gaps of silence.

The praying mantises whined as they came to life. They stood on their feet, stretched their spines and arms and rose with a loud screech that made some men in the crowd whistle while one or two looked away. The birds on the branches held their peace. They were waiting for us captives to mount the backs of the beasts and ride into the sky.

I saw the first man lifted slowly. There was a little struggle, his legs momentarily twitched but his neck, like the soft stem of a flower, promptly gave in and leaned to one side. He was high in the sky, higher than the horizon, dangling from the fingertips of the crane. The sun rose slowly and glimmered behind him. He looked like a diamond, like a medallion of a resurrected saviour swaying on the end of a chain. The wind played in his white shirt, saliva dripped out of his mouth. He seemed at peace, like a hungry loner who had fallen asleep on his legs, who dreamt about a hot, mouth-watering meal.

Ciao bello, ciao. Bask in the light my friend; let the high wind caress your hair like your mother had done before tucking you in, and hold the spring's fragrance in your lungs like that of a lover who had once kissed you. You are in a better place.

"Why are you smiling?" asked the last friend I'll ever make. "What are you looking at?"

"Look there," I said, facing the sun behind the elevated men. "It's so beautiful, it's breath-taking."

"Four hanged men are breath-taking?"

"No. Look more closely. There, can't you see it?"

"Where?" she said and searched the sky more carefully. "What?"

"Azadi ... Look!"

Look. Up there!

Freedom!

# Acknowledgements

To mom and dad: thank you for being the best.

To my siblings: thank you for your love and inspiration.

To my wonderful editor Michael Mirolla: thank you
for believing in my book and for your patient
and gentle guidance.

To David Moratto: thank you for your openness
and for the great job you did on the cover.

To Sinan Hussein, my friend and stellar painter
whose beautiful art adorns this book: thank you for
your kindness and for wanting to be a part of this.

To my friend Rahil (Ranjha): thank you for
being so intelligent and for your constant
encouragement and support.

To anyone who has read bits and pieces of this
story and offered guidance, kindness
and criticism: thank you.

➲ ABOUT THE AUTHOR

A passionate and dedicated writer, Ava Farmehri presently lives in Canada. But she grew up in the Middle East surrounded by books, cats and war. She loves books. She loves cats. She hates war. She really hates war. This is her first published novel.

Printed by Imprimerie Gauvin
Gatineau, Québec